MIMIKA COONEY

Mind Reader

Sensibility Romance Series (Book 1)

Mimika Media

Dedication
To my teenage sweetheart and dashing husband, Michael.
I'm so honored to be your partner on this journey called life.
Your unfailing love has made me a true romantic.

To my Grandmother, Yiayia Cleo.
You taught me that love was shown with time, care and affection.

Contents

Foreword

In the age of new discoveries, let's not lose sight of discovering ourselves.
-Mimika Cooney

In Memory

The figure skating community will never forget the skaters and families who lost their lives in the Potomac River mid-air collision on January 29, 2025.

Invitation

Grab the free Book Bonus when you join our email list.
Visit https://www.mimikacooney.com/mindreader

I

Mind Reader

1

Chapter 1: The Pitchathon

Cleo

I said yes because Megan insisted.

What she didn't mention was the couture battlefield of hyper-competitive egos in designer suits and the TED Talk energy. It's like Shark Tank and the Met Gala had a baby and raised it on caffeine.

"It'll be fun, Cleo," Megan had said. "It's a satire event. Faux apps, fake elevator pitches, a charity auction, and some schmoozing. A mocktail with a cute paper umbrella. It's not real unless you win, of course."

She also swore the room would contain at least one eligible billionaire, but I'm not here for that.

Stilettos tap across the marble. Heads flick my way, measuring. I cross the space the way I learned to enter the ice rink, calm, measured, polished.

The Tribeca Art Gallery gives high-gloss Bond villain hideout vibes. Exposed brick, curated lighting, and just

3

enough hush in the air to make you think something expensive is about to explode.

Then I spot him.

He pauses near the entrance as a waiter nearly loses control of a tray. He says something low to the kid.

Almost anyone else in this room would have stepped aside and let the crash happen. Free entertainment for a room full of competitors.

Heat pricks along my skin, sudden and inconvenient.

This is Dillon Whelan, the mind behind iSight.

Early thirties. Sharp jaw. Broad shoulders. A tailored Armani that signals quiet wealth.

He's the kind of man who doesn't walk into a room so much as alters the air inside it.

I tell myself it's just presence. Confidence. The sort of thing investors train themselves to project.

Still, the room feels different now.

Seriously, Cleo. Get a grip. You don't get flustered by suits.

He scans the room once, like he's cataloging variables before making a move. Then his gaze lands on me.

Not lingering. Not looking away either. Just assessing, as if he's already decided the room is worth understanding before engaging with it.

Recognition clicks a beat later.

Forbes 30 Under 30. Founder of iSight. Tonight's judge.

He adjusts his glasses with smooth precision and slips his hands into his pockets. Nothing about him feels accidental.

Interesting.

Let's see what he does with that.

A hostess appears beside me with a blueberry mojito mocktail. Crushed mint over pebbled ice, the scent drifting up like some rooftop cabana I definitely don't have time for tonight.

"Bold drink choice," he says.

That voice. Low and confident, the kind that slides under your skin.

I take a sip and nod. "I like to stay sharp."

It lands flatter than I intended.

Ugh. Should've gone sassier.

Dillon lifts a brow, like he clocked the same thing.

"Over engineered," he says, studying the glass. "Garnish overkill."

I blink.

Did he just critique my mocktail like it's a startup pitch deck?

He studies the glass the way I study people.

Okay, gladiator. Slicing through cocktails now? Bold move, even for this crowd.

He's close enough now that I catch a faint trace of cedar and citrus, clean and understated in a way that doesn't try to be noticed but is anyway.

I chuckle. He looks me up and down. Slow, deliberate, like he's dipping a toe into shark-infested waters just to see if I'll bite.

I sip more, wishing mint plus sugar could quench this odd flutter.

"I don't think we've met. New around here?" His eyes, ridiculously blue, flash something. Amusement? Or calculus wrapped in charm?

"Something like that." I maintain eye contact, testing the temperature.

Dillon doesn't blink.

My grip tightens on the glass even as my smile stays easy.

It's either going to be catastrophic, or fascinating. I can't tell which yet, and that unnerves me.

"Mrs...?" he says too casually. Is he baiting me?

Something about the way he says it, low and loaded, zaps straight through my ribcage like static.

His jaw tension, blink rate, and voice cadence trigger my internal lie detector radar.

"It's Miss."

Let him chew on that.

"Miss, excuse me. No plus one?" he asks, voice casual.

"Not tonight." I shrug. "But tomorrow's still open for applications. Assuming the applicant knows how to stick around."

A queen's mic-drop move.

For a split second, his gaze flickers, like I hit a nerve. A blink, a pause, and then that smile resets.

I've cracked something, even if I don't know what.

The emcee calls contestants to the stage just as the rhythm shifts, disrupting our banter.

Dang it, this was just starting to get good.

"Catch you later," Dillon says as a closing move. Like he's already seen the final scene and knows I'll be in it.

Something about the way he studies the room tells me this is not a man who loses often.

I catch my reflection in the chrome statue, shoulders squared, expression composed.

All right, Cleo. No mistakes, not here, not tonight.

My name tag reads Veg-A-Find, which is ridiculous on multiple levels, because apparently ferns need a wingman, and tonight I'm it.

Finally, recognizable faces.

Maximillian O'Sullivan adjusts the rose lapel on his tux with mob-boss theatrics.

His date looks like she's deciding whether to invest in a startup or marry one.

Near the hors d'oeuvres table, Ethel Baxter from *The New York Ladder* stands crisp in emerald tailoring, pearls draped like warnings.

One good PR feature from her team could put me on the map.

Rows of ghost-white chairs face a low-lit stage framed in golden drapes, where five judges perch on stools like skeptical critics.

Tonight's Pitchathon is part satire, part gladiator show.

Founders sell faux startups to investors while real venture capitalists and the media watch the mayhem.

A golden brain trophy, a viral clip, and enough ego fuel to start a turf war over brunch.

This room hums with that particular New York energy, where everything feels half performance and half test.

This is New York's tech-meets-art bloodsport, where reputation is the currency and everyone's net worth is contingent on who's watching, and suddenly I'm very aware of exactly where I'm standing.

If I tank this, they won't laugh it off, won't brush it aside as part of the act.

They'll file my name under "forgettable" and move on, and in a room like this, that's worse than losing.

Officially, I'm here for a client.

One of those discreet, high-net-worth types who bankrolls from the shadows.

He wanted quiet eyes and instincts on the players.

Unofficially, I've got skin in the game.

We built Calypso Consulting's reputation on reading people for a living.

That's how we change the way power communicates.

I don't love competitions, but I love reading people.

On second thought, maybe I do love competitions.

It's less about logic and more about intuition.

My gut knows something's off long before my brain computes what I'm seeing.

The crepe Vera Wang dress fits flawlessly. Sleek black, sharp neckline, off the shoulder for a little sass.

I feel like I'm cosplaying my own CEO Barbie edition in these three-inch Blahniks.

While I'd normally prefer less skin showing, this is a branding decision. My fashionista sister will be proud.

I swore I'd never be part of this play. Slick smiles, sharper contracts, men who can sell sand in a desert and still forget to come home for dinner.

The emcee introduces him as he takes the stage. Everything sharpens. The voice, the charm, the intent tucked behind that maddening expression.

Dillon stands near the judges' table, sipping his drink like this is a pool party. I'm just a few feet away, and yet it feels like miles.

Dillon finishes his introduction. The applause is still fading when the spotlight sweeps the stage as the hostess gestures me forward. I smooth my dress and channel every ounce of confidence.

I've rehearsed this spiel a hundred times. Workshopped it in a day with Megan until she threatened to hide my laptop.

I plant my weight evenly, like I'm about to land a triple axel. This, I know how to do. I'm ready.

"Cleo Ambrosia," the host announces, "founder of Calypso Consulting. An emotional intelligence consultancy for high-impact leaders."

I hate how much I want to win this. But as I scan the expressions and analyze the micro movements, my nerves steady.

A man behind me murmurs, "You teach CEOs how to cry or something?"

Typical. Coward hidden by ego.

"No," I say. "I teach them to stop bleeding talent."

I straighten my shoulders and move toward the podium, reminding myself who I am. I take my place beside the other hopefuls, mic in hand.

It's showtime.

Dillon steps up to his mic, the spotlight catching the sharp cut of his suit like he's doing PR for Armani. Not rushed, not hesitant, but deliberate. Tiny, precise movements are the kind that don't show as nerves, only readiness.

"Tonight, I bring you MeowMoney. A platform for investing in the internet's true celebrities: cats. We finally have a way to monetize the memes that already rule your screen time."

He takes a breath.

"The truth is that your 401(k) might crash, but that tabby cat with a short man syndrome offers a solid ROI."

The audience roars. The air is electric as everyone leans in to see who caves first. He sells it like a late-night infomercial pitchman, only smoother. Every move is calculated, composed, magnetized. Flawless, without notes or a teleprompter.

Dillon's not just selling his idea. No, he's selling himself.

And the audience is eating him up.

He leans into the spotlight like he belongs there.

Game on, peacock, I think, the competitive switch clicking fully into place.

The next thirty minutes are a blur of fast talking and applause. We volley like we're in a startup version of *Jeopardy!* One by one, the competition dwindles. Each quip lands with the snap of a tennis volley, precision over power.

I haven't felt this energized since I stepped on the ice to compete before everything fell apart. The tension coils like a double axel, tight, fast, and about to launch.

What began as a lighthearted game of darts has turned into a low-key war of wits and words.

"At first glance, you think our app is a cute cat meme," Dillon says with confidence. "But behind the fluff is a real-time emotional analytics engine. We've gamified mental health check-ins using pet-based humor. Why? Because dopamine works. Give yourself a hit of cuteness with every scroll."

It sounds too legit, which means I'm already off-brand for this event.

"Interesting premise," I say, keeping my tone neutral. "But what's the actual utility beyond dopamine scrolling?"

"If utility is your metric, you'll love our AI-driven tracking backend," he replies smoothly. "We monetize engagement through mood mapping. Even skeptics smile at cats." He takes a jab at my app. "It might work with talking plants."

"At least mine doesn't require a litter box," I fire back.

The audience laughs. We don't.

I'm in the zone. Calm, focused, the way I like it. I grab the mic without missing a beat. "Adorable. But while your investors are chasing laser pointers, I'll be matchmaking houseplants."

He volleys back with, "If your plants drink the mojito mocktails you're so fond of, they will go home alone anyway."

Another wave of raucous laughter sounds out. One judge even snorts.

The air between us crackles like the Wi-Fi jumped to 5G.

Dillon leans toward his mic. "Yes, Veg-A-Find. Because clearly, house plants have been lonely for too long."

"They deserve love," I say. "They photosynthesize, they thrive in silence. Basically, they're ideal partners. Unlike some startups I could name."

I catch the smallest glint in his eyes behind those glasses. Like he's doing a silent calculation. Analyzing, adjusting, recalibrating. No wonder he's winning.

"Low maintenance and good at oxygen exchange," he says. "Basically me."

The audience laughs again.

Ugh. I hate how smooth that landed, like he knew exactly when to drop it.

I cross my arms in defiance, keeping my tone light. "At least my users don't require flea treatments."

His hand lands on his chest in a theatrical gesture. "Wow. Harsh. You wound me, Mrs...?"

I raise my mic. "It's still Miss."

There's a beat of charged silence. He flashes a confident grin. But something in his eyes isn't smug, it's searching. I realize he's not intimidating me or gloating. No, he's studying me.

I don't flinch. But every nerve ending registers that spark, like I'm touching a live wire. For the first time, I feel disarmed.

"Final lightning round," the host announces. "One-line

elevator pitch, no pauses. Go!"

Dillon steps forward. "MeowMoney: turning fur into fortune, one meme at a time."

I follow, voice crisp. "Veg-A-Find: because succulents deserve a chance at true love."

I freeze. Not visibly, but inside. That one lands differently. Lower, heating my insides.

After a pause, a ripple of laughter sounds, followed by applause.

Dillon and I glance at each other across the stage like dueling royalty. That's when I realize this isn't a sparring match. He's got under my skin and in my head. He parries with words like he's fencing.

Every beat, every micro pause, timed with maddening precision. Somehow, he's turned this ridiculous charity pitch into a duel I didn't agree to, but one I can't stop fighting.

I'm used to being the one in control. The one with the sharper tongue and the cooler head. He's matching me step for step.

His smug almost-smile makes me think he already knows how this duel ends.

And the worst part?

I don't know whether I want to win this round or watch what happens if I let him.

Dillon keeps sneaking glances. Like he's silently daring me to go bigger. "That all you got?"

Whatever. Let him look.

That smug confidence is what's throwing me off. Too arrogant, too calm. Far too dangerous for my liking.

I land one flawless zinger, clean and sharp. Silence. Then slow applause, like the crowd's catching up. But he's not. His eyes say he's already three moves ahead, waiting for me to close the gap.

He makes his last offer of the night. He nails it. Of course, he does.

The host announces the winner. Of course, it's him.

I want to roll my eyes at the fluff, but I can't deny it. His pivot was clever. Smart, even.

And judging by the VC nodding like a fool, I'm not the only one who saw it.

My stomach sinks. I can feel the heat rising to my cheeks, but I lock my expression into neutral.

I've met someone just as good. Or better than me.

That smirk. That stupid, infuriating, arrogant smirk.

But why can't I stop thinking about it?

Dillon steps forward, accepts the trophy, and thanks the panel. He takes the win with the grace of someone who wins often.

Dillon offers me a hand to shake. His warm palm jolted something in me when we briefly shook hands, something I wasn't prepared to feel. It's uninvited, electric, and worse, it lingers. Not on my skin, but somewhere deeper. Somewhere I swore I'd locked down.

"Strong presentation," he says as we shake. "Your opening hit hard. But somewhere in the middle, it tilted a little more toward show than structure. Still, impressive."

What? Did he just analyze me?

Even my failure came with footnotes.

I narrow my eyes as I pull my hand away. "Enjoy the win. I don't lose twice."

He beams like he's already penciled in our next match. "You don't strike me as someone who quits easily."

Is he goading me?

"Maybe not." My voice is cool, but there's an edge to it I didn't mean to let slip out. "It's been real."

I shift my weight to ground myself. My pulse is steady, my smile still plastered in place. Three weeks of prep, down to the cadence of my opening joke. Gone in a breath. But I'll swallow that sting before I let it show.

But my pride? Torched.

Fingers fumbling, I grasp at my clutch.

I glance back once and catch him watching, calm, unreadable.

He might think this is about the loss, but it isn't.

That is why I never trust charm. It always looks like control until the moment it isn't.

I came for a mocktail and a PR boost. Instead, I walked away rattled, and curious.

I set the empty glass down beside the tray.

The thought lands harder than it should. I straighten my shoulders like posture alone might seal the crack.

I glance back once and catch Dillon watching, calm and unreadable.

I did not lose to Dillon.

I lost to someone who thought he saw through me.

2

Chapter 2: The Analyst

Cleo

Ice crackles under my blades, shattering the hush of morning. For one quiet hour, the Wollman Rink is mine.

I couldn't sleep after losing to Dillon. I needed air. Somewhere my body remembers what to do when my mind won't stop racing.

Here, I breathe.

The ice waits, a glassy canvas asking to be carved. Above me, the skyline looms, silhouetted against the blush of dawn. Fall lingers, with streaks of green, gold, and crimson flashing through the canopy.

New York's trees hide secrets I'll never know.

Each cut of my blade shaves something tight from my chest, and with every deeper carve, my thoughts come into focus. If I can move fast, I might be able to escape the noise within.

Okay, that got deep. Ugh, I definitely need caffeine.

I move to a rhythm that's sharp and graceful. The overhead

speakers play Vivaldi's Winter with a modern twist.

Classical music always calms me, the way it did when I danced ballet. Precision drilled into my bones.

Miss Sadie was a drill sergeant with a perfect bun, spotless shoes, and abs of steel. But floating across the floor was the part I loved, and it translated well into figure skating.

I let the music carry me, and I stay inside the moment. I pivot into a spiral, then a lunge. My hip falters for an instant, but muscle memory steps in to fix it before I can think. When I overthink, I tense up, and the mistakes follow.

I hate how much I need this to feel steady.

It's been years since I competed on the ice. The memory of Coach Olga's glacial stare still raises goosebumps on my arms. She never raised her voice because she didn't need to. A single look could freeze you mid-movement, breath locked, body braced for correction. She built champions. No excuses. No softness. Overcoming her felt like earning a medal. Even when I resented her methods, they carved something unshakeable into me.

Those years under Olga trained me to hold a pose anywhere. From the ice, through the boardroom, to facing verbal ambushes. Stillness equals strength. Wobble reads like weakness.

There was a plan once. A future mapped in clean lines and earned precision. It ended suddenly, leaving me to relearn who I was without the structure that defined me.

For a long time, I stayed off the ice. When I finally laced up again, it wasn't to chase medals or prove anything to anyone else. It was to remember that muscle memory doesn't forget what ambition taught it, even when everything else goes quiet.

I only feel like myself when I'm on the ice. Out here, I don't have to read people. The ice doesn't lie, and it doesn't ask me to fake a smile.

When I warm up and run the choreography, surrendering to the music, my mind finally stills. Perfectionism pauses in the moment when passion outpaces pressure. That's when the edges of my skates rip through the ice. The crunch tells me the edges are deep enough to slice through the noise in my head.

It's the same in consulting: tight lines, clean execution, no room for error, because I don't pitch clients as much as I perform.

Every word and glance calibrated for impact.

I didn't wake up one day knowing how to read people. I grew up learning which emotional landmines to avoid. I tracked the flick of my dad's jaw before a blowup, and I caught my mom's fingers twitching right before she shut down. Survival made me observant, and the patterns came first; the language followed.

Later, I formalized it with degrees in behavioral science and training under Dr. Levine, an FBI lie detection expert. I specialized in micro expressions, those split-second facial tells, and decoding emotion through cognitive empathy, because truth always hides in plain sight.

My methods aren't magic. They're trained instinct. I track patterns like delayed responses and tiny posture shifts, and I read the cues most people miss.

And once you know what to look for, the truth is rarely silent.

Back at the bench, I grab my water bottle and notice the gold medal at the bottom of my bag. I haven't touched it in years. I turn it over. It's heavier than I remember. It used to mean I'd made it. Now it just reminds me how far off the mark I am.

I toss it back in my bag as I notice my phone light up. A voicemail from Megan and six unread messages in the *Sensibility Sisters* group chat.

Seven girls, one thread surviving breakups, burnout, career detours, and one unforgettable beach trip.

Tia's my sister, Megan's my BFF and business partner. Separated by cities and time zones, Shiloh, Mia, Nicole, and Alexa still find a way to stay in touch.

We met in college and stuck together through finals, first jobs, and life's many curveballs. An unlikely group of Jane Austen personalities who, against all odds, still coexist.

We joke about renaming the chat *Emotionally Complicated*, but *Sensibility Sisters* stuck. Tia feels everything, Megan can smell a lie a mile away, Shiloh's taste is impeccable, Mia hears what's not said, Nicole sees the fault lines before they crack, Alexa sees your spiral coming and has snacks, strategy, and a pep talk ready. And I see it all coming before anyone else.

I scroll through the chaos. Of course, the girls have weighed in, and even when I don't reply, I'm thankful for their noise today. It reminds me I'm still tethered to something real, not just algorithms or contracts.

SENSIBILITY SISTERS: (*6 unread messages*)

Tia: *Cleooo!* If you're alive, blink. If not, I'm sending a glitter bomb to your apartment and a singing telegram. Possibly shirtless. 👀

Shiloh: She's either skating in a vengeance spiral or baking sourdough with angst. I approve of both.

Mia: Leave her alone, girls. She'll talk when she's ready. Just no Insta stories, okay? We don't need this trending.

Nicole: If she doesn't respond in ten minutes, I'm filing a Missing Sanity Report. Also, I brought pie charts. And pie.

Alexa: Someone get her real food. She's not fine, but she will be. And she doesn't have to do it solo.

Megan: She's not unraveling. She's recalibrating. Let the system reboot. I've got her. Give her time. And space. And chocolate.

I click on the voicemail from Megan. "Cleo, my love, it's me. Sorry to bug you this early, but it's urgent. Call me when you get this."

I sigh. I hate being rushed, but it looks like today is going to be one of those days. I yank off my skates, wipe the blades, and put on the soakers that keep them dry. Dread fills my stomach, cold and sharp, settling just behind my ribs.

We didn't fulfill the contract. Now, to untangle this ball of spaghetti.

Friends and colleagues think I'm crazy for being the one who runs toward the fire. To me, real life sounds like a broken record when I don't get to pick the soundtrack. Mom says I think and talk fast, but I say others think and talk too slow.

I slip into my sneakers and reach for my phone. Just as I'm about to hit return, Megan's name flashes across the screen.

"Hey girl," she says. "Sorry to interrupt your me time, but what happ—"

"I'll save you the rant," I say, rubbing my temple.

"Yes, yes. How could I let it happen, yada yada. I don't need to hit repeat to know it's bad."

A client complaint risks ruining our reputation, and a roomful of New York's finest witnessed my meltdown.

Great, just great.

Megan sighs. "I can hear your pacing."

I stop.

"I don't pace," I lie.

"Uh-huh, right. You know, normal people plan before they act."

I shrug. "Normal people waste time. But I know. Last night was embarrassing. We need a plan."

She huffs. "More than embarrassing. It's a potential disaster. You could at least pretend to think things through."

"Where's the fun in that?"

"Cleo, my love, I know you were giving it your best shot. I wish it hadn't ended like *that*." The tension in her voice tells me everything. This isn't just about losing my cool and damaging my reputation. It's about survival.

"It was unavoidable. I saw red, forgot why I was there, and let my frustration bleed into a professional room, which is ironic, considering I teach people not to react." I say.

"I panicked the second I saw the email. But I know you were doing your best." Megan says.

If only I'd forget how a simple smirk got under my skin.

I went in planning to pitch my client's idea, and the second Dillon walked in, the air shifted and I forgot everything except proving I belonged.

"Bad news travels fast in this industry," I mutter.

"The client's already sent a notice of intent to terminate," Megan says, voice tight. "Thirty-day clause. But we both know that means the door's closing."

"I could've thrown a mocktail, and it would've gone viral in a good way, right?"

Megan lets out a loud sigh. "Instead, you got the boardroom version of an open-mouthed gasp and five LinkedIn articles about 'grace under pressure.'"

I pinch the bridge of my nose. "I know. This week proved unexpectedly challenging."

Two clients pressed pause. One wants to 're-evaluate strategic alignment.' Translation: We made them feel things, and that's scary in corporate.

"Well, I've been up since three a.m. racking my brain. There's a possibility, but it's a bit of a mess…" Megan trails off.

My stomach tightens. With my bag over my shoulder, I pick up my pace, crossing the road and narrowly dodging a biker. My pulse syncs to the static in my head. "How messy?"

"More than enough to keep us afloat. If it works, we won't have to gorge ourselves on Ben and Jerry's. So, my new Prada jeans won't cry."

I can work with that.

"But Cleo, we can't make another mistake."

"I hear you loud and clear. See you at the office."

New client. No name. No safety net. While others hesitate, weigh the risks, and second-guess, I survive by staying three moves ahead. I don't crave safety. I crave the fire.

Maybe that's why I hunt the hardest clients. It's the same thrill as a jump with a blind landing, where you either stick the landing or kiss ice. But however it ends, at least you flew.

* * *

Sitting in the back of a taxi, my phone lights up. It's my sister Tia calling from England.

"Cleo, darling," Tia singsongs. "Are you free Friday night?"

I narrow my eyes. "Why?"

"No reason. I'm coming to town. A small dinner. A few friends. And oh, would you look at that? One of them is single and charming."

Ugh. I need carbs and a reality check. In that exact order.

I groan. "Tia, stop. I don't need you to set me up."

My last relationship ended in a whimper, not a bang. Three months of fake compatibility and mutual ghosting. Before that? Nothing worth a scrapbook.

"Remember that time I saved you from that disastrous networking event by texting you fake emergency messages? Consider this me cashing in that favor."

I rub my temple. "I'm too busy for relationships. I'm swamped and have an urgent project to deal with."

"Are you married to your job? You know your bank account can't keep you warm at night. Take some time off. Meet me over here for a multi-city adventure. Just you and me and my camera."

"T, I can't follow you around taking photos for your influencer thingy. Find someone local to be your butler. Why don't you ask your BFF Shiloh to go with you?"

"Nah, Shiloh can't make it. But, Cleo," Tia says, sweetness dripping like honey, "you know I trust only you to capture my essence. How about we go on my travel trip, then spend Christmas with Mom? You know you want to."

"No promises," I say. "And I've arrived for my meeting. Tell Mom I love her and will call soon."

"Don't be alone again this Christmas. A little romance wouldn't hurt."

I snort. "Says the woman whose last so-called soulmate lasted, what, three weeks?"

"Fine, mock me. But someday, you're going to fall, and it

won't be on ice."

* * *

Steam curls around me as I step into the office's fabulous white marble locker room shower. The scalding water eases the tension in my shoulders.

Corporate warfare is more polished than chasing criminals, but it isn't exactly safe. My stint consulting for the FBI started as a thrill until one insight cracked open a cartel case, and my name ended up in places it didn't belong. When a burned-out car showed up near my house, I got the message.

After that, I chose corporate clients instead. Messy, but at least corporate drama doesn't come with death threats. You only need a flicker of doubt to see through a bluff. People don't say what they mean. But their bodies do. I get paid to translate subtext into strategy. If I can't carry it solo, I don't trust it'll hold. Control freak? Guilty, and I make it work.

I armor up with a crisp white Calvin Klein collared blouse, gray high-waisted fly skirt with jacket, and blue accents. I pat on the tinted moisturizer and apply mascara. Tia, my fashionista sister, goes nuts when I refuse her make-over sessions. No time for that nonsense.

I'm halfway through my protein bar when I step off the tenth-floor elevator and spot Abby. "The client moved up the meeting and wants a meetup tomorrow at their office."

"Abby, you've been with me four-plus years now. When have you ever seen me pander to a client having a hissy fit?"

"Never. But this is a huge project. Your team has collected everything you need." She hands me an iPad.

"I'm not rushing anywhere until I've had time to review the materials."

Abby flushes. "I know, Cleo, but they insist they need a quick turnaround."

"Please get back to them and set it up for later today." I hang my jacket on the back of my white leather chair. "Also, please replace the locker room hair dryer. I'm having to go for the poofy look today."

"Noted." Abby nods. "Let me order you an omelet to last you past noon. A car can't run on fumes, right?"

I wave a hand. "I can handle it."

Abby gives me her classic eye roll. She knows by now it's pointless to waste energy arguing with me.

I glance at the iPad, then shift my bag higher on my shoulder. "If a chocolate croissant ends up on my desk, I might pretend it's for you."

I see her shoulders ease, just a fraction, and I pretend not to notice.

She smirks. "You remembered?"

"Please. You lit up like Christmas the last time I shared one."

Abby shakes her head, but her smile lingers.

I do not correct her, rush her, or ask for more. Right now, this is enough.

People work better when they feel safe.

"And Abby?" I pause. "Thanks. For keeping me running. I don't say it enough."

She gives a small nod. I don't wait for more.

"Oh, and don't forget the updated P&L from accounting," Abby adds.

I wave her off. "I'll look at it later."

Later usually means never. I've built Calypso on instinct

and grit, not spreadsheets. Numbers make my head hurt.

Sitting at my desk, I pick up my tiny New York City snow globe and shake it. I collect them from cities I've lived in or passed through, small worlds under glass.

Watching the replay recording feels like scraping skin across sandpaper. It was only a charity event, a little showcase with a silly glass brain trophy, overcooked canapés, and bragging rights, and I keep telling myself that.

But the sting? Still there. Sharp, throbbing, beneath the surface.

Dillon beat me, smoothly without missing a step.

And I let him.

Some part of me, deep down, thought I had it. That this was my moment. That I'd finally get to stand in a room full of power players and not belong, but lead.

I watch as I walk to the mic with polished confidence. Calm. But I see how narrowly I held the line. The tightness around my eyes, the flicker of nerves I thought I'd masked.

And then Dillon, striding onto the stage like he owned the room. Charismatic and elegantly poised. That stupid knowing smirk, like he'd already seen the ending and knew how it played out.

And the worst part? He timed it flawlessly.

I watched, rewound, and replayed it again, like somehow I'd missed the part where I will lose.

Because it mattered. Because winning was essential, whether ego or survival, it yielded the same result.

My company needs momentum. A short-term contract, a high-visibility win, a client willing to vouch for us in public. More than enough to boost our street cred. Calypso doesn't struggle because we're unqualified. We struggle because we work behind the scenes, fixing what other consultants miss. Our clients don't give testimonials. They make us sign NDAs.

We're the whisper fixers, the ones execs call when the issue is too delicate to go public. High-impact, low-visibility, and that's a hard pitch in a world that values loud.

Why do intelligent people struggle to understand the impact of EQ on their overall achievements?

I swipe through our latest proposal drafts and pause at the red margins on the budget sheet Megan flagged. Our services are solid, more than solid. It's difficult to translate emotional intelligence into ROI in a world obsessed with data and analytics. We've proven results. Behavioral shifts. Retention wins. But until someone influential says it's worth it, most execs treat EQ like a side salad.

That's why landing iSight matters, because if we can make Lucid's AI more human, we're not just relevant. We're essential.

But Dillon got the applause. I got a polite smile. And polite doesn't pay invoices.

I sit back, eyes burning not with tears but with frustration. Shame, that awful, aching feeling of *almost*.

I rub my temple.

Reframe it, Cleo. Learn. Move. Next play.

But today? It still hurts.

I'm mid-scroll, eyes blurring as they scan over a proposal, when Megan pops her head into my office like she owns the place.

Megan glances at the snow globe on my desk and nudges it with one finger, sending another quiet storm swirling over Manhattan.

Her eyes gleam. "You know, you don't have to be perfect to

be powerful."

A half-laugh escapes before I rein it in. "Trust me, I once built a whole brand on pretense. Want to know how that ended?"

She snorts. "Want a Floriography reference?"

I roll my eyes.

"Maybe just a reminder that some things grow better once they're pruned."

I laugh out loud. "Huh! You and your flower language, always finding a way to sound poetic, even when I mess up."

"It's okay, darling. Flowers get to bloom again every year. They get do-overs without judgment."

I pause. She's right. I need a do-over.

"You only spiral when it counts, you know that?" She says it casually, but there's something in her eyes. Like she understands the stakes even when I pretend I don't. "It's not a flaw," she adds. "It's just you want things to mean something. That's not a bad thing. Just be kind to yourself."

I stare at the proposal on my computer screen. I've skated through pressure before. Judges, sponsors, lights. This is no different. Less glitter, more suits. Same expectations. Same tightrope between control and collapse.

I dab the corner of one eye before the mascara smudges, then blot the skin dry.

I feel a sharp sting behind my sockets. It creeps down my temples like a vise grip. The hum of the air conditioner has become too loud, the overhead lights too bright. Even the weight of my own thoughts exhausts me.

Some people burn out staring at spreadsheets. I burn out from analyzing people, from patterns and masks and tiny tells, and my brain never cools. It loops, it analyzes, it rewinds.

Tia says I'd rather face ten thousand raging suns than ask for help. Mom says it's a shame I sacrifice the creative parts of me on the altar of success. Whatever that means.

I exhale and close the file.

If I want different results, I need tighter execution.

I need to lead from the front.

My phone buzzes on the desk.

A calendar notification flashes across the screen.

Client Meeting: iSight Software.

3

Chapter 3: The Shark

Dillon

The ceiling fan slices the silence as I toss for hours. My brain won't quit. So, instead of wasting time, I run. When my brain runs fast, I run faster.

My feet hit the pavement in a steady pattern I've kept since college.

Running used to clear the static, but not today.

I pass a vendor cart being wheeled into place. This is New York City. You can always find someone awake at this unearthly hour.

A kid in a red puffer coat trails behind a woman juggling coffee cups and a stroller. Her shoelace drags behind her. She trips. I stop.

"Hey," I say, crouching before she can get up on her own. "Want help?"

She nods, cheeks pink from cold or embarrassment, maybe both.

"Double knot?" I ask.

She nods back.

The mother rushes over, flustered. She apologizes for the chaos of mornings.

"No worries. She's got solid survival instincts," I say.

The kid grins. "He talks weird. But he's fast."

They laugh and walk off toward the pier.

"The knot will hold," I think automatically. "At least until she runs again."

I watch them for a second. More than I should have.

Something tugs in my chest, and I don't have a name for it.

Not loneliness. Not envy. Just something I keep outrunning.

I shake it off. This city makes you sentimental if you stand still.

I run again, faster now. My feet pound the pavement. I'm short of breath. Normally this rhythm relaxes me, but it isn't working today.

The incline looms ahead. I push through the pain, my thighs, and lungs on fire. Pain is simple. It doesn't ask questions. It settles them.

I blink, struggling against a gust of wind that stings my eyes with beads of sweat.

Keep moving. No stopping.

Stopping means thinking.

Running is the closest thing I have to silence.

Thinking means spiraling again.

My company's hanging by a thread. Investors want guarantees. The team wants certainty. I have neither. Because the first time I didn't catch that in someone, it cost me everything. I didn't stumble into success. I built it, piece by piece. While other students partied, I coded all night and cold-emailed industry leaders until someone gave me the time of day.

My first startup wasn't flashy. Just practical.

A tool that read market trends in real time by watching tiny shifts in the industry. I launched it with two dorm mates, pitched it at the university's business competition, and landed a mentorship with a retired venture capitalist who pulled strings and opened the right doors. The sale was modest, but enough to prove I wasn't another kid with a far-fetched idea.

My father offered few details then. A monotone "congratulations" and a spreadsheet correction I didn't ask for. But months later, one investor mentioned how Robert Whelan had vouched for me.

The wind bites as I cut across the trail, data still looping behind my eyes. The event. The woman.

She flinched. The glasses noticed, though it was so subtle that most wouldn't have.

A fractional twitch in her left brow. Pupils dilating. Mouth tense before she masked it. Skepticism.

That's when I shifted and ditched the stats, softened my tone. Hit the emotional note. Let just enough imperfection through to sound real.

She blinked, brows eased, confirmation.

Maybe that's why I built it. Not to read *them*, but to protect *me*. My strengths lie in data, not emotions. Lucid Lenses does the thing I can't. It catches the wince before the lie. The tight smile before the fallout. The hesitation before the betrayal.

I didn't just win that pitch. I adjusted, recalibrated, and watched it land.

And the glasses worked. Mostly.

But her face was distinct. Harder to read.

She didn't blink when the room turned on her.

Cleo Ambrosia isn't like the others. That makes her dangerous.

I'll need to tweak the system to account for how people differ.

I round the bend too fast, almost clipping a guy walking his dog.

"Watch it, man!" he yells.

I look back and wave. I push harder. Sweat dripping down my shirt. The team thinks we're close. I know better—we're miles off. That last five percent? That last stretch is the gap between good and great.

I see it like a crack in glass, small, but fatal.

The vision isn't the hard part.

Convincing everyone else to see it is.

Twelve weeks, that's all we have.

I run harder, my breath coming in sharp bursts. My lungs burn from the frigid air.

They see headlines and clean branding. What they don't see is how close we are to folding. One bad demo, one misstep, and I'm another startup flame out with a glossy pitch deck.

If it crashes, I lose the only proof I ever mattered.

And I can't let that happen. There is too much riding on this. The product works ninety percent of the time. We're close, but not close enough. That margin of error could ruin us.

We have twelve weeks to get this perfect.

And we're already behind.

I let out a pent-up breath.

If we crash, I don't lose a product. I lose the proof.

The river fades behind me. Time to suit up.

There's a boardroom waiting. And a woman with eyes like

X-rays I can't stop thinking about.

* * *

The file slaps the table. Papers scatter. Let them feel it.

"The software failed," I say, voice sharp and flat. "We're out of time. Fix it."

No one moves. Sweat trickles down the UX engineer's forehead. He freezes whenever I look at him. It looks like he's melting into his chair.

Noah leans back like he's bracing for impact.

Silence fills the space. Tension strangles the air. Someone swallows.

They know what's at stake. They don't need me to spell it out.

I plant my palms on the table. The tension creeps up my arms, coils around my chest. If I don't keep myself grounded, I'll start pacing.

"The rim vibrated, subtle muscle tension. The system flagged doubt based on a micro expression. The glasses glitched during the scan. Froze. Error codes. Total shutdown." My jaw ticks. "No data, no way to reset the system. It took five slow minutes for them to come back online."

I breathe out.

Noah's eyes flick up. He knows I don't win like this, not without the tech.

Every morning, I wake up wondering if today's the day the illusion cracks.

"The investors are watching us like hawks. We have twelve weeks to get this working before FounderCon, the biggest startup showcase in the country. If we show up with a half-baked prototype, we're done." I shift my weight. "They'll pull their money, and we'll be another cautionary tale of a potential startup that choked."

Noah exhales through his nose, measured. "What triggered it?"

I push off the table and pace. "You tell me."

"Dillon." His voice is steady. "Take a breath. Tell us what went wrong so we can fix it."

Ringing cuts through the silence.

"Mr. Whelan." Cynthia's voice crackles through the conference speaker. "Abby from Calypso Consulting is on line one."

Of course, it's her. Right on schedule. I need Cleo Ambrosia working for me, not against me.

I pinch the bridge of my nose. "Put her through."

A crisp, professional voice. "Mr. Whelan?"

"Speaking."

"Hello, it's Abby, Miss Ambrosia's assistant from Calypso Consulting. She has an opening at noon tomorrow. Will that work for you?"

The consultant. The human lie detector.

I shift my weight, glancing at Noah. He's eyeing me. "Yeah. Send her to my office."

Noah folds his arms. "Wait. You brought her in now?"

I nod. "Cleo saw the glitch in real time. She's already asking questions we can't afford to ignore."

I want Cleo inside the system, not in my head.

His brows shoot up. "We agreed to bring her in after the next phase."

I rub my jaw. "Had to. The glitch at the event changed

everything."

"Yeah, well, now we're in crisis mode. And she will not play nice."

"I don't need nice." I retort.

"Good. Because what you need is someone to see past your God complex."

Around the table, no one speaks. Six pairs of eyes flick between us. A leather chair groans as someone shifts in their seat.

"Readings were accurate. Real-time feedback confirmed it. When I shifted tone, her skepticism dropped by seven percent. That's how I knew I had her. The glasses worked fine, until they didn't."

Noah scrutinizes me, raising an eyebrow.

I hesitate to keep talking, but I do. "She was different. Something didn't compute. The tech stopped, and maybe I did too."

Noah frowns. "Different, how?"

Something flickers within his gaze. Understanding. Possibly even recognition. Like he's been there too.

"Not just in how the tech reacted. In how I did." I rake a hand through my hair. The system had already processed all contestants before her. It recalibrated, read their reactions, and spit out the data. Then I got to her, and it stopped working."

Noah taps his pen on the table. "That was not supposed to happen. A two-second scan isn't enough to crash the system." He pauses. His gaze sharpens. "What if it wasn't her? What if it was reading *you*?"

I stop pacing. "What?"

"The tech doesn't just read faces, it tracks physical reactions too. Heart rate, body temperature, even stress signals."

I stare at him. "You're saying the sensors were reading me, and I was the glitch?"

Noah doesn't blink. "Yes. It's not just data, it's a mirror. She triggered something. But the system wasn't ready."

I let out a forceful breath. A lead weight settles behind my ribs.

I scoff. "I don't glitch."

Noah shrugs. "Wouldn't be the first time emotions messed up tech."

My pulse pounds. "This is exactly why I don't do emotions." I shake my head, then spin back to Noah. "And you didn't flag that in pre-check?" It comes out sharper than intended. "Do you realize if this had happened at FounderCon, we'd be out of funding?"

Noah blinks but doesn't back down. "I get it. I messed up. But that oversight gave us the key to fixing the problem. It won't happen again." He lets out his breath. "It was a controlled test. I forgot to shut off the sensors that track body heat and stress indicators. But honestly? This is a win. We caught the problem now, and not at FounderCon."

I clench my jaw. He's right. It gave us insight we didn't have.

He's got a point. But I'm still annoyed.

The biggest variable in the room wasn't the tech, it was *me*.

"No one leaves until we fix this," I say flatly. I point at Noah. "And yes, coffee breaks count."

Groans sound throughout the room.

Let them complain. Obsession builds legends.

Someone mutters, "Figures."

Another says, "This is why no one invites him to happy hour."

Noah smirks faintly but doesn't defend me. He never does. Not because he agrees, but because he thinks I need the feedback more than the comfort.

"Exactly."

I'm not here to be liked.

I'm here to win.

Period.

And tomorrow Cleo Ambrosia will be sitting across my desk.

The one person in the room who already knows where the cracks are.

4

Chapter 4: Unmasked

Cleo

Two nights ago, I was sipping mocktails and mocking elevator pitches. Today, Megan, my best friend and marketing manager, has me scheduled for a last-minute consult.

She said it was urgent and NDA-laced. The calendar invite said iSight, which usually means a tech founder trying to look mysterious.

The usual glass-and-steel tower flexes above Midtown, New York's unofficial temple to ambition.

The receptionist smiles like she hasn't had her caffeine yet, then points me toward a glass-walled boardroom gleaming with chrome and surgical precision.

Two men sit at the table. One in the center like it's a throne.

I can only see half of his face, but he looks composed. His fingers dig into the glass table a little too hard. Control must be his armor.

But then I see the jawline. The watch. The smirk half hidden

38

by concentration.

So it's him.

The Pitchathon. The mocktails.

Dillon Whelan.

I walked in expecting another puffed-up startup founder drowning in acronyms.

I did not expect Mr. Stealth Wealth and Smolder to be running the meeting.

For half a second, my breath hitches.

I blame surprise, not the inconvenient fact that he is distractingly put together.

Dillon sits at the head of the table like he owns the place.

Because, of course, he does.

His Daniel Wellington peeks from a crisp cuff, understated but intentional. Everything about him hums with the kind of confidence you can't fake and wouldn't dare challenge.

Dillon doesn't flinch when I walk in. No blink of surprise. Just quiet satisfaction. Like he got exactly what he asked for.

So the calendar notification wasn't just logistics.

He asked for me.

The other guy in the room stands and offers a hand. "Noah Carter, co-founder of iSight. And this is Dillon Whelan, CEO and co-founder."

Dillon slowly stands and reaches for my hand. But his eyes? They're saying he remembers. I feel a chilling déjà vu as our hands touch.

A jolt shoots up my arm. His skin is warm, and his grip is confident but not too tight. I file it under irrelevant and move on.

This is a job. I've walked into higher-stakes rooms with cooler heads. I'm not rattled, I'm just under-caffeinated.

"Static," I lie, pretending I didn't just feel whatever that was. I notice how he subtly rubs his thumb. Did he feel it too?

His gaze flicks to my mouth, intentional. A classic non-verbal play designed to spark a reaction. Textbook tight jaw, subtle shoulder tension. Stress cues under the surface of that too-casual lean. Most people wouldn't catch it but I do.

That does not make me immune. Just aware.

"Thanks for joining us," he says. "Appreciate your time."

As soon as I'm seated, Dillon leans back and launches into his pitch. "Our tech startup is like the cool kid of the business world."

There's a slight hiccup in his voice when he glances at me, like he's testing for a spark and clocking the results.

"Like any other tech company," he goes on, "we want to create and monetize a novel idea quickly. But I'm not your standard-issue CEO."

I've seen this pitch before. It comes with a demo and delusions of grandeur. He's reciting buzzwords like they're Shakespeare.

"Others chase growth for investors. I'm here to change how people think—literally."

He's not selling a product. He's selling a revolution, with himself as its leader.

Wow, he even brought notes to explain startups. Cute.

Dillon keeps going.

His voice is smooth, too smooth. He's performing. "We're designed to scale quickly," he says. "Start small, test a basic version of the product, the MVP, and iterate fast."

I nod slowly with an arched brow, letting him finish. He doesn't notice. Or maybe he assumes I've never heard the term before. Classic.

Noah winces like I've insulted his baby. But Dillon? Totally unfazed. The man has built-in emotional noise-canceling headphones. There it is, a flicker of real amusement before the mask settles back in place.

"We use technology, like the cloud, to handle sudden user growth without crashing. We challenge industry norms and rewrite the rules."

"It's like a lie detector and intuition booster rolled into one," Noah inserts.

I don't need a lie detector. I carry one in my head, calibrated by survival, sharpened by behavioral science and Bureau-grade training. Truth leaks through the pauses.

Dillon offers a half smile, like this is a mic-drop moment. His confident image, holding the golden brain trophy, is seared into my memory. I log it, just like I used to do in the field.

A mental pattern sheet: rigid posture, evasive eyes, a smile too symmetrical.

Something is off. He is saying the right things, but the tension in his jaw does not match the script.

He leans forward, elbows on the table. Not aggressive, not relaxed, then charges back into his pitch without missing a beat. "What separates me from the vanilla CEOs is a scalable infrastructure. That's the backbone of our business."

I bite my lower lip. This is his shield, and I'm dying to see what happens when it dents.

"Fascinating." My voice carries polite boredom.

"People call it emotional intelligence. But what I do is closer to forensic empathy. Less about feelings, more about patterns. Truth disguised as instinct."

The tech is impressive, cold, and calculated, a mirror of him.

But every now and then, a flash too fast to catch makes me wonder what else he's hiding.

Noah whispers something to Dillon. Dillon looks up, wide-eyed. "My apologies, Miss Ambrosia. You must be wondering why we asked you here."

"I'm guessing a lesson in startups isn't the reason, so let's skip the sales pitch," I say.

He raises an eyebrow, smiles, and steeples his fingers. He's baiting me, testing if I'll crack first. The impeccable hair and Armani suit don't fool me. Neither do his controlled mannerisms. Sitting all nonchalant but crisp as cashmere that went through the drier.

I mirror his posture, chin lifted. The skater ballerina in me knows how to hold a pose.

And there you have it, folks, a standoff.

If Siri wore Armani, she'd be this guy.

He didn't just remember me.

He recruited me.

Game on.

"We need your expertise for a top-secret project," Noah says. "Your track record in human behavior analysis speaks for itself. Your work with executive emotional strategy has come highly recommended."

Oh, so they did their homework. But I've heard this kind of spiel before. If I had a dollar for every time someone lured me with "top secret" and "game-changing," I'd be rich.

I'm curious what those eyes are not saying. Tilting my head, I say, "Interesting. But I still don't get why you need me."

Dillon keeps his eyes locked on me. "Like he said, it's top secret."

My patience barometer flatlines. I've heard this kind of

vague, ego-stroking pitch before.

I push away from the table and stand. "Sorry, gentlemen. Secret-mission vibes sound fun, but I'm out."

I turn to head for the door.

Noah rushes toward me. "Wait! Please let me explain."

Dillon stands, looking surprised. "Miss Ambrosia, please. I have a lucrative proposition for you."

Rolling my eyes, I place my hands on my hips. "Three minutes. That's all."

Noah looks between us, then diffuses the tension by sliding a folder toward each of us. "We need help fine-tuning the software," he explains. "Without an NDA, we can't disclose the exact details. Your background makes you ideally qualified."

My pulse spikes and my stomach flips. I hate the reaction.

"What you did at the Pitchathon impressed me," Dillon adds.

My eyes flick to Dillon. He was paying attention; he just hid it well.

I look between them, egging them to go on.

Dillon shoves his hands into his pockets. "Noah, show her."

We resume our seats.

Noah opens his laptop and turns the screen to face me. When the short video ends, I say, "So, tell me what you're *not* saying."

Noah says, "Lucid Lenses processes emotional data in real time, loops the feedback, and learns as the wearer interacts with the software."

Dillon stands, the glasses glinting between his fingers. "Lucid Lenses is like a truth translator for your face."

My stomach flips. He was wearing them at the Pitchathon. That's why his reads were so perfect. He was analyzing me, not just sparring. And that's cheating. It wasn't instinct, it was tech!

"Most people think they're good at reading emotions," he continues, "but they miss the micromoments. Our glasses pick up those tells and translate them into real-time emotional feedback."

"So, you made X-ray glasses for feelings?" I say. My pulse is betraying me. Of course, it is.

Maybe it's the room, the pressure, the million-dollar stakes. Not him, surely?

"Think of it like this: if traditional body language is a blurry mirror, Lucid Lenses is 4K emotional clarity. Whether you're pitching an investor, de-escalating a tense conversation, or helping a child with autism navigate social cues, it gives insight into what's really going on beneath the surface."

I glance at Noah wriggling in his chair.

"This," Dillon says, sliding the sleek frames onto his face, "is what separates us from every emotion-reading algorithm on the market." He turns to Noah. "Ready?"

Noah half grins. "Hit me."

Dillon taps the side of the glasses. A faint blink of light, then his voice sharpens. "You said you're relaxed. But your left brow twitched a millimeter, indicating masked discomfort. You forced an asymmetric smile. Stress response. And the pitch of your last word rose by two hertz. Subconscious defense."

Noah rolls his eyes. "Fine. So, I'm a little tense."

Dillon looks at me. "Lucid Lenses can't decode full thoughts. But they catch what the conscious mind hides."

"And their weakness?" I ask, crossing my arms.

"Highly trained individuals like actors, sociopaths, and professional liars know how to mask."

I watch the frames glint in his hands. A sleek weapon of perception and power.

"So, it's like built-in AI with face recognition?" I clarify.

"Precisely. The applications cross industries and markets. We provide the software and build the brain, while others build the body."

"So, you have the potential to expand exponentially in simultaneous markets without doing much else. Do you plan to license the software?"

Both men nod.

"If this software is so intuitive, why do you need me?"

Noah points to the printout. "Right now, the software struggles to accurately match emotions to expressions. According to this data, it still struggles to match expression to emotion with consistent accuracy. We've heard that is your signature expertise."

"We need you to show us how to better integrate human responses without waiting a year for engineers to close the gap," Dillon inserts.

I look between the two men. "Okay, I get it now."

I pause, measuring their responses. I clock anticipation and hope.

I cross my legs too fast and knock my knee against the underside of the glass table.

Smooth, Cleo. Real smooth.

"I'll give you three months. If we don't get it up and running by then, I walk. But I get the full payout no matter the outcome. Agreed?"

I hate how much I want Dillon to say yes. It's not about the deal; I've walked away from better. But something in me wants to outmaneuver him. Or unravel him.

I should look away. Say something. Break the moment. But I do not. My mouth forgets how to move, and that annoys me.

Dillon tilts his head and smiles. "What number would make this worth your time?"

I consider his question. I'll admit, it's fascinating tech. Useful in boardrooms, interrogations, and probably even therapy sessions. But it's not foolproof yet, and it takes more than gadgets to read a room the way he did at the Pitchathon. That took instinct. Not tech.

I study him. I want to see what he thinks I'm worth. Not the rate, the signal.

That'll tell me more than any number of zeros on a check ever could.

I mirror his body language and smile back. "Assuming you plan on an IPO, what is your current valuation?"

His gaze holds mine, steady. Too steady.

Dillon says, "We've raised $30 million at a $100 million valuation. Once the product is viable, that valuation moves toward $1 billion. Good enough for you?"

He's a smug CEO with a billion-dollar ego.

"So, if the product doesn't work, your billion goes to zero?"

His smile falters for a split second. "Correct. But with you involved, we increase our chances and probability."

"What is my expertise worth to you?" I say, locking eyes with him.

"We're prepared to pay you $250k for a quick turnaround."
Is he for real?

I know my value. And $250k is pocket change. Especially for a guy whose shoes probably cost more than my monthly rent.

That's the kind of number you toss at someone who you think is desperate. I'm not. And even if I were, I wouldn't show it.

I scoff. "That's what you offer someone you assume needs a job."

Both men look at me, perplexed.

"One million for three months is fair," I counter. "Half at signing, plus 1% equity."

Dillon tries to hide it, but there's the faintest tick in his jaw when I mention equity. Not annoyance, but something else. Intrigue, maybe?

"That's a steep price for theory," Dillon says. "The 1% equity alone is an additional ten million. What's your ROI?"

"Sounds like you have some expensive glasses," I say. "Eleven million out of a billion doesn't sound unreasonable, does it? Without my help, they could be worthless."

He leans back, but his fingers drum once on the table before he stills them, a weakness he didn't mean to reveal. "Sure, if we get to a billion, it's no problem."

"If I give you the missing 5%. That's a bargain at 1%, right?"

"Let's talk first about the retainer. How about $500k for three months?" He looks at me like he's trying to solve something.

Not the pitch, me.

"No."

"You're not paying for three months."

"You're paying to skip three years of mistakes."

I let the silence hang.

When our eyes lock, Dillon holds my gaze a second too long.

Not in challenge. In curiosity.

"Let's shake on a million." I extend my hand.

Dillon doesn't move at first. His fingers tap once on the table. He's calculating valuation, timeline, and risk.

"That's a steep ask," he says, voice neutral. "How about 750k?"

I tilt my head. "You're not buying my time. You're shortcutting your way past a minefield."

He holds my gaze. "And if we don't hit the target?"

"You still pay. That's how consulting works. I don't offer refunds on insight."

Behind the frost, I'm annoyed. Not by the stakes. By him.

Noah coughs lightly. "Dillon, she's right. We've already spent that much time chasing the wrong metrics."

A beat. Then Dillon sighs and finally stands. He takes my hand. "One million. But I want results fast."

I flash the kind of smile that says *checkmate*. But my palms are still warm.

"It's a million," I say. "Plus equity."

He shakes my hand, firm and steady. That's confirmation enough.

***

Sitting in my car, I open our company group text messages to see what drama I missed this morning:

Megan: Riverstone execs canceled again. Citing 'momentum fatigue.'

I sigh and roll my eyes.

Cleo: Translation: They're afraid we'll call out their CEO's man tantrums.

Megan: Pretty much. Also, medical startup wants another

round of onboarding interviews.

Cleo: But we just delivered a full report.

Megan: Yes, but they want it with more "emotional alignment." Whatever that means.

Cleo:

Megan: You okay? You sound extra dry.

Cleo: Just spent an hour sitting through an explanation of facial recognition tech like it's a TED Talk for toddlers.

Megan: Mansplained again?

Cleo: With graphs.

Megan: Yikes! I know you're anti-VC-funded scaling, hun, but please think about it.

Cleo: Won't be a cog in someone else's machine. Not giving up control over ethics. #Sorrynotsorry.

The truth is, I hate what this tech could become in the wrong hands. If I'm on the inside, I can steer it. Maybe even challenge Dillon in ways no one else will.

Megan: Let's figure something out. I'm sending backup espresso. Or wine.

Megan: You're like a skater in stilettos. All grace and precision on the surface, but I know you're gripping for balance underneath.

I laugh, but it catches in my throat. She's not wrong.

Years of muscle memory make it look easy, even when I'm falling apart.

Cleo: Bless you. Back in a few.

My phone pings. Emojis light up the screen. It's a text from my sister. Her timing is impeccable.

Tia: I want DEETS.

Cleo: Met the client. Infuriating. Smug. Good to look at, but I'm debating homicide. Also, my pulse is still recovering.

Probably the caffeine. Probably.

Her reply pops up instantly, complete with a cartoon blinking hearts GIF.

Tia: Oooh, you're rattled. Is he cute? But what did he *say*? I need DETAILS.

Cleo: Tough shell, glossy finish, probably has daddy issues. Cracking in progress. Updates pending.

Tia: Meme of a melting Barbie under a sunlamp with the caption "British Summer, 2022 Edition"

I snort out loud. Trust my sister to always bring a smile to my face.

Our summer in London included the hottest day on record, the tarmac actually melting from the heat. Tia was convinced we'd become human popsicles on the sidewalk.

I'd forgotten how much we laughed on that trip, before our lives got so heavy. That week was ridiculous. And perfect. My people.

Cleo: Still hotter than this pitch meeting #neverforget.

Tia: Barely. Remember the Tube that day? We all emerged like croissant dough.

My smile lingers. Okay, maybe I can survive today.

Tia: This is going to be SWEET! I'll bring the power tools. Luv ya loads. TTFN. Mwah!

I lean my head back into the car seat, close my eyes, and exhale.

The next meeting with Dillon will either be worse or interesting.

After exiting the car, I roll my shoulders back and adjust my blazer.

I walk in like I own the building.

Because today, I need to.

5

Chapter 5: Ladies Who Lunch

Cleo

Late afternoon light spills across Midtown in sheets of gold, catching on taxi roofs and the glass fronts of every building trying to look richer than it is.

My favorite Greek restaurant, Avra, is the best place to reset. The grilled lemon and oregano hit me the moment I step inside, and my stomach rumbles. The low hum of conversation blends with the clink of cutlery and the soft swish of waiters in black aprons gliding between tables. A flash of silver trays, the faint scent of garlic butter, and cool marble floors polished to a shine.

I shrug off my coat and place it on the back of my chair.

Megan looks up from her phone. "So, Cleo, my love, how did it go?"

"Let's just say the tech's smarter than it looks, the paycheck made me blink, and the CEO is equal parts irritating and distracting. But the deal? Strategic. It opens doors I never thought we could knock on."

"Well, somebody's ready to set things on fire," Tia, my sister, teases.

"I heard the CEO crowd didn't handle being emotionally X-rayed." Megan hands me a glass of water.

I sigh. "It went poorly. One client ghosted us after a media leak. His idea of conflict resolution was waiting for the internet to forget."

Tia winces. "Oof. Did you read his soul too fast?"

"Calypso was brought in for reputation strategy. He expected a PR spin. I gave him a mirror."

Megan chuckles. "Let me guess, he didn't like the reflection."

"He didn't like that it wasn't centered on him."

"This contract vaults us into the right rooms. So, if decoding a walking ego trip gets us there? I'll bring the popcorn."

Megan sets her phone down with a sigh and a secretive little smile.

"You're grinning," I note with suspicion.

"I am not."

"You totally are. Spill."

She shrugs, the action too casual. "Just my favorite Reddit pen pal being clever again. He sent a meme about tech bros trying to explain emotional labor using pizza charts."

Tia perks up. "Ooh, the crush strikes again!"

"It's not a crush," Megan says. "It's witty professional banter."

"With emojis," I deadpan.

Megan tries to look unaffected but fails.

"You're practically in a digi-relationship," Tia teases. "One emoji away from eloping via encrypted chat."

Megan rolls her eyes but can't stop her cheeks from flushing. "Anyway. Another VC-backed firm just slid into my inbox asking if we can guarantee their next round will close faster with better EQ."

I arch a brow. "Let me guess, they want a 'soft skill' discount?"

"Naturally. Because reshaping toxic leadership patterns isn't real work."

We share a look. We've had this conversation before.

"We're not failing," I say quietly. "We're just ahead of the curve."

Megan nods. "Then we better make sure the curve bends our way. Fast."

Tia claps her hands. "You two have so much fun at work!"

Megan and I exchange knowing glances.

"Sooo how was Mr. Armani Ego?" Tia asks.

I blink, caught off guard. "You've been stalking my calendar again, haven't you?"

"Puh-lease. Megan spilled. Now dish the deets."

Of course she did. My best friend and my sister are co-hosts of a gossip podcast I never agreed to be featured on.

"Tough nut," I mutter, situating my napkin on my lap.

Megan looks between the two of us. "I'm looking forward to this."

"He's good," I admit. "Too good. I hate that I noticed. Usually, I read people in seconds. But this guy? He threw off my timing. That never happens."

Tia squeals. "So you like him."

"I said he's good. Not *that* good."

Megan leans in. "It must be major if we're celebrating at Avra. You only order lobster when you've crushed someone's soul or secured a seven-figure deal."

"Why not both?" I deadpan. "Add prawns. We're going full

seafood domination."

We laugh. For a minute, I let myself enjoy it. The sound, the company, the feeling of being seen but not judged.

We order our drinks, and Tia and I head over to the fresh buffet. The chef asks how we like our lobster cooked. In unison, we say, "With lots of lemon!" Giggling, we head back to our table.

Megan swirls her wine glass. "So, globe-trotter, when do you fly out?"

"Before the sun's up," Tia groans. "Hotel at Fifth Avenue tonight. Client's paying, so I'm milking it."

"Dessert at Grace Street Café?" Megan asks.

"Obviously. I need my Korean shaved snow fix before I escape this concrete jungle." Tia waves dramatically.

"Sure, let's walk off our lobster as we check out Koreatown."

I reach for the bottle of wine, pouring with a practiced hand. "Spill. What mysterious luxury gig has my sister excited now?"

"Took them a hot minute, but I'll hear about my six-week Europe stint soon. They're finding a filmmaker to go with me. Since the client is paying the big bucks for a multi-product endorsement deal, they want someone legit. Anyway, I've been bored, so I've been moonlighting doing a few gigs for the rich and infamous," Tia explains, sipping her wine.

"Ooh, you're going to meet someone mysterious and brooding in a bookshop," I say.

"If he brings you peonies, you're in for a romance. They symbolize romance, happy marriage, honor, and prosperity," says Megan.

"Wait, is that another flower thing?" Tia asks. "What if he brings lavender?

She leans closer. "Then you have a keeper. Lavender means

purity, calmness, devotion, and serenity. I'd marry him."

"I have layers. Like a peony. Soft. Abundant. Dangerously dramatic," says Tia.

"That's fitting! I know this one. Tulips mean love, affection, and fame. We all know that is right up your alley, T," I say with a laugh.

"Ooh, do tell. I'm on the edge of my seat!" Megan says, leaning forward with anticipation.

"Can't drop names, NDAs and all that jazz, but let's just say one client hired me to tone down his looks. Imagine a Tony Stark situation with too much hotness."

Megan giggles. "So, you gave a billionaire a budget glow-down?"

I shake my head. "Only you could turn de-glamorizing the rich and famous into a thriving side hustle. But I get it. Here in the city, everyone has secrets. They will pay top dollar not to let them out of the bag."

"Exactly," Tia teases. "When this gig's over, I'm introducing you to Faux Tony. He's charming and single."

I groan. "Please don't. Dating's like Russian roulette with more lip gloss. And I'm out of emotional ammo."

"Cleo, you never give anyone a chance!" Tia huffs.

"Last time you 'introduced' me to someone, I ended up blocking him on three different apps."

"Not all men are gamblers or womanizers. Don't close your heart to the possibility of love." Tia gives me a warm smile.

"I can read people faster than they can finish a cocktail. And half of them lie before dessert anyway. Back at Quantico, we call that deception drift," I mutter, raising my glass. "The longer someone talks, the more their truth slides sideways."

I used to believe I could separate heart from instinct. Then a certain colleague proved me wrong with charm, secrets, and a burner phone that nearly blew open an entire case. It never made the press, thank heaven for sealed records, but it made a mess of me. Since then, I read fast, decide faster, and keep my walls up.

Tia makes kissy noises. "Girl, your heart's not a fortress. It's solitary confinement."

Megan nods. "You spend all your energy protecting yourself. But who's protecting you?"

Tia tsks. "Bitterness doesn't attract bees, babe. You want a catch? Try honey, not vinegar." She throws her hands up. "And you are a catch, so stop downplaying it. This whole 'tough chic' ruse and armor of yours is getting old. You know I love you to bits, but it's exhausting!"

I rest my chin on my hands, elbows on the table, and let out a long sigh. I haven't stopped thinking about the way Dillon said my name.

Ew. I should never say that sentence aloud.

"You can't keep punishing the next guy for what the last one did," Tia says gently.

"Yes, Captain Obvious. I hear you. You constantly play matchmaker, even when you're uninvited. But this party animal prefers to stay home and watch K-dramas in my comfy PJs. It's far less risky than putting my heart out on display. Thanks, but no thanks."

"Uh-huh. You wear that ice queen mask so well, people forget there's a person underneath."

"Exactly," I whisper.

"I'm not giving up on this, and you know it!" Tia points her index finger at me like she's aiming a pistol.

Megan reaches over and squeezes my hand. "Love's not a

liability, Cleo. It's the one thing you don't have to control."

"What she said!" Tia echoes. She snaps her fingers. "Wait. I know what you need. A break. Switch off that busy brain of yours."

"You know she's right," Megan says. "You've been working non-stop and deserve a break."

"Forget about a break. Tell me more about this messy client," I say, pleading with Megan with wide eyes to change the subject.

Megan takes the cue. "Now that you've landed iSight, we need to map the engagement before Dillon turns this into a pressure cooker."

"Ooh, biometric software. One of the brands I'm partnering with plays in that space," Tia says.

"What's the messy part?" I say, waiting for the punchline.

Megan grimaces. "He burned through three consultants last year. He's got quite the reputation."

I blink. "I can deal with that kind of messy."

I grab my phone and start outlining the next move.

"Can you slow down for, like, two seconds?" Tia says, clearly annoyed.

"Nope."

Megan squints at my phone screen. "Cleo, we haven't even finished step one and you're already on step five?"

"Seven."

Megan groans. "You know most people process information at a normal speed, right?"

I slap my phone on the table. "And that's why most people are still stuck at step one."

Megan shakes her head. "One of these days, you're going to burn out," she says with more concern than judgment.

I glance up. "One day, you'll trust that I understand my own boundaries."

She frowns. "You don't have to push all the time."

Just in the nick of time, a sizzling platter arrives, steam curling with lemon and thyme. The shell cracks under my fork, releasing that briny, buttery aroma. For a fleeting second, it all feels justified, every risk, every red flag, every skipped lunch.

The waiter sets down our coffee, a delicate leaf poured into the foam. Megan turns the cup slowly, studying the latte art like she always does.

Tia and Megan's chatter washes over me, and I laugh too loud at something ridiculous. I feel full for the first time in weeks, and it's not just from the lobster. The seafood, the sass, the shared history.

No masks, no reads, no negotiations. Just girls, and garlic, and gratitude.

This is my happy place, where I remember what safe feels like.

6

Chapter 6: The Boardroom

Dillon

Bryant Park buzzes as steam rises from grates. Taxi horns slice through midtown noise. New York doesn't bite. It cuts. The weak fold. The smart adapt and keep moving. You don't bet on luck. You plan the view, then make the skyline prove you right.

The elevator opens to my office with a ding, revealing forty feet of glass and chrome. Hudson to the west and the Empire State to the east. The skyline frames everything because I planned it that way.

I set the Golden Brain next to my MIT diploma. A flicker of satisfaction passes, but I don't linger. In this industry, momentum is everything. Stop moving, and you're obsolete.

I check my watch. Cleo Ambrosia is due any minute. Emotional intel specialist. A smart move bringing her in, at least on paper. Let's see what kind of edge she brings.

She's late. I straighten my cuffs and refocus.

Then I hear her.

Heels click across the floor, her pace confident, unhurried, deliberate. She walks in like she belongs here, eyes bright, lipstick bold, blouse sharp enough to pass for armor.

Cleo Ambrosia, the human lie detector.

"Nice view," she says, glancing out the window, then straight at me. The same razor-edged aura as before.

I don't smile. "You're late."

She places her notebook on my desk like she's used to taking over other people's turf. "I'm on time. You're early. You strike me as someone who hates being kept waiting. Noted."

"You're profiling me."

She leans against the glass table. "I'm a professional profiler. It's my job to judge you." She crosses her arms. "I'm not here to unpack your childhood or make your staff cry in a trust circle. I'm here to observe your leadership team and help you integrate real human behavior into your system."

I bristle. "My system doesn't need therapy. Neither do I."

"No, maybe not," she says, flipping her notebook open. "But your leadership team might."

I straighten slowly, buying myself a second.

Most people unravel under pressure, but she seems to thrive on it.

"Mr. Pitch Perfect turned CEO," she says, goading. She glances at the Golden Brain trophy sitting on the mantel. "I guess it takes more than an MIT degree to outsmart a computer?"

Her gaze tracks mine, not flirtatious but clinical, like she's logging patterns she hasn't named yet.

"I'd say you like provoking arguments." I reach for my iPad.

"I appreciate the confidence, Mr. Whelan. But I'm here to

work with you. Not against you."

"Let me guess," I say. "You think we're emotionally stunted and that our communication breakdowns are sabotaging performance."

She shrugs. "More or less. Or maybe I just think you've gotten too good at pretending emotions don't matter because data is easier to control."

My jaw tightens. "Relax. I will not coddle anyone. Especially not you."

She stares a beat too long. Cool, amused. Like she already has me pegged.

I turn toward the window. "We start in five minutes."

"Perfect," she says breezily. "Just don't flinch when I speak the truth."

***

Cleo Ambrosia stands across from me in the conference room. Her arms folded, that signature glint in her eye. She wears chaos like perfume and speaks fluent interruption. She's already made herself at home. Notebook open, questions locked and loaded.

We've made it through the first thirty minutes of the onboarding session, and it already feels like a cross-examination. Cleo is quiet but not passive, scanning for flaws we haven't said out loud.

There are six of us around the glass table: me, Cleo, Noah, Jemima from ops, an engineer from the dev team, and Sarah, our analytics lead. No one speaks except for Cleo, of course.

Noah hooks up his laptop and projects it onto the sleek, oversized touchscreen at the front of the room. The lights dim.

Putting on the glasses, I adjust the frame and tap twice on the right earpiece. Everyone watches as the real-time interface feedback lights up.

Jemima, Noah's assistant, steps into the frame. "Scan complete: Green ring, open posture, normal."

The engineer in the corner murmurs.

I turn to look at him. "Scan complete. The red indicator shows elevated stress. Defensive body language. Signs of discomfort, a twitch in his lip and a blinking rhythm slightly off."

I smile. "Watch this."

A yellow flicker replaces the red ring. The readout pops up in the right corner of the glasses: elevated stress, defensive posture, concealing disagreement.

Confidently, I say, "The lenses don't guess. They reveal what you want to hide."

I click to the next slide. Lucid Lenses pulses across the screen in minimalist font, clean and confident like the product itself.

"We're targeting early adopters, top-tier sales teams, investor pitch rooms, and negotiation trainers. Basically, anyone who's willing to pay for an edge."

I notice her eyes flick to the budget slides, my weakest section. I didn't fudge the numbers, just glossed them over. It's fine. People don't invest in decimal points. They invest in vision.

She taps her pen, frowns slightly. Of course, she notices.

I scan the room. Most faces are nodding. Curious. Calculating. One face differs.

Cleo tilts her head. "An edge or an unfair advantage?"

The question slices through the room. I pause. She doesn't blink.

"You said 'interpret user intent,'" she adds. "You're teaching a machine to guess someone's motive based on their face. Do you know how facial cues can be misread across different cultures?"

I try not to react. "The model's adaptive. It learns."

"That's not the same as understanding people," she counters. She leans forward. "What happens when someone's autistic? Or from a culture where maintaining eye contact is disrespectful? Or they just had Botox?"

I frown. "So you're saying it won't work?"

"I'm saying it *will* work," she says, voice low. "That's the problem."

My breath hitches. She's not just testing the product. She's testing *me*.

This challenge reminds me of my father. He built empires out of spreadsheets and skepticism. We haven't spoken in six months. His choice, not mine. After I turned down his offer to fund iSight in favor of scrappy angel investors, he'd said, "Fine. Let's see if you can build without my backing."

"You want to read people," she says softly, "but you're forgetting that people aren't formulas. They're stories. And if you're not careful, your tech won't just misread them, it'll rewrite them."

I built a system to control risk. She flagged the risk in me instead.

The room goes quiet.

I exhale. Then, surprising even myself, I smile. "That's why we need you."

She raises a brow. "To fix your ethical dilemma?"

"No," I say, holding her gaze. "To make sure we don't build something smart that ends up stupid."

She gives me a look. It's not one of approval, but something softer. Smarter. Her mouth curves before she catches it.

Okay. She might have figured me out. But that doesn't mean I'm backing down. She came to test the system.

"The tech's solid," Noah inserts. "But it's the application that gets tricky."

I fold my arms. "Clarity matters when the stakes are high."

She doesn't back off. "You say clarity. I say control."

"It's not about controlling people. It's about reducing uncertainty fast enough to act," I say.

Noah lifts both brows. "I say let's not start World War Three in the first hour."

I shoot him a look. That wasn't a joke. He's supposed to back me, especially in front of outsiders. If he had doubts, we should've hashed them out in private.

"What you're describing is misuse," I say. "That's not our intention."

"Your intentions may be good," Cleo says, flipping a page. "But this tool could easily be misused. That's what I'm here to assess. How your team's culture handles ethical ambiguity."

"We're a strategic and measured team."

She exhales like she's amused but doesn't want to admit it. "So far, I've seen an overworked assistant, a partner who braces himself for conflict, a finance exec who can't make eye contact, and a junior dev team that flinches every time you walk by."

Noah coughs into his mug of coffee.

I stay still.

"They're efficient," I reply coolly.

"They're afraid," she says, just as coolly.

There's a painful pause.

"You're here to improve performance, not teach empathy," I say, breaking the silence.

Her expression doesn't falter.

"I don't pitch unless it's worth the emotional bandwidth," she says, calm but direct. "Most companies don't want mirrors. They want applause." She glances at the demo, then at Noah. "And how's your retention rate in R&D?"

He winces. "We've had some turnover in R&D."

She nods. "What you've built might show more than your backers are ready to face."

I say nothing.

She lets the pause stretch, then finishes with this: "The way people communicate *is* performance. Especially when no one's watching."

My jaw ticks. "We don't micromanage, we set expectations and expect results."

Cleo nods. "Innovation needs trust. Micromanagement kills it. They're performing, but are they thriving?"

We're quiet again.

She closes the notebook slowly with a deliberate pause. "You built something brilliant," she says softly, finally meeting my gaze with something other than a challenge.

For a second, I hate how right she is. No one in this room saw that flaw. Not even me.

I notice the faint citrus note of her perfume before I remember we're supposed to be arguing.

My curiosity brews.

"Brilliance without boundaries is chaotic. Control without trust?" She shrugs. "It's dangerous."

I tighten my fists. Dangerous is manageable.

"You're not under attack," Cleo says gently. "You're under pressure. And your team knows it. They're looking to you for regulation, not a volatile reaction."

I don't respond because she's too close to something I have let no one name. Something in my chest tightens.

"We brought you in for this reason. You flagged blind spots. We're listening."

"Are you?" she asks, voice calm. "Because from where I'm sitting, it sounds like you want emotional intelligence that doesn't ask uncomfortable questions."

Her words hang in the air like smoke.

I glance at Noah. He meets my gaze, then looks away. That's when I know. He's not with me on this, not fully.

I shift my gaze back to Cleo. Her expression is unreadable now. I can't tell, and that bothers me more than it should.

Noah clears his throat.

"Why don't I give Cleo a full walk through of the dev floor and let you both cool off."

"No," I say. "I'll do it."

Cleo raises a brow. "You sure? I wouldn't want to risk disrupting the flow."

I level her with a look. "Don't psychoanalyze anyone in the hallway."

She grins. "No promises."

I gesture toward the glass doors. "Let's start with R&D in five minutes."

Jemima glances at the wall clock. "You two sure you want a tour this late? Most of us are heading out."

I shrug. "R&D doesn't sleep. Neither do I."

With that, my team leaves the room. The air feels different

now. Like Cleo rocked something beneath the surface. And now everyone's pretending not to feel the aftershock.

***

Noah lingers and waits for the door to click shut. He checks his phone absently, thumb hovering like he's expecting something. A half-smile tugs at his mouth, then vanishes. He pockets the device.

"She's not wrong," he says.

I stiffen. "We're making progress. You saw the pitch response."

"That's not what I mean." He rests a hand on the back of a chair.

I cross my arms. "So now you think it's unethical?"

"I think it's powerful," he says carefully. "Which means it can be misused. And you know what happens when we don't build in safety brakes."

"You think I haven't thought about that?"

"I think you're too used to being the smartest guy in the room to admit when someone else sees more than you do."

I scoff. "Are you saying Cleo does?"

He doesn't answer right away. Just walks to the window, looks out over the skyline. "She sees you. That's why you're reacting like this."

That lands harder than it should. Noah reads silence better than most people read words.

"Careful, Noah," I say, trying to keep the edge out of my voice. "You sound like one of her case studies."

He turns back to me, unfazed. "Maybe that's what we need."

A long beat passes between us.

67

"Do you think she'll walk?" I ask.

"I think she'll stay if you let her challenge you," Noah replies. "She makes this whole thing uncomfortable. But maybe that's the point."

I replay Cleo's words. Not the ones the team heard, the ones she didn't need to say out loud. I was the target. And she didn't miss.

The glasses flagged her as confident, neutral, and non-threatening. But I saw something different. A quiet certainty. Unfiltered conviction. And the one variable I hadn't accounted for.

Behind me, Noah stays by the window a beat longer. His reflection lingers, half lit, half shadow. Always watching, always weighing. He doesn't say goodbye. Just looks at me with a knowing smile, and I see the mischief in his eyes.

Cleo taps on the glass door, breaking my focus, gesturing to the R&D department. I nod and walk out. She falls into step beside me without asking.

If she's here to poke holes in my system, she'll have to understand it first.

But she's not just here for the software.

She wants to decode the man behind it.

I'm curious to learn more about what makes her tick.

She wants in.

And I don't know if I want to stop her.

7

Chapter 7: Locked In

Cleo

The office is quieter than it was an hour ago. The lights are dimmed, and most of the desks are cleared. Only the hum of machines and the echo of my heels on the concrete remain. After hours always strips a place of its polish.

"Is that where the magic happens?" I ask.

"Not quite," Dillon answers. "The real magic's downstairs in the basement."

We step inside the elevator. The hush is the kind only overachievers and server banks recognize. Before we exit, Dillon swipes his security clearance card, and the doors open.

"I thought you'd like a private tour without the distractions."

Blinking lights greet us, and the hum of servers lines up like soldiers. The space feels part boot camp and part lie detector.

"Interesting place," I say. "Smells like shoe boxes and metal."

He grunts. "Yeah, it's not the most pleasant aroma. The servers stay cold to avoid overheating."

"So why is this your magic room?" I ask, nose scrunched.

"It's where we process data at lightning speed and spit out spot-on results. Noah used to sneak in just to drop a dad joke or fake a breach to see if I'd flinch."

"Like a *Star Wars* thing, only insiders get it?"

"Exactly. But don't get Noah started. He'll trap you with Yoda impressions and a monologue about Jedi leadership theory."

"Noted. Avoid *Star Wars*."

He gestures to a *smorgasbord* of buttons, lights, and beeps. "This is our central command panel. It keeps everything running."

"Looks like the cockpit of a spaceship," I muse.

"It's sacred ground to Noah," Dillon says, half-smirking. "He'd live in here if I let him."

"Doing what, exactly?"

"Creative chaos. Data stress tests. Harmless mischief. Unless you count the time he rigged the fridge to text motivational quotes."

The server room door shuts behind us with a heavy click. Dillon swipes his keycard. The panel flashes red, and he tries again.

I lift my brows. "Is that supposed to happen?"

"No." Dillon frowns and swipes again, slower and more deliberate. Still locked. "Must be a system error."

Something shifts in the air. A faint mechanical hum stops. My skin prickles, and I glance over my shoulder. It is too quiet.

"Error? What error?" My voice stays steady.

"The system is supposed to reset after hours so we don't lock up."

"Dillon, speak English." I shoot him a look.

"The security system auto resets."

My mouth falls open. "You're kidding, right?"

"Do I look like I'm joking?" he mutters, not meeting my gaze.

I start pacing. I dig my phone out of my bag and hold it up like a lifeline while I scan for a signal.

"Let me guess, no signal?"

I'm not panicking, not exactly. But being boxed in with no exit and no leverage is another story entirely. I don't like surprises.

I stop and glare at Dillon. "So, we're actually stuck?"

"It's a secure floor," he says, rubbing the back of his neck. "Limited access. Didn't think it would reset this early."

I cross my arms, scanning the room like a hidden exit might magically appear. "Do your genius glasses predict this kind of irony?"

He glances over, a smirk tugging at his lips. "They're not clairvoyant. Yet."

I lean against the wall and exhale slowly as my eyes adjust to the dim red glow of the emergency lights. "So we wait?"

"I'll try the override," he says, already moving toward a panel in the corner.

I watch him work, noting the tension in his shoulders even under that crisp button-down.

"Tell me something," I say, trying to cut the tension. "Was this your idea of a team-building exercise?"

"If it were, there'd be a whiteboard and color-coded sticky notes." He doesn't look up, but the edge of his mouth twitches.

I tsk. "Disappointing. I was expecting escape room-level drama."

"You're not far off. The clues are encrypted, and a firewall is the villain," he mutters.

I laugh, letting it slip out without permission.

A shared glance shifts the atmosphere.

I break eye contact first. Dillon types again, the screen blinks, then goes blank.

"How long will it take to escape?" I ask.

"Hard to say. Security might reboot in twenty or forty minutes. Depends on the update cycle."

I sigh. "And here I was hoping for a graceful exit."

He hesitates, then approaches, leaving a respectful distance between us.

"This wasn't a system glitch," Dillon mutters as he squints at the override log. "Someone did this deliberately."

I step closer, reading over his shoulder. "Meaning?"

"Meaning someone with top-level clearance did it on purpose." He pinches the bridge of his nose. "This is a test-only floor, cut off from our live network. Only three people have that clearance. And one of them has a history of playing mastermind with the server logs."

Dillon's jaw tightens.

"What?" I ask.

He shakes his head once, too quickly. "Nothing. Could be a glitch."

But the way his mouth twitches makes me think he knows exactly what, or who, caused it.

"Well, that's not cricket." The British slang slips out when I'm annoyed. I plant my hands on my hips, shift my weight, then slip off my heels.

Dillon scrutinizes me. "Got any gum in that oversized purse of yours?" he asks, gesturing to my leather messenger bag.

I lean against the icy wall and rummage through my bag, pulling out gum, chapstick, and a hair tie. Dillon's gaze tracks me like a laser.

I twist my hair into a messy bun, swipe on chapstick, then hand him the gum.

He looks at me like he's never seen a woman do that.

"I take it you don't have any sisters?" I say, looking up at him, amused.

His eyes widen, then he follows my lead and sits on the floor as he takes the gum.

"Nope, just me and my dad. You?"

"Yup, one. My sister Tia, short for Althea, and my mum and me. Just the three of us."

"Well, let's get comfortable. It's going to be a long night," he says, leaning his head against the wall.

I lean back against the wall with my legs stretched out. Dillon drums his fingers on his knee.

"So," he says. "Behavioral profiling. That's your thing?"

I smile. "Among other things."

"People fascinate you, or do they frustrate you?"

I glance at him. His tone is casual. But there's an edge of testing in it. Like he's trying to categorize me before I can categorize him.

We let the silence stretch. He waits. Not many people do.

There it is, a twitch in his jaw. He is not as at ease as he wants me to think. Progress.

"Fascinating," I say. "Frustration usually comes later."

That earns a small smile. Not smug. Just acknowledged.

"You read me at the event, didn't you?"

I tilt my head. "Would you like me to confirm it?"

"Only if you're brave enough."

I shift, facing him more directly.

"Honestly?" I say. "You didn't say enough."

His eyebrows lift. "No guesses?"

I wave a hand. "Guesses are lazy. I prefer patterns."

"And?"

I tilt my head. "You're careful. You speak in three-second delays. It means you think faster than your mouth moves. But you've also read just enough psychology to protect yourself from being read."

Dillon exhales a quiet laugh. "And here I thought I was subtle."

"Oh, you are," I say. "But you blink faster when someone mentions your personal life."

That stops him for half a second.

"I was waiting to see if you'd offer to analyze it."

I smile again, and this time, it's genuine. "Now *that* is subtle."

I sigh and tilt my head back. "So this is how we die. Blinking lights and burned circuits."

Dillon grins. "I think we'll make it out alive. But if not, at least we won't die alone."

I roll my eyes, but a smile tugs at my lips.

Charged air hangs between us in the forced proximity, but we both pretend not to notice it.

"So, you really hate feeling boxed in?" Dillon's voice is casual but laced with curiosity.

"Yup. The only boxes I like are Amazon boxes."

He chuckles.

I pause, weighing my words. "It's not the walls. It's the feeling of being contained. Like someone else gets to decide my limits."

Something about the quiet, the way he's not pushing,

loosens a thread. I feel brave enough to take the first step toward honesty.

"I guess it started with my dad," I say. "He lived without boundaries, roots, or rules, just motion. Always chasing the next shiny thing. I hated the instability and the chaos. But I hated the labels people tried to put on me even more. Like I was destined to drift too."

I pull in a breath. "So, I overcorrected. Built structure and became a control freak. The second someone tries to put me in a box, I want out fast."

Dillon watches me attentively.

"I promised myself I'd be different. That I'd build a life of my own choosing where no one could limit me."

Something flashes in Dillon's gaze. Interest, or perhaps surprise? I don't know, but he doesn't pry.

"I get that," he says, nodding. "Let's just say my father never tolerated uncertainty."

He sighs.

After a beat, he says, "My dad's the opposite. He's obsessed with control, schedules, and results. He ran life by a checklist: elite schools, quantifiable wins, zero margin for error. Anything less than perfect wasn't acceptable."

I understand that kind of perfectionism.

I study him. "And you followed it?"

His jaw ticks, and he lets out a humorless breath. "For a while. Until I couldn't breathe in his prison anymore. So I started building something of my own."

I know that feeling of being trapped in someone else's script.

"I used to study his face like it held a hidden algorithm, but nothing cracked the code." He swallows hard. "People think Lucid is about optimization. But it started with a boy who couldn't decode the man sitting across the dinner table. I built an algorithm where love had a signal. If I couldn't read my dad, maybe the data could. That's why I code. You can't disappoint a machine."

"So Lucid was your rebellion?" I ask, tilting my head. "Emotional insight, something you didn't get much of growing up?"

He nods. "Sophomore year. Noah and I coded our first prototype between midterms."

A soft smile tugs at my lips despite myself. "Did you succeed?"

He quirks his lips in triumph. "We sold it eighteen months later, just before graduation. I bought a Porsche with my payout."

My eyebrows shoot up. "Of course you did."

"I told myself it was about freedom," he adds with a shrug. "Or maybe I just needed to escape."

The mood isn't uncomfortable anymore. It's something else, something deeper. We're standing at the edge of something unspoken.

We both step back as if retreating from a dangerous ledge.

I hear shuffling somewhere outside the utility door. Faint, but real. Like the moment just gave us both permission to breathe.

I flash a teasing smile, pushing the tension aside. "Next time we get locked in somewhere, you better have an escape plan."

He mirrors my tone, smiling with deliberate mischief. "Noted."

He laughs at the exact moment I bite back a grin.

I narrow my eyes. "Are you reading me with those things?"

He lifts a brow. "Would it bother you if I was?"

"It will bother me if you think you need them."

He doesn't reply.

"So, you don't do feelings unless they come with a data set and margin of error?"

"You say that like it's a bad thing," he says, amused.

"It's not. Just human emotions aren't algorithms."

"They should be. At least then, they'd make sense. And people wouldn't lie."

I study him. He doesn't elaborate.

It dawns on me. "So that's what this is about. The glasses. You don't want to understand emotion. You want to predict it."

A tick in his jaw tells me I touched a truth he didn't mean to show.

"You keep profiling me," he says.

"Habit."

"Consulting style?"

"Behavioral strategy. I named my firm Calypso for a reason."

He exhales a half-laugh. "You ever scare yourself with how accurate you are?"

"Only when I like the person I'm reading."

Whoops. Did I just say that out loud?

The second I say it, I regret it.

The tension eases, but the moment lingers as the hours pass. We settle into an uneasy rhythm, the tension shifting into something lighter. Not quite comfortable yet, but not hostile either.

"Just to be clear," Dillon deadpans, "this wasn't my fault."

I glance at him. "You designed a server vault with no manual override. That's not protocol. That's a power move."

He shrugs. "You wanted to see the backup system. I was

being accommodating."

I snort. "You were flexing. 'Welcome to my blinking, beeping, bulletproof man cave.'"

Dillon grins. "State-of-the-art. Practically escape-proof."

"Says the guy who flinched when the lights dimmed."

"System stability check."

"Sure, CEO."

He chuckles. It's low and unguarded, and for a second, I forget we were on opposing teams a few hours ago.

I lean back against the wall, arms crossed. "Okay, survival question: We're stuck here for seventy-two hours. We each get three things. Go."

He tilts his head, pondering. "Power bar, satellite phone, and obviously, my Porsche."

I blink. "How is your Porsche helping us in here?"

He shrugs. "Morale boost. It's beautiful."

I laugh. "You can't drive it inside, Dillon."

He raises an eyebrow. "Can't I?"

"Fine. My turn." I hold up a finger. "One: my noise-canceling headphones to tune out your smugness."

He sets a hand over his heart dramatically. "What? I'm wounded."

"Two: a massive thermos of good coffee."

He nods in approval. "Practical."

I pause for effect. "Three: a crowbar. For the panic button you should've installed."

He grins. "Remind me never to trap you in an elevator. You'd take out the wiring with your hairpin and start a coup."

"Exactly." I nod. "Okay, next challenge: Worst room to be stuck in. Go."

He doesn't miss a beat. "The DMV."

"Classic."

"Have you ever seen the inside of the Midtown DMV at lunch hour?"

"Unfortunately, yes."

He tilts his head at me. "How about yours?"

"Chuck E. Cheese, the kids' indoor playroom," I say without hesitation. "Babysitting a group of screaming five-year-olds is plain torture."

Dillon winces. "Brutal. You say that like you have experience."

"Endless screaming. Constant resentment. Passive-aggressive lighting."

"And no actual exits," he adds. "Just doors that lead to more rooms."

I snap my fingers. "Exactly."

He looks at me with amusement.

"I promised myself back then that when I became a mom, you couldn't pay me enough to go there. I would rather watch paint dry than take my kids to that germ-infested cesspool." I shudder.

Dillon chuckles. "I assume your mother took you there when you were a kid?"

"Um, no. My mom loves me enough to know that germy places like that give me that major ick. What about your mom? You close with yours?"

His expression falters, and I detect a shift in his mood.

"Not anymore," he says. "She passed a few years ago. But it's okay, I have great memories of her." His expression softens. "You ever feel like, even when you're not boxed in, that you're still stuck?"

We share an understanding. What it means to be trapped.

To perform, to endure the noise, the expectations. I don't answer right away. I just slowly nod.

"You ever talk about it? Your mom?" I ask quietly.

He hesitates, just for a second. "Not really. Talking about it doesn't change it."

The silence returns, not heavy this time, but thoughtful.

Dillon glances at me. "So, why this line of work?" he asks. "Behavioral analysis, microexpressions. What made you want to dig into people's heads?"

I shift, caught off guard by the softness in his voice. Most people ask what I do, rarely *why* I do it.

"I've always been observant. Not just expressions, but the minor stuff. How someone shifts their weight when they lie. How their eyes avoid certain truths." I smile faintly. "When I was seven, I knew this guy was conning my dad before he even said a word."

Dillon raises a brow. "Seriously?"

"Oh yeah." I stretch out my legs, warming to the memory. "This flashy Cypriot guy showed up one day. His blazer smelled like cheap cologne and empty promises. He shook my dad's hand with both of his like it was a wedding proposal. Claimed he had a connection in Mali, West Africa, and wanted to partner with my dad to sell emeralds. Said millions were available for mining."

Dillon leans in. "I assume there were no emeralds?"

"Oh, there were emeralds, but no way to get them out of the ground. My dad was starstruck. He only saw money, and the guy's charisma captivated him. Meanwhile, I'm sitting inside the car and watching their exchange. The guy was too polished, too still. Smile didn't quite reach his eyes. I knew he was a con."

"You read all that at seven?"

I nod, a little sheepish. "I didn't hear a word. Just watched. I told my dad and explained what I saw."

"Did he believe you?"

I exhale. "He laughed. Said I was cute. A month later, the guy vanished with an 'investment deposit' and left my dad drowning in debt."

Dillon says nothing for a moment. He watches me.

"After that, I stopped trusting first impressions. Maybe people altogether."

I spot something unreadable behind his eyes.

"That's wild," he finally says. "So, you've basically been a human lie detector since grade school?"

"More like a walking warning label no one wants to read," I mutter, half joking.

"You ever get it wrong?"

The question catches me off guard. "Not often," I admit. "I believe in others because I want to believe in them. That's the dangerous part—when your heart overrules your instincts. Our body knows before our brain does."

He studies me, something sharper in his gaze now. "I get that."

Our eyes meet, gazes lingering. Suddenly, this doesn't feel like a conversation anymore. It feels like a line being drawn and then blurred.

I study him. He doesn't elaborate.

"So that's what this is about," I breathe. "The glasses. You design systems that predict behavior. Read the room before you enter it. Stay five moves ahead. You're not trying to build empathy. You're trying to *control* it, right?"

His jaw tenses. He doesn't answer. But his body language

speaks volumes.

I glance at him. "I've seen it before, that edge-of-the-cliff focus. It starts early."

His brow lifts faintly. "Define 'early.'"

"Parents. School. Something that taught you being vulnerable meant falling behind."

Still no denial. A beat lingers too long.

I wave a hand. "You don't have to tell me your childhood memoir. I'm just saying, you read like someone who made himself bulletproof because someone once made him feel like a target."

A breath. Not a laugh. Not quite a sigh.

"That's dangerously close to profiling."

I smirk to cover the feeling of discomfort in my chest. He's getting too close, too fast.

"It's not a profile," I say. "It's an impression. Based on posture. Precision. The way you pause when someone asks about your 'why.'"

He watches me, unblinking. "You get all that from body language?"

"Not just body language." I gesture between us. "From moments like this. When you flinch slightly at sincerity."

"You're not wrong," he murmurs.

It's not a confession. It's a crack. A shift. The first one I've seen. And I don't push it. I shouldn't be telling him this. It's too much too soon. But the words slip out anyway.

"I used to skate. Trained like it was life or death. It felt like control. Until the one thing I couldn't control wrecked it."

"What happened?"

He waits, giving me space to answer or not.

I shake my head, brushing off a memory that cuts too deep.

"Doesn't matter. That was another lifetime ago." I pause, looking away.

"Cleo, you okay?"

I nod, but it's a second too late.

"You don't have to be," he adds.

I say nothing, toying with the edge of my sleeve.

"I used to have a partner," I say. "In ice dance. We trained for years. You learn early that one mistake can cost everything. I got used to hiding nerves behind perfect posture. Make it look easy, or don't bother getting on the ice. That's what this room feels like. A performance stage. No room to fall."

"You're not performing now," he says gently.

I finally look at him. Our eyes hold. Not sharp, not playful, just present. At some point, our jokes fade. I don't remember leaning in. But somewhere between the banter and the quiet, our shoulders brush. His jacket caresses the silk of my blouse, and neither of us moves.

I should pull away. Reestablish boundaries. But I don't. Neither does Dillon. He just stays there, breathing steady, our heartbeats in sync.

The air between us shifts.

When I glance up, I find Dillon already watching me. Not with his usual intensity. This isn't a challenge or a calculation.

It's something else. Something still, quiet and dangerous.

His gaze drops to my mouth. And just for a second, my heart stumbles.

He notices. I know he notices.

Then my eyes do the same, dropping to his lips before lifting back to his eyes.

We hover there in the space between what we want and what we're afraid to want. I can feel the heat between us, low and magnetic.

My pulse answers before my brain does.

He leans in just slightly. A breath closer. And I do too.

It's not a kiss. Not really. But it's the moment right before one, when time freezes.

Dillon's hand fidgets like he wants to reach out and touch me. And for a second, I forget who I am. Forget the rules, the layers, the reasons I don't let people in.

But then, he stops.

Like he made the decision a second too late.

Just like that. One heartbeat short of too much.

His breath catches, and mine stumbles after it. We break apart, not suddenly, but quietly. Like being pulled out of a dream you don't want to admit you were having.

I straighten. He shifts back. No words. No apology. Whatever that almost was, we pretend it didn't happen.

He looks away and runs his hand through his hair.

I clear my throat. "What time is it?"

"Nine thirty," he says, looking at his wristwatch.

I nod, focusing on the blinking lights instead of the heat still curling in my chest.

Neither of us speaks. The moment lingers, stretched thin and trembling like a live wire. Not quite touched, but far from forgotten.

***

An hour later, we hear the console beeping. A green light pulses at the door. We jerk apart, blinking heavily. The door beeps and swings open. Light spills in, and there's Noah, grinning like a satisfied cat, holding two bags of takeout and

84

his laptop charger.

"Server room sleepover, huh? Want me to start the gossip now or wait till lunch? Figured you two might be deep in conversation. Plus, my test is complete. You guys pass. I'm so proud of you."

Dillon glares. "You triggered a server lockdown just to play therapist?"

Noah shrugs.

"Isolated floor. QA test for the lockdown script."

He grins.

"Also, the emotional reboot was overdue. You're welcome."

I cross my arms. "You locked us in to play couples therapy?"

"Oh, please. I knew you'd crack it. Eventually. Also, you two were tense. Figured twenty square feet of blinking servers might help." He holds up the bag. "Besides, I brought Thai food. That's got to earn me partial forgiveness."

"I hate you," Dillon mutters.

"You love me. Like a fungus."

I stand up and straighten my jacket. "Okay," I say, mustering a smile. "I'll pretend this didn't happen." Even if my pulse hasn't caught up yet.

Dillon's gaze lingers on me. "This is mild. Noah once faked a fire drill just to get me to ask someone out."

I straighten, brushing imaginary lint off my blouse, while Dillon rubs the back of his neck.

I clear my throat. "Just working through a situation."

"It was a professional crisis," Dillon clarifies.

Noah chuckles but steps aside to let us out. I walk ahead, spine straight but bracing for impact.

Later, after fresh air and much-needed space, we find ourselves in the breakroom. Dillon stands a few feet away, pretending to check his phone. I lean against the counter, stirring my tea.

After a brief pause, I feel Dillon's gaze on me. Something unreadable in the air.

"Noah is lucky he's brilliant," he says. "And my co-founder and best friend. Otherwise, I'd kill him."

I chuckle. "It's okay. We survived."

Dillon groans. "Noah thinks he's Lucid's in-house Yoda. Always meddling, never apologizing."

I smile. "Remind me never to wander in a server room again."

8

Chapter 8: Competitive Fire

Dillon

The conference room hums with curated calm. Controlled lighting, chilled water, buzzing smartwatches. Everyone is playing their part.

It's been three days since the lock-in. Just enough time to pretend it didn't happen, yet not nearly enough to forget. Cleo and I haven't spoken since, outside of clipped logistics and meeting invites. But my body remembers the electricity of almost, the weight of what could have been. The way she leaned in like she didn't mean to, and how I didn't stop her.

I know the warmth of her breath when she hesitated. I've tried to shake it, but I can't seem to. Something shifted. I felt it in the way Cleo glanced at me, like she was rethinking her original analysis. And I found myself second-guessing mine.

I stand at the head of the table. My slides click forward on cue. The tone is polished, just casual enough to look unrehearsed. Lucid Lenses gleam between two mugs like a prototype centerpiece, exactly where I want them.

Every stat and every phrase has been pressure-tested. This is the apex of weeks of data. I'm delivering it like I was born for this because this is what I was built for.

Everyone's listening. But Cleo does not look at me once.

She's watching them. That's how I know it got to her too. Her posture is perfect, but her foot taps half a beat too fast. Her fingers drum on the blank notepad.

I finish the pitch, and the room exhales in polite interest.

And then Cleo speaks. "What's the error margin on microexpression recognition across cultural profiles?"

The air stills. Even Noah looks up.

Cleo picks up the glasses like they're loaded. The way she exhales, slow and controlled, tells me she's not just assessing them.

I don't blink. "It's adaptive."

"But trained on Western expression sets, yes?" Her tone is casual, but her eyes are serious. She's gauging the space between us. The one we both pretend isn't charged.

"We're expanding the dataset weekly."

She nods slowly. Then, gently, she sets the glasses down. "Until then, you're handing people a lens that might misread someone entirely." She meets my gaze, unflinching. "That's not understanding. That's guessing in disguise."

The silence that follows isn't awkward, it's sharpened.

I hold my ground. I say nothing for one beat too long. My jaw flexes.

She sees it. Of course, she does. She came to assess the tech, but she's also dissecting the man behind it.

My fingers twitch, and I clasp my hands to still them.

"Interesting," I say evenly. "So, empathy's manipulative

now?"

Her head tilts slightly. That look that says she's already picked me apart. And when her gaze drops for a second too long, to my mouth and back, it sparks like static under my skin.

My chest tightens. She's just one person, yet something about her gets under my skin.

"You're skilled at reading people. But have you ever let someone read *you* without dissecting them first?" she asks.

The boardroom tension could be bottled and sold by the ounce.

I cross my arms. "You're betting on instincts. Data doesn't lie. People do."

She tilts her head, watching me like I'm part of the case study. "Yet you flinch every time someone says 'emotions.' Fascinating."

She crosses her arms, but her eyes soften for just a second, like she's trying to read past my defense.

I straighten my spine. "That's irrelevant."

She leans forward. "No, it's not. You built a machine to do it for you. But here's the problem: machines miss what actually matters."

I keep my hands flat on the table. Calm. Unmoved. "Such as?"

"Subtext," she says, flicking her gaze around. "Your head of finance just clenched his jaw when you mentioned quarterly projections. He disagrees with you, but you didn't notice. Your assistant checked her watch twice. She's anxious. Probably about something you dismissed earlier."

My father used to say emotions were the enemy of efficiency, that they made you weak. Now Cleo's sitting here, dismantling my framework with a smile and a few offhand observations. I hate how close to the mark she is.

"Your numbers are clear," Cleo goes on. "But your people are trying to tell you something, and you're not listening."

I process every word like data, but it refuses to compute the way I want it to. She's not wrong, and I hate that she knows it.

I keep my hands flat on the table.

She shrugs. "I expect you to stop pretending that intuition is weakness."

Silence settles. Noah leans back in his chair, fingers steepled over his mouth, doing a poor job hiding his amusement.

Jemima glances at me, then Cleo. Team Disruptor wins another vote.

One of the newer staff members shifts in his seat. "To be fair, emotional intelligence has been trending in leadership studies," he says cautiously.

I shoot him a look that silences any follow-up. But the damage is done.

Cleo waits, letting the silence take hold.

Noah clears his throat. "Well. This just got interesting."

Cleo's eyes flick to mine. She knows she's won the exchange. But she's not finished.

"You think reading people is a party trick?" she snaps. "Many of us have lived lives misunderstood by systems, strangers, and presumptuous men."

I lean back, stunned. She's never dropped her armor like that before.

"You know what your problem is?" she says, smoothing her skirt as she stands. "You don't know your team. You know their metrics, their projections, their performance indicators.

But not how they think under pressure."

"I'm not here to babysit their emotions. I'm building a Formula One team."

"No, but if you can't read them when things go sideways, you'll miss the critical moves before they happen."

Noah lifts his head, clearly entertained. "She has a point, and I never say that."

"You asked for feedback. If you don't want honest input, don't invite a consultant to the table," she says.

"I want results. Honesty is only useful if it leads to a solution. Can you provide one?" I ask.

With a smug smile, she steps closer. "Already did. You just didn't like it."

Silence. I'm processing the data.

Cleo grins. "So, let's test it."

I narrow my eyes. "How?"

"Escape room. This evening. You. Me. Your team. No data. Just instincts."

I blink. "You're joking."

She's got that look again. One eyebrow raised, the corner of her mouth twitching like she's enjoying this. Like this is sport, and maybe it is. The nerve.

I've handled hostile takeovers. But this woman, all nerve and zero fear, is my most unsettling opponent yet. The way she steps into my space without blinking. The way she gets under my skin without trying. She's not intimidated one bit. And part of me wants to lose, just to see what happens.

"You're deflecting again," she says. "You do that when you're cornered."

"No, I do that when people start analyzing me like a case study."

We stare each other down.

Lucid Lenses would be lighting up like Times Square right now.

My pulse spikes. My jaw clenches. Her pupils dilate just slightly, like she's preparing for impact. Or maybe for retreat. But no glasses needed. I see it. I *feel* it.

We are both scared, just about different things.

"You're scared," she breathes.

I let out a dry laugh. "Hardly."

"Then prove it. If your team surprises you, if they outperform because you stop micromanaging and I win the game, you let me drive your Porsche for a week."

Noah chokes. "That's his baby."

Cleo doesn't break eye contact. "What's the matter? Scared I'll stall it?"

I stare at her. She's baiting me, and it's working. "You drive stick?"

"Well enough to handle a Porsche. Especially under pressure."

I glance at Noah. He mouths, *"Don't do it."*

Cleo just stands there, radiating nerve and a little mischief that makes her intriguing.

She knows exactly what she's doing.

Then something inside me gives way.

"You're on," I say.

Her smile is triumphant. "I called in a favor, an old client owes me. Private room, no waitlist. See you at seven."

She turns and walks out without looking back.

Everyone rises, gathers their things, and makes a fast exit.

Noah groans. "What did you just do?" He crosses his arms and shakes his head. "You're seriously putting your Porsche on the line for a dare?"

"It's not a dare, it's a challenge. And I don't back down," I say.

"You sure? Because it looked a lot like pride. Or something else."

I glare at him. "Say it."

"She gets to you."

I snort, and it falls short. "She annoys me."

"Right. I annoy you too."

I look back at the door Cleo exited.

"You brought her in to balance the system. But the moment she pushes back, you go into lockdown. You don't want a translator; you want a mirror that flatters you."

I look straight ahead.

"Just watch yourself," Noah cautions. "She's sharp."

I don't answer. Saying it out loud would make it real, and real is messy. Real carries risk.

My phone buzzes. It's a forwarded message from Oscar:

"Intriguing dynamic in today's meeting. Would love to see a tighter leash on consultants in investor-facing rooms."

I stare at the text. What's that supposed to mean, a tighter leash? Oscar wasn't even in the room.

My jaw tightens. It's subtle, but it's there. A warning. Not about the product. About Cleo. He's never liked variables he couldn't control.

And Cleo is uncontainable by design.

As I head back to my office, the thought sparks under my skin. I'm not thinking in numbers anymore. She's not a variable. She's the anomaly. I'll crack her before she wrecks me.

She thinks it's a game? Well, I don't play unless I win.

And the Porsche? Just the opener.

The real win is figuring her out before she tears me down.

I head to the lounge to reset, but before I get there, my phone buzzes.

Robert Whelan. No subject line. Just one sentence:

"I heard about the pitch event. Be careful who you trust. Some smiles are weapons."

I stare at the message. No greeting. No pride. Just a calculated shot across the bow.

I walk inside the break room, the space with low lighting, polished wood, and curated silence that whispers expensive.

The faint smell of espresso lingers in the air.

It's designed for decompression.

I don't need it, but my nervous system does.

I pour something clear into a glass. Vodka-free. I just need the ritual.

I haven't spoken to my father in two years. Not since I turned down his capital and built Lucid without him. He called it reckless; I called it freedom. He's still bitter. Says I embarrassed the Whelan name by playing startup roulette instead of building a dynasty.

No congratulations. No pride. Just a surgical jab to the gut. Classic Robert. He doesn't text unless he's sniffing out the sharks in the bloodied water. And even then, it's not conversation. It's commentary. One-sided and surgical.

I start to type a reply, then stop myself. Because as much as I hate it, he's not wrong. He's not just throwing shade. He's warning me about backers with sharp smiles, about the ones I let too close.

I've been so focused on the product that I forgot the rule he drilled into me at thirteen: Build with trust, protect with suspicion.

And lately, I haven't protected anything.

Sharp, intentional footsteps sound, and I don't have to look to know who's coming. Cleo steps into the break room. She doesn't turn, doesn't acknowledge me. Just leans against the bar, nursing a drink she clearly didn't want.

I speak first, keeping my tone measured. Neutral. "You don't hold back."

She doesn't flinch. "Not when someone puts emotion on a spreadsheet and calls it data."

She's closer to the truth than I'm willing to admit.

I move a little closer. Close enough to be felt. Still far enough to keep the peace.

"You were right about the training bias," I say.

She turns, finally. "But?"

I hold her gaze. "I still think what we're building will change the way people connect. Help them understand each other."

She tilts her head, eyes narrowing. "Do you believe that, or was it just a strong closing line?"

A small smile breaks through my strategic defenses. "I believe in removing guesswork. In equipping people to read what's already there."

She studies me, and I know what she's doing. Reading me like I'm a walking contradiction she can't decide whether to trust.

"Funny," she says. "You're not as unreadable as you think."

Her words hit like a soft punch. Intimate, yet disarming. Like she sees more than she should and isn't sure what to do with it.

"Oh?"

"You track people constantly," she says. She watches me

carefully, like she's watching to see if I'll deny it or admit she's right. "You gauge tone, posture, eye contact. You walk into a room and analyze its emotional climate before you speak."

I keep my expression blank, but internally, I freeze. Because she's right. That's exactly what I do.

"And what does that say about me?" I ask.

She doesn't hesitate to answer. "That you're afraid of misreading someone who matters."

The silence hits hard.

I stare at the ice in my glass, like it might buy me a second of insulation. But there's no buffer left.

Cleo sets her drink down. "But here's the thing," she says, her voice dropping. "The more you rely on tools to tell you what people feel, the less you'll be able to feel it for yourself."

That one lands deep.

I step back. Not out of defeat, just to regain my frame. Professional mode reboots.

"That's why we brought you in," I say. "To translate. Not derail the vision."

She smiles, razor-edged. Returning fire with composure. "Then maybe you should clarify what kind of translator you hired."

She walks out. Doesn't look back.

And the room feels quieter without her in it.

But I do, just for a second.

Not to win. Not to understand. Just to feel the space she leaves behind.

Because whatever we are doing, sparring, testing, circling, it stopped being business somewhere along the way.

And I cannot help but wonder if I just met my match.

9

Chapter 9: Escape Room

Cleo

The door shuts with a metallic click. A hiss of compressed air. Then darkness settles, tight and pulsing. A dim red glow blinks from a corner bulb like an old horror movie.

We all go still.

"Was that supposed to happen?" Jemima asks.

When I was little and scared of the dark, I used to whisper that old Psalm Yiayia loved. The one about the shepherd and not being scared. I don't remember all the words, but the rhythm still calms me.

I let out a breath. "I think so. That lock was real."

Jemima gives a nervous laugh.

Noah claps once. "Let the chaos begin."

Dillon stays silent.

Somewhere, a timer counts down from thirty minutes. No pressure.

We split into pairs. Jemima and Noah head to the opposite

corner, where a console glows faintly. Dillon and I have been paired. It's team building, after all.

The tech is innovative. Hidden clues in the walls, pressure-sensitive panels, and motion-activated locks. Part ancient crypt, part sci-fi bunker. Every puzzle forces cooperation. Smells like ozone and locker room funk.

I blink, waiting for my eyes to adjust to the dim lighting. The faint outline of a bookshelf takes shape, then a crate.

"There must be an exit button somewhere, or a switch or lever."

I brush my fingers along the edges of the books, searching for anything unusual. Then I see a lantern tilting, inviting me to touch it. Twisting the handle causes a small battery-powered bulb to flick on.

"Found a light," I say.

Dillon glances over, his silhouette finally visible. "Of course you did."

"Trial and error." My voice comes out tighter than I want it to.

We pass a metal filing cabinet, a wall poster from the seventies, and a fake safe with a keypad. Using the lantern, I scan the walls. Luminous glow-in-the-dark words sprawl across a wall map, reading, "Staying Alive."

I pause. "A nod to the Bee Gees?"

Dillon steps so close that I feel the heat of him near my shoulder. "You okay?"

I nod. "I don't like being cornered."

"Physically or emotionally?"

I arch a brow. "Both."

He smiles.

A riddle appears on the wall: "Truth hides behind the false

door. Time is ticking."

I squint. "False door?"

We work side by side. I touch all the surfaces, moving the items and turning them upside down. We slide tiles into place like competitors in a mental sparring match.

The tension between us hums.

I flash back to the server room. The heat between us. The pause before we didn't kiss. The pull that still lingers in my chest like a pent-up breath. He's been in my head ever since, and I hate that I notice how close he stands. How his voice lowers when no one else is listening to us.

Dillon raises a brow. "You've done this before?"

Our eyes lock for a second too long. I force myself to look away. My eyes revert to the map on the wall. My gut urges me to touch it. I walk up to it and rip it off the wall.

Dillon turns to me in surprise. "Easy, tiger."

I grin. That got his attention.

Holding the lantern up to the now empty space, I see it.

"Got it." I exhale. Taped to the wall is a key.

"Impressive," he says, and I can tell he means it.

"Four questions," I say, arms crossed. "That's all I need to crack your code."

Dillon glances at me, amusement beneath that razor-sharp calm. "You think you can crack me like a code?"

"I'm confident in my abilities." I lean in. "Extrovert or introvert, intuitive or observant, thinking or feeling, judging or prospecting."

"What are you talking about?"

"It's a personality type system. Tells me how you process the world. You're the classic ENTJ command-and-conquer type. Craves control like oxygen. Efficient. Feelings are optional."

He glances at me again, more curious than smug. "And what about you?"

"Me?"

"Yes, Miss Profiler. Profile yourself."

"ENTP. Chaos in heels. Intuition first, questions later."

He lets out a short laugh. "So basically, unpredictable."

"Spontaneous," I correct. "Adaptive. Vision-oriented. Annoyingly curious."

"I'll give you 'annoyingly.'" He flashes a self-satisfied smile.

"I'll take it as a compliment."

The overhead voice booms loudly. "T-minus five, four, three, two, one."

Mid-step, we hear a click. The lights go out, plunging us into deep darkness.

Dillon goes completely still. No flinch, no reaction at all. I wait for him to say something, to break the tension with a snarky comment or bossy instruction. But nothing. The silence stretches as the air tightens.

If I had to guess, he is not afraid of the dark. He's afraid of what it strips away. His edge, his read on the room, his control. And being dependent on someone else. This is his worst-case scenario playing out in real time.

I shift slightly, careful not to startle him. "Hey," I whisper, soft and steady. "It's just a game. We're fine."

A faint tremor in his voice catches me off guard. It's not panic, exactly. But there's something there. Tight, guarded, like his body remembers something his brain won't name.

"Sorry. Just needed a second." He lets out a shaky breath. "I assume this is part of the game?" he mutters.

I grin. "Or the power failed, and we're trapped forever. Either way, watching you navigate without a visual feed is going to be the highlight of my week."

"Not helpful, Cleo."

"Allowing me to lead will be helpful. Since, you know, I have actual instincts."

A beat of silence.

"Fine. But how do you expect me to follow you when I can't see anything?"

"Hands on my hips. I'll guide us."

He doesn't move for a second. Tension rolls off him in heavy waves.

"You're kidding," he drawls.

"Do you have another option?"

Dillon hesitates again. This time, his reluctance sounds closer to fear. The quiet kind that doesn't scream, but clenches. I've seen this in clients. Not claustrophobia exactly. It's what happens when control freaks are dropped into sensory blackouts. They lose their edge, and the panic creeps in sideways.

Dillon Whelan doesn't lose control.

But I'm watching it unravel, one shallow breath at a time.

Hesitantly, almost like it costs him something, his fingers find my waist.

His grip is firm, warmer than I expected.

Not competitive tension this time. Something else.

I stay still.

"Relax, Whelan," I murmur, keeping my tone light. "I don't bite."

"That's not what I'm worried about." His voice is soft, not teasing like his usual MO.

I don't press. Instead, I move, leading us through the dark.

Then it hits me: this isn't his usual tension.

My voice becomes the compass. Each step is careful.

His grip intensifies every time we stop.

Every time the room unexpectedly shifts. It's subtle, but I feel it.

I glance over my shoulder, though I can't see him. "How are you doing back there?"

He doesn't answer. He's struggling.

"Dillon?"

Another pause.

"Fine."

Except he's not. His silence is brittle. His usually certain movements are now slow, and his steps faltering. And his hands, still on my waist, feel like they're holding on for more than balance.

I don't push him. My intuition says that will aggravate the problem. So, I keep going. We round a corner, and a low light shines from beneath a door, illuminating the corridor.

A sharp gasp breaks the silence. We both still.

We see Jemima and Noah. She's pressing herself against the wall. Her breaths are fast, panicked.

Even in the faint light, I see Dillon stiffen. Something tight or haunted. Then, just as quickly, he masks it.

"I—I can't—" Jemima rasps.

Before Dillon can move, I'm already crouching down in front of her. "Jemima, hey, I've got you. Listen to me." My voice drops into the calming register I use with clients on the brink. "Breathe with me. Four counts. Ready? In two three four. Hold. Now out."

She nods, mimicking my breathing. Her shoulders begin to relax.

Behind me, I expect movement, a command, *something*. But

all I hear is silence. Dillon and Noah both stare at me.

"Just breathe. It's a reaction. Your body's doing what it's supposed to," I say. "I used to teach agents how to spot panic before it exploded. That doesn't mean I'm immune to it."

For a beat, Dillon goes rigid. His jaw is locked tight.

I notice something almost raw in his expression.

It's gone in a blink, but it was there.

A crack in the armor.

The faint light returning to the room illuminates his tense posture.

He stares at Jemima, but his eyes are distant.

Unfocused. Haunted. I've never seen him like this.

"Dillon?" I ask gently, not letting it slide this time.

He blinks. He doesn't answer.

But a beat later, he moves.

I stand up slowly and step toward him.

"You shut down in there."

I say, voice low but steady.

His jaw tightens.

But he doesn't argue.

"It wasn't just Jemima. You went somewhere too. And it wasn't here."

A shadow falls across his features.

"Was I?" he asks, but there's no denial in his tone.

"You were," I say simply. "And it's okay. Just, don't gaslight yourself about it."

A muscle jumps in his jaw. "I don't like not knowing what's coming next." The words are quiet, clipped. As close as he's come to admitting fear.

"Control feels like safety, doesn't it?" I murmur. "Even if it isn't."

He steps beside me, lowering himself just enough to meet Jemima's eye level. But his gaze flicks to mine first. And to my complete surprise, he reaches for my hand. It's brief, almost reflexive. But not nothing. It's a tell.

His fingers close over mine.

For a second, neither of us moves.

I don't pull away.

A jolt runs through me, sharp and immediate. It's not romantic. It's not calculated. But it's real. And my traitorous heart responds like it's been waiting for this.

I stay still, pretending it doesn't matter. The desire to protect someone who won't let themselves need it. It's clearer than before. This isn't fear. It's memory. And for someone like him, that's worse.

Something about this moment is familiar to him. Too familiar.

There's history in that silence.

Bigger than this room.

No control, no light, just the fear of not knowing what's coming next.

And I think he's been running from that feeling ever since.

I could let it slide; I've done it before. Let the tension fade, let him reset. But if I do that now, we're just back to where we started.

And I'm tired of almosts.

I turn to Dillon, lowering my voice. "I meant what I said back there."

He glances sideways. "About what?"

"You froze. And I saw it."

He doesn't answer. But he doesn't deny it either.

"If you want me to help, I need to see the cracks. Not just

the steel."

"You're not what I expected, Ambrosia."

I smile, but it's softer this time. "That makes two of us."

"Thanks," he says, voice low, like that word cost him.

I nod. I don't need to ask what happened. Because, for the first time, I'm starting to understand. This isn't about puzzles or power. This is about something much deeper. And whatever it is, it scares him.

The light flickers back to full brightness, and the moment shatters. Dillon pulls his hand away, smooths his shirt, and stands like nothing happened. But something did happen.

After we all exit the room, we step outside for fresh air. The team members are discussing what to do next.

Dillon glances at me first, like he's waiting for my read.

"Alright, team. Night's still young. We've reserved two hours at Make & Bake. The good news is we get to make our own pizza tonight," I say.

A few whoops sound, then the rest of the team gets the memo. Free food on management.

Dillon looks at me and furrows his brow. "Are you saying there is more torture tonight?"

"But of course. We are only halfway through our team-building exercise," I quip.

"Hey man, take a chill," Noah chimes in. "It's going to be worth it when everyone sings your praises tomorrow."

Rolling his eyes, Dillon puts his hands on his hips and inhales a slow breath.

"I saw that," I say, giving him a wink.

Wait, did I just wink? Abort mission!

But it's too late. Dillon saw me eyeing him, and he noticed my wink. The corners of his mouth curl up into a satisfied grin.

"Still chaos," he says, but there's something warmer beneath it. Less armor, more curiosity.

I lift a brow. "Still trying to crack me?"

"Lead the way, Miss Ambrosia." He gestures to the road.

I walk ahead without turning, but my pulse skips. Something's unraveling between us.

Something I'm almost afraid to want.

For the first time since I met him, Dillon isn't watching the room.

He's watching me.

10

Chapter 10: Measure By Heart

Cleo

The scent of tomato sauce, garlic, and sugar hangs in the air of Make & Bake, a do-it-yourself cooking studio.

The ovens hum softly, interspersed with the laughter of patrons and the clang of metal baking trays. Warmth radiates from the brick pizza oven, and flour dust glitters under the overhead lights like fairy dust.

Jemima and Noah have claimed the corner booth, working on their dough with exaggerated care. Jemima is quieter than usual, her eyes still a little too glassy, forcing herself to laugh at Noah's teasing. He bumps her shoulder gently, trying to lighten the mood, but there's a lingering stiffness in her posture.

Dillon notices it too. He hasn't looked her way since we walked in.

I perch on the edge of the kitchen counter, my legs dangling. Dillon stands at the counter beside me, sleeves rolled up, meticulously measuring flour.

I jiggle my feet against the cabinets, itchy to say something to snap him out of his focus. "I'm tickled pink that they have gluten-free options."

"Gluten, hey? When did that become your nemesis?" Dillon asks.

"Since I discovered my food hangovers stemmed from an immune disease. Thanks, Grandma, for that."

He looks at me quizzically.

I love throwing him off balance.

"Wow, this place is da bomb. Wait, do people still say that? I feel like I time-traveled back to the nineties."

He's trying to hold back a smile. This Mr. Serious has got to go.

Then it happens, he laughs.

Not the restrained half-smirk I'm used to, but a real, quiet laugh that hums under my skin. The kind that sneaks in before you can brace for it.

It's just a laugh, a flicker, a brief break in his armor. That's all it is.

Except, there's a warmth to it I didn't expect. A sense of safety I did not ask for.

"Yeah, you did," he deadpans. "With Michael J. Fox in his DeLorean."

I chuckle. "Along with Vanilla Ice. But I digress."

He lines up the ingredients like he is practicing for a test.

I pick up a whisk. "Here's a serious question: If you were stuck on an island with only one kitchen utensil, what would it be?"

Dillon arches a brow. "Is this like a survival scenario or a gourmet Chef Ramsay experience?"

"Your choice, but choose wisely. The fate of your culinary future depends on it."

He sets the measuring cup down. "A cast-iron skillet. Versatile, durable, and you can fend off aggressive coconuts."

"Coconut defense. Excellent choice. But a cast-iron skillet?" I lift a brow. "We're counting that as a utensil now?"

He smiles at me warmly.

I take a sip of my matcha tea, studying him. "You're really into this baking thing, huh?"

"It's just chemistry." He wipes his hands on a dish towel. "If you follow the rules, you get predictable results."

I tilt my head. "So, you're saying if someone doesn't follow your exact rules, the whole thing falls apart?"

He gives me a sideways look and taps the measuring cup twice before leveling it off.

I keep my tone light. "That escape room kind of proved your rule-following theory."

He doesn't respond, but his jaw ticks once.

I tilt my head, studying him. "It must've been hard. Not having control. No visibility. No Plan B."

Still nothing.

He measures too carefully, like if one grain is off, the whole recipe will collapse.

"I mean," I say, dusting off flour caked to my fingers, "some people panic in chaos. Others adapt. Neither is wrong. Just different wiring."

His shoulders tighten ever so slightly. "I didn't panic."

"I never said you did."

He doesn't look at me, but I feel the weight of what's unspoken settle between us like the steam rising from the oven.

And I don't press. I let it hang. Because sometimes the most honest moments are the ones you don't name out loud.

I pluck a pinch of flour from the counter and toss it lightly at him, a playful cloud catching his shirtfront. "Or maybe you're just scared of unpredictable things. Like imperfect cookies. Or imperfect people."

He shakes the flour off his shirt with exaggerated movements. "Unpredictable means chaotic. I prefer things reliable."

I lean in a little, grinning. "You know what they say about best-laid plans, Whelan."

He pins me with a look, half challenge, half something else I can't quite name. And for a second, the air between us tightens.

Then he huffs a laugh, breaking the moment. "Let's just get the cookies right before you start psychoanalyzing my pastry skills."

I laugh, bumping him lightly with my shoulder, testing the spark I've been pretending isn't becoming a flame. His arm brushes mine in return, and neither of us moves away. The brief touch ignites my senses.

I tell myself it's nothing. Just two people sharing a kitchen. Static and flour and coincidence. But my body doesn't believe me.

"Fine," I concede. "But just so you know, you're officially on cookie probation. So, be honest. Could comfort or nostalgia be the reason? Maybe a certain someone who taught you how to bake?"

His hand freezes on the sugar container, and he looks straight ahead.

"I'm not profiling," I blurt. "Okay, I'm profiling a little. It's what I do."

He shakes the container, avoiding my eyes. "It's just something to do."

I lean my elbows on the island, cupping my chin. "You're not fooling me, Whelan."

Dillon lets out a rough laugh and rubs the back of his neck. "Fine. My mom. She taught me. We used to bake when my dad worked late." He glances at me. "She said baking made people feel cared for."

He keeps his eyes fixed on the mixing bowl of batter. There's a stillness in him I haven't seen before. Not silence from calculation, but from something gentler underneath. Like maybe this matters more than he'll say. Like maybe sharing this memory, this ritual, costs him something.

My heart squeezes. "She sounds like she was pretty special."

"She was." He clears his throat. "I haven't baked since she died."

The rawness in his voice catches me off guard. Not because I pity him, but because I know what it costs to say that out loud.

I press my fingers into the counter, grounding myself. He's not just baking cookies; he's breaking a rule. One I never expected him to bend for me.

I set my mug aside and reach for his hand. My fingers rest over his, light as sugar dust. Harmless yet encouraging. That's all I mean by it. At least, that's what I tell myself.

He doesn't pull away, doesn't flinch, doesn't mask the way his fingers shift to meet mine. I feel it anyway. This moment threads its way under my skin, and I let it.

"You know," I say, keeping my tone light, "my Yiayia would say a prayer as she cooked. She said thanking God and making things with love made everything taste better."

"Yeah? Who is Yiayia?"

"She's my Greek grandma. Taught me everything I know about cooking."

"Sounds like an awesome lady."

"She was. Her spanakopita was delicious. The trick is using feta made with goat's milk for the best taste, then making the sign of the cross before popping it into the oven."

"Well, I don't think God cares much about perfectly made food."

"But I think He cares more about the people who make them."

Dillon looks down at the dough and stills. "I'm not sure God's really interested in hearing from me these days."

"I think you will be surprised." I nudge him. "Start with the cookie prayer."

He huffs out a laugh. "What's that?"

"Simple. You pray your cookies turn out well. If they don't, you trust God has a sense of humor and a lesson in store for you."

He shakes his head but smiles. "You're impossible. You know that, right?"

"Oh, and charming. And insightful. And always right."

He grins at me before rolling out the dough on the counter. We move in tandem, reaching for the same spoon. Our fingers brush, our hands touch, and we pause. We don't quite pull away.

It's just cookies, Cleo, not chemistry.

But I feel it. That tiny breath he holds every time I get too close.

We work together in seamless synchronicity, placing the dough balls on the tray. Dillon slides the tray into the oven.

"So?" I say expectantly, looking down at his hands.

He hesitates, then places both dough-stained hands on the counter. "Okay. Uh God. Please don't let these cookies burn. Amen."

I grin. "Solid start, Whelan."

He glances at me, his usual guarded expression softening.

"Yiayia once burned the baklava because she got too passionate talking about Greek politics. Said the smoke gave it character."

He chuckles. "We better use the timer."

The delicious aroma of baking cookies, pizza, and doughnuts fills the room.

Pride warms my chest. Another point for Team Cleo.

Ten minutes later, the oven beeps, and Dillon pulls out the tray of cookies. Perfectly golden. He breaks one in half and offers it to me.

I take a bite. "These are amazing. Seriously."

"Told you. Chemistry."

For a moment, time seems to stop. Our eyes say more than we will admit.

"Nah." I nudge his arm. "That's all heart."

His eyes meet mine. He smiles, really smiles, his eyes creasing. Like he's asking a question without saying a word.

My breath stutters, and I look away.

We gently remove the cookies from the baking sheet onto the cooling rack.

"So, about that bet. You know I won fair and square, right?" I say, pointing to his Porsche key fob.

"What? You'd really take my Porsche from me?" he says, clutching his chest, faking a wounded heart.

"Dillon, dear, you can't be so attached to things. You can

replace things. Not the people who matter."

"That your life motto or just today's wisdom?"

"Things depreciate. People are like a fine wine. We increase in value with age."

"Let me guess, that's your view about aging, too, right?"

"How did you know? I plan to age gracefully. And while I'm at it, I plan to have the most fabulous time!"

He raises a brow. "Fabulous? Who uses that word?"

"It's a British staple! Fabulous is a fantastic way to celebrate life," I say, waving my hand.

"Sounds very British. Wait, are you British? You've got this half-accent thing going on."

"Well, darling, it's strategic. Depends on whom I'm speaking to. The rather fabulous accent comes out when I'm dining like the queen, drinking my favorite Earl Grey tea, and nibbling on biscuits. The sweet British kind of cookies, not the dry things Americans call scones."

Dillon chuckles and shakes his head. "You've said fabulous, like, three times."

I give him a crooked smile. "Born and raised in the UK, polished in the States. The accent is a patchwork, refined but slippery."

"So that doesn't explain your half-accent," he says, raising a brow.

"I'm getting to that. Be patient, grasshopper."

He chuckles.

"If you must know, me mum lives in the UK. When my parents divorced, we moved to York. My sister, Tia, lives there too. Well, mostly, when she's not flitting her way across the globe doing her Instagram PR influencer thingy and styling celebs."

He looks at me with bated anticipation.

"I moved to the US when I was twelve. I ditched the British lilt somewhere between algebra and afternoon tea. Prep school kids don't exactly embrace difference, so I perfected my own flavor. One part rebellion, two parts don't-mess-with-me."

"Really?" he says, brow raised.

"What can I say? I like to keep life interesting." I grin.

I start stacking the cookies into a take-home dish.

Dillon studies me for a beat and then his mouth quirks in amusement like he's solved half a puzzle.

"So, an international mystery woman with a flair for drama and cookies?"

I lift my mug and clink it against his. "They're biscuits, not cookies. And yes. Absolutely, darling."

I shift a little closer, pretending to reach for the parchment paper.

My hip grazes his. He doesn't step back.

Instead, he angles toward me, just a little.

It's nothing. And, it's everything.

Leaning against the counter while folding his arms, Dillon responds, "Miss Ambrosia, you could be an international spy with all the places you have lived."

I mimic his pose. "Well, Whelan, how do you know I'm not a spy?"

"I suppose you'd have to kill me if I revealed your identity?"

"Maybe not kill you. But I might have to give you amnesia," I say, tucking a strand of hair behind my ear.

His gaze dips to my mouth. I pretend not to notice.

I do. Oh, I do.

A slow current shifts between us, one neither of us seems

ready to cross.

For half a second, I almost lean in, just enough to blur the line between teasing and something real.

But then the woman on the loudspeaker interrupts the moment by blaring her announcement. "Please start cleaning up your stations. We close in twenty minutes."

The spell breaks. We busy ourselves with the clean-up. Neither of us says another word, but I know what he's thinking. Because I'm thinking the same thing. There's something about baking cookies with a man who's allergic to feelings.

It wasn't a date, I tell myself.

Just because it was warm and good and real in a way that sneaks up on you when you're not looking.

As we gather the leftovers, his fingers brush mine again. No apology or awkwardness. Just that quiet awareness.

And for the first time, I wonder if we are still pretending to be on opposite teams, or pretending we are not already falling.

***

On the drive home, Dillon's words loop through my mind. *She was the heart.* And suddenly, I feel the hollow space in my chest where worry settles.

I pull out my phone to text my mom but stop. It's past midnight her time. I scroll through my messages. Nothing. She'd sounded tired last week. Weather, a headache, one of those vague parent things that never quite sits right.

I start typing. Then stop.

"Hi, Mum, just wanted to check..."

Delete.

I toss the phone into my bag. Overthinking is my Olympic sport anyway. But even Olympians know when to trust their gut.

Dillon's mom taught him that baking made people feel cared for. My mom just wanted a phone call. Sometimes showing up doesn't require an escape room. Just a check-in.

I'll call her first thing in the morning.

***

My phone pings as I slide into the back of my Uber. The Sensibility Sisters chat is exploding again, dings, emojis, the usual chaos.

SENSIBILITY SISTERS:

Tia: Emergency!!! Just passed my ex. He smirked like we shared a Pinterest board and not two months of emotional trauma.

Cleo: Want me to send a glitter bomb to his coworking space with a confetti invoice?

Nicole: I got something better, a custom mug that says, *"Her ROI improved without you."*

Shiloh: Can we not talk about exes before lunch? I need carbs and someone who gets feelings.

Alexa: Someone get her a real breakfast. And maybe delete the apps. Soul > swipe.

Mia: Or at least stop matching with guys who list "banter" as a personality.

Megan: I'd like to formally retire from modern dating. Someone find me a florist in Paris.

Tia: Honestly? I'm done. Apps, bios, ghosting. It's all unpaid emotional labor.

Nicole: Burn them. And their voice notes.

Cleo: Plot twist: Your soulmate is in Tuscany with no Wi-Fi and a dog named Zucchini.

Megan: Preferably fluent in espresso. And honesty.

Tia: And not allergic to commitment. Or pants.

Shiloh: And can make a decent risotto. Or at least pronounce "bouillabaisse."

Alexa: Take the trip. Change the view. The right guy won't need translation.

Mia: And won't ghost if you ask about his actual feelings.

Cleo: Still voting for our Paris branch. With croissants and no spreadsheets.

Megan: And lavender ice cream. And flower stalls.

Tia: And men vetted by Megan's peony test and Nicole's risk matrix.

Nicole: I already started the form.

Alexa: Add a loyalty clause and emotional availability clause. I'll enforce it.

Megan: Then I guess I'm finally safe to fall in love.

I smile at their chaos, but something tugs beneath it. Maybe we're all just holding out for the thing that makes us feel chosen.

For a second, everything feels a little less heavy. Dillon saw something in me I wasn't pitching. And that might be the scariest and most hopeful part of all.

Maybe what matters isn't how we show up. Maybe it's being seen. Really seen. Not for what we project, but for what we carry.

Megan's always believed in wildflowers and wild dreams, especially the kind that bloom on Parisian balconies with men who actually listen.

And Tia? She taught brands how to be seen.

But sometimes, I wonder if anyone really sees her.

I sigh.

Maybe that's all any of us want.

Someone who reads between the lines.

11

Chapter 11: After The Escape

Dillon

The building is quiet when I finally step outside. Most of the team is still inside, laughing over leftover cookies and boxed-up pizza, trading inside jokes. From a distance, it probably looks like a win to anyone watching. Team unity, corporate trust-fall energy, the kind of evening HR loves to brag about.

But I'm not thinking about optics.

I rub my thumb along my jaw, letting the cold night air steady me.

I keep thinking about the moment the lights went out and the door sealed shut with a soft click that echoed louder than it should have.

It wasn't the darkness that got to me. It was the memory it carried with it.

It snaps me back to a childhood hallway and news that changed everything.

For a breath, I was no longer in the escape room. I was

ten years old, holding my mother's hand when she got the devastating news.

I froze because my body remembered before my mind caught up.

And Cleo, she saw it. She said my name like she meant to steady me.

My fingers curl, nails pressing into my palm.

That was what caught me off guard. Not the panic or Jemima's spiral, but her.

She walked toward the chaos, not away, and I followed.

I draw a sharp breath.

I pull out my phone to check the time.

Incoming call: Robert Whelan.

I stare at the name. Two rings, then decline. I don't have space for that tonight. I slide the phone back into my pocket.

Cleo's voice echoes in my head.

I still don't know what possessed me to go to that baking class. All I know is that I stood in a room that smelled like vanilla and garlic, watching her toss flour at me like we were old friends instead of two people who had spent the week pushing each other's buttons.

When I mentioned my mother, she stayed steady in a way I didn't expect.

Just steady. Just there.

I run a hand through my hair.

When I admitted I hadn't baked since she died, when I said God probably wasn't interested in hearing from me, Cleo didn't argue. She didn't offer platitudes. Just that look. That steady, soul-deep presence that made me feel, unguarded. And for the first time in a long time, I didn't resent it.

In my world, vulnerability equals danger. With her, it didn't feel like that.

What am I doing?

Focus, Whelan. Get control. This is how people get distracted.

I keep thinking about the way Cleo's fingers brushed mine when we reached for the same measuring cup. She didn't pull away. Neither did I. Just the soft graze of skin, barely anything, yet it short-circuited my focus.

Then she leaned in too close, laughing about cookies and chaos, her breath warm with matcha and spice. I caught the scent of something floral and earthy. It hit like a memory I didn't know I missed.

One look and everything in me went still.

This is a bad idea.

Cleo is off-limits. Wanting her doesn't change that.

I drag a palm over my face.

My hand hovered near her jaw. I saw it flicker in her eyes, too, want colliding with restraint. And just like that, the moment passed.

It is just a reaction. I will move past it. I always do.

The crusted cookie dough on my hands feels more human than any investor handshake I've had in a year.

I'm not used to being seen like that. Not without strategy. Not without conditions. And the part that unsettles me most is that I did not mind it.

Lifting my head at the sound, I shove the thought down.

Noah's footsteps scuff the rooftop. He slides a whiskey tumbler toward me, then drops into the chair beside mine with a groan. "That was something," he says, tipping his head back. "Remind me why we thought corporate team building was a good idea?"

I take the glass. My fingers curl around the chilled surface.

"She handled it well," I say after a beat.

Noah glances sideways. "Cleo?"

I nod. He says nothing, but the corner of his mouth lifts. "She was calm. Efficient. Surprising."

"That time Jemima had a meltdown and Cleo played therapist, right?" he asks.

"She didn't hesitate. I did," I confess.

"And you froze." He says it like he's reporting the weather.

I stiffen. He's not wrong.

My fingers tighten around the glass.

Memories I'd buried tried to surface. For a split second, in that escape room, I locked up. Not because I didn't know what to do, but because I did.

Because I remembered my father's temper. His steel-edged voice. *"Boys don't cry. Winners don't show weakness."*

Ketchup had splattered down my temple at dinner. I didn't move, didn't wipe it.

He looked once and walked away. There was no comfort. No apology. Only silence.

I sat at the table for an hour.

Noah watches me. Doesn't push. "What's the story with you and her?"

"Nothing," I say.

"Sure," he says, drawing out the syllables.

I glare at him. He doesn't flinch. "She's good at reading people. It's her job."

"And you hate being read. So what makes her different?" Noah asks, crossing his arms.

"She doesn't flinch," I say before I can stop myself. "Most people try to impress me or avoid me. She does neither, she pushes."

"You put your hands on her hips and followed her through the dark." He wiggles his eyebrows. "That's not nothing."

I take a long drink. He's not wrong. "It was a trust exercise."

Noah chuckles. "Looked like a chemistry lab from where I was standing."

Cleo's voice cut through the black, grounding me. "Dillon. Talk to me." Not fear, not weakness, but grief dressed up as control.

I shove the memory down, but it presses against my chest like a weight.

Maybe that's why Cleo got under my skin. She didn't freeze. She didn't falter. She jumped in like it was instinct. I didn't want her to see me like that. But I didn't want to be alone either.

I clench my jaw. "She helped Jemima breathe," I say, steadying my voice. "It wasn't just technique. It was her presence. She knew what to say. How to be."

Noah nods. "You weren't expecting that."

I don't answer, because yes, she surprised me. No metrics. No overlays. Just her laughter.

"It caught me off guard," I admit. "She wasn't the version I'd pegged her for."

"And that scares you."

Fear is predictable. Data is predictable. She isn't.

I stare at the skyline, the cold glass in hand. "I don't have room for distractions."

"Dillon, you don't have to treat life like a chessboard."

I shrug. "That's how I stay in the game."

"But winning might not be the point."

I look down at my hands. I haven't scrubbed the crusted cookie dough off.

I have had chemistry before. Charisma, strategy, flirtation. But this was not about spark. It was about safety. About being seen and still standing.

The thought that she might matter in a way that doesn't fit my equation? That's dangerous.

Cleo Ambrosia doesn't want to win me. She wants to understand me. And I can't afford that.

***

I barely slept and spent the night tossing and turning. I checked my phone twice this morning, waiting for a reply that never came. I hadn't even messaged Cleo.

It's nothing. Just habit. Just proximity fallout. These things fade. Except it hasn't.

When I walk in the office the next morning, Cleo's already working in the lounge. She sits cross-legged on the sofa, laptop open. Her hair's up, eyes focused on her screen. She looks nothing like the woman who guided me through the dark without hesitation. Because this Cleo is real.

There's a faint trace of something floral, jasmine, maybe, or whatever lives on her skin. I should be focused on grabbing the file, but my gaze catches on the curve of her neck where a strand of hair has fallen loose.

I clear my throat.

She looks up. "Morning, Whelan."

"Ambrosia," I reply.

She waits.

Say it.

I pick up the file I left yesterday. I could simply leave, claiming that as my sole purpose for visiting. But I don't.

I hover. "You handled last night well."

She blinks, then shuts her laptop. Harder than necessary. "That's your version of a thank-you?"

"I said you handled it."

"Let me guess. You Googled thank-you phrases for alpha males."

I exhale through my nose. "I Googled nothing."

She snorts. "Well, there's your first problem."

We fall quiet. Sunlight catches in her eyes.

"I wanted to acknowledge that you didn't have to step in," I say.

"You mean, when you didn't?"

I don't respond. I can't tell if she is joking or criticizing.

She softens. "That's not a crime, you know."

I shift my stance.

"It feels like one anyway."

She studies me. "You're not used to freezing."

"I didn't freeze."

"Sure. And I love spreadsheets."

My lips twitch. I sit next to her. The pause stretches out. "What do you want me to say, Cleo?"

"Nothing. Unless you want to. But I want to know something."

"What?"

"Why is control the only thing holding you together?"

I exhale a long, slow breath. She watches and waits.

"Because it is," I say.

She nods, almost imperceptibly. "I know what that's like."

I meet her eyes. She doesn't elaborate. But I remember her voice last night. Her stillness. Her presence.

Cleo's gaze drops. Mine does too. She shifts. Clears her

throat. "We should get to the meeting."

I stand. "Right."

I turn to go, then pause. My fingers twitch against the file. I could walk out, pretend last night didn't rattle me. But the words claw their way up my throat anyway.

"Cleo."

She looks up.

I take a breath. No armor this time. Just truth. "Thanks."

Not just for Jemima. Not just for the room.

Cleo's smile is genuine.

And it hits like warmth cracking through concrete.

***

Noah stands outside the conference room, coffee in one hand, typing fast on his phone with the other. That familiar half-smirk plays on his face. I don't ask. Probably trading business memes with that Reddit pen pal he refuses to admit he's half in love with.

Looking up, he asks, "You good?"

"Fine," I say.

"You briefed her yet about the weekend?"

I shake my head. "Not yet."

"Oscar requires all top-level executives and consultants to attend."

I arch a brow. "Since when do we let Oscar dictate a guest list?"

"Since he doubled his investment and he is hosting the fundraiser at his Country Club," Noah mutters, clearly not thrilled.

"We can't afford to turn that kind of exposure down. We've

already presented it to investors as a strategic off-site. But a guest list?"

"It's Oscar. You know he's going to showboat. Just don't let him rattle you."

"He won't."

Noah tilts his head. "Then tell Cleo she's going. Preferably before we're halfway to the lake house."

I nod, but my jaw tightens. Cleo won't enjoy being blindsided. I'll tell her.

12

Chapter 12: Lake House

Cleo

I veer off the mapped route. Dillon's jaw tightens.

"I had it all figured out," he says.

"Exactly why I'm driving. I won the bet, so my rules." I grin, easing around the curve. "Time to loosen the tie, Whelan. Spontaneity won't kill you. You know," I say lightly, "they never tell you in founder school that success can take you down faster than failure. Calypso's scaling too fast."

Dillon raises a brow. "You worried?"

I shrug. "Only when Abby starts using words like 'burn rate' and 'runway' like we're about to crash-land."

"By the way, I still don't know what I'm supposed to be packing for. You said weekend. That's all I got."

Dillon smirks but doesn't look over. "I didn't get the full details until this morning. We weren't sure it was happening, but Oscar locked in the event very last minute."

"And you didn't think I might need, I don't know, shoes?"

"I solved the shoe problem. You'll see."

I hit the gas pedal while maneuvering around a sharp bend.

Dillon shakes his head. "You're a handful. Where did you learn to drive like this?"

"What, is not being in the driver's seat too much to handle?" I smirk. "I did an advanced driving course during college. "They say the secret to handling tight corners safely is not to hit the brakes when it gets scary, but to hit the gas."

I look over my shoulder at a wide-eyed Dillon. He tries to hide it, but I read the intrigue in his eyes anyway.

As we drive the windy mountain roads, I glance at him wryly. "You didn't expect my special brand of awesome."

Dillon laughs, muttering, "No, but I'll be prepared next time."

"So how about you give me more intel about why we are going on this weekend trip?"

Dillon straightens in his seat and clears his throat. "We've been preparing to pitch Damon Oscar from Finn Financial for months. He's hosting the fundraiser at Mohonk Mountain House. Stone fortress meets curated legacy, perched on a cliffside lake like it owns the view. Very Oscar. Very optics."

I clock the venue choice instantly. Oscar's not just throwing a party, he's staging a curated scene. Influence wrapped in charm, power disguised as generosity.

"He's an angel investor who likes young blood startups. Noah and I figured it's the perfect time to get on his radar."

"I'm guessing iSight is a sponsor?" I ask.

"Two tickets. Diamond dinner. Fifty grand a seat," he says like it's just logistics. But the smug glint tucked at the corner of his mouth is the real tell. He's holding a winning hand, and he knows I just realized it.

"Just two tickets? Why wasn't Noah here?" I ask with a straight smile. Then it clicks. "Hang on, is this dinner a black-tie event? You didn't tell me. I have nothing to wear! "I packed like I am going hiking, not hobnobbing with billionaires," I say, a flicker of panic creeping in.

"Calm down, I took care of everything. There was no time for shopping, not for this level of formality. And I figured you'd hate asking for help."

Speaking of last-minute events I remember that Tia never texted back. She'd been juggling some last-minute styling project this week. Something for a "very particular" client, she'd said. Probably a brand shoot or a corporate thing. I didn't ask. She gets cagey under NDA and usually vanishes into glam land until it's over.

"Noah thought Oscar wouldn't open up to two bros. Besides, we need your expert skills in observation." Dillon flashes me a wry smile.

"What cause are they raising funds for?" I say as I check the rear-view mirror.

"It's for his Entrepreneur Incubator University. Oscar likes to find talent in obscure places so he can groom and nurture promising students into successful startups."

"He likes to *groom* talent?" I deadpan.

"Yeah, he likes to spot talent so he can be the first on the ground with new ideas. Because the tech industry moves so quickly, new products that are first to market tend to gain lots of attention.

If Oscar's idea of "grooming talent" means puppeteering people, I'll be watching him like a hawk.

We stop at a gas station to fill the tank. To give my hands something to do, I pull out my phone and scroll through old texts. Nothing from Mom. That's strange. She hadn't sounded great the last time we spoke. Tired, distracted.

A thread of unease tugs low in my chest. I push the worry down; I have enough problems without inventing new ones. She's fine, she has to be.

I add a mental sticky note to text her later.

Thirty minutes later, we enter a gated community. I slow down as Dillon leans forward, scanning house numbers. "We're here. Turn in there, park in the driveway."

I turn the car down the steep driveway. A spectacular view unfolds in front of us.

"Wow!" I exclaim. "It's beautiful here."

I park, and we both jump out of the car. I grab my phone and start snapping photos. Every frame is a painting. As I turn to my right, I stop, and our eyes meet. Dillon's not looking at the lake. He's looking at me with a smile that lights up his entire face.

"Glad you like it," he says as his eyes brighten.

The tension thickens, and I look away first.

"Let me grab our bags. You head inside," he says, handing me a handwritten note.

I unfold it and read the door code numbers. His handwriting is cute, but deliberate. Pocketing the note, I head to the front door, punch in the code, and step inside. I stand stock-still in the entrance hall, my mouth agape.

The entryway opens into a space framed by massive glass sliders. A chic wooden deck overlooks a panoramic lake.

The view looks like an architecture digest spread with the glassy water surface reflecting the trees. The high ceilings with wooden beams give it a modern yet welcoming feel.

"Wow," I murmur, delight slipping out before I can stop it.

Dillon is calm and steady. "Yeah, the lake's spectacular this time of year.

The ache lingers longer than I want, threading through the edges of my excitement like a frayed stitch. I cross my arms, pressing my elbows to my ribs, grounding myself before it shows. I don't want Dillon to see it, the girl still waiting for broken promises to be fulfilled.

"Are we the only ones staying here?" I ask, glancing around the open-plan living space like it's too good to be true.

"Just us," he confirms. "Oscar and the other guests are booked at the club resort down the road. I figured this place would give us some breathing room. We each have our own room."

I raise an eyebrow. "You booked us a whole lake house. For strategy?"

"And quiet," he admits. "Noise does not help me think or sleep."

"Right," I say, a flicker of emotion tightening my expression. "Me either."

Dillon leans in over my shoulder and murmurs, "You planning to admire the view all day or help me carry these bags?"

I'm suddenly aware of every nerve ending as his breath skitters across my neck. My breath hitches, and I feel ridiculous because I can't move. Shivers shoot down my spine, and I'm hyper-aware of every muscle in my body.

Dillon walks past me and sets the bags down on the floor. Looking back, he beckons, "Come look outside."

I force a smile, chasing the breath caught behind my heart. "Yeah. Coming."

I follow Dillon outside to the deck, the cool air biting at

my skin, a reminder that some aches follow you even into the prettiest places.

The lake is framed by trees, most of their branches bare, with only a few stubborn leaves clinging in shades of russet and gold. Fallen leaves scatter across the shoreline and float on the water's glassy surface, catching the fading light.

We watch the sun sink behind the ridgeline, its reflection rippling across the lake.

"Ready for more?" he says, gesturing toward the house.

"Sure. Lead the way."

He turns to head inside, and I follow close behind. The house has three floors, exquisitely decorated with tasteful furniture. Gold and blush accents adorn a plush tan leather sofa. An interior decorator with carte blanche must have created this. The designer selected every painting, vase, and décor piece to accent the high-end aesthetic.

We take the stairs to the lower floor. Another wall of floor-to-ceiling sliding doors shows off the lake view. It reveals an open plan, a fully equipped home gym, and two kayaks.

"Wait here a sec," Dillon says, pausing outside a closed door. "I solved a problem for you."

I raise an eyebrow. "What kind of problem?"

"The kind you didn't realize you had until now."

Turning the light on, Dillon holds the door open, and I step inside. The room glows warm and gold. I gasp and hold my hand over my mouth. It looks like a Neiman Marcus showroom. Three beautiful gowns hang on racks, shoes in labeled boxes, everything pristine and arranged like something out of a luxury boutique. There is a table laid out with unopened makeup, hair products, and styling brushes.

"I didn't know what color or style you'd like, so I called in a little help," Dillon says with a wink.

I stand there, stunned.

"Dillon…"

He shrugs. "You said you had nothing to wear."

I glance at the labels. Every single one is my size. Not even close.

Which means what, he guessed? Or bribed a stylist with CIA-level data access?

I don't know.

But somehow, that feels more intimate than if he'd kissed me.

"Cleo? I've never seen you speechless before. It looks good on you," Dillon says with a wink.

I press a hand to my chest. "That's not fair. You don't get to be thoughtful *and* smug about it." "How did you know my size?" I ask, surprised.

His smile deepens. "I'll take that as a thank-you."

Warmth spreads through my chest, and my heart pounds. No one's ever done something like this for me.

"I have my ways. I told you, I'm good at solving problems. Please, take your time. This space is all yours."

I stand there, blinking, overwhelmed, and touched. I want to say something witty, something breezy and dismissive, to brush off the knot rising in my throat. But nothing comes.

Dillon watches me from the doorway like he is still evaluating my reaction. Filing it away in some mental Excel spreadsheet labeled 'Cleo: Emotional Data, Inconclusive.'

"How did you manage to get all of this?" I finally ask, fingering the hem of a deep sapphire gown.

"I told you," he says with a faint smile, "I solve problems." He says it like it's simple. Like the logistics and precision it must have taken to pull this off isn't impressive. As if expecting what I might need and want isn't personal. But it is.

We lock eyes and exchange loaded smiles.

It takes everything in me to stop myself from launching myself into his arms for a hug.

For the first time, I don't see a gruff exterior.

This man is a truffle!

Polished armor hiding something unexpectedly sweet and gooey in the middle.

What is hidden underneath is a heart that just might undo me.

I don't know what game he's playing, but it's not one I know how to win. And maybe that's the point. This isn't strategy, it's intention. And for the first time in a long time, someone saw my need before I even named it.

"Take your time. Just holler if you need anything. We leave by 6:45." He takes one last lingering look, then closes the door behind him.

I hear the click. The sound reverberates in me. I stand in the center of that room for another full minute, staring. Everything Dillon's done, everything he wasn't saying, bounces around in my head like ping-pong.

For the first time since I met him, I'm not sure how to frame him. Was this calculated? Generous? Just strategy? Or was this something else?

I run my fingers across the smooth silk of one dress and let out a slow breath.

He's not the only one struggling to interpret signals.

A dress I didn't choose, hanging in a closet I didn't expect. In a gorgeous house with a man I don't quite trust yet.

Yet somehow, he knew my size, my style, like some kind of

bespoke fairy godmother with a superiority complex.

It should creep me out, but mostly, it makes me feel seen.

No one has ever anticipated my needs before I spoke them.

This kind of vulnerability is scary.

If Dillon sees me, really sees me, then he might see the parts I've worked so hard to conceal.

Okay, enough spiraling. No more time for self-medicated therapy, Cleo.

I glance at the clock. Two hours to go. Time to suit up. We have an expensive dress, questionable guests, and a CEO who looks at me like I'm either his biggest threat, or worse, his biggest craving.

I glance at the note card on the makeup table. "Go slay," it reads in unmistakably bold cursive. My heart skips. It looks like Tia's handwriting.

I pull out my phone to call my sister. It goes to voicemail. I shoot her a text.

Cleo: CEO man surprised me. Personal shopper + glam squad moment. Everything I need, in one room. I'm shooketh.

The three grey dots pulse. She's seen my message.

Tia: It's midnight. Can't answer your call. And OMGosh akamazing!! 💃✨

Tia: CEO man has good taste

Cleo: Did you have something to do with this?

Tia: Can't say for sure. Now hush and slay. Sending you a hair curling video. Text me a photo. xoxo 💋

Perching my phone on the shoe box, I watch the tutorial and follow the steps. Let's hope it turns out without needing hairspray, glue, or duct tape.

Twenty minutes later, I hear a knock on the door.

"Two more minutes! I'm almost finished!" I exclaim.

I glance at myself one final time. This dress is perfectly form-fitting, yet tasteful. I feel a little exposed with how low the back is, but the built-in bra fits for comfort. The soft silk finish and flowing skirt make me feel like Cinderella, ready for the ball. So, this Oscar night by Oscar is going to be a little less pretentious, I hope.

I snap a quick photo and text it to Tia.

I slip my feet into the slingback heels. They fit. Grabbing the matching silk purse, I switch off the light. I ascend the stairs, clutching the front of my dress. Let's hope I can make it through the evening without falling over myself.

I round the corner, and I hear a gasp. Dillon holds a hand over his mouth and stares at me with wide eyes.

"Looks like it's your turn to be speechless. It's a good look on you, Mr. Whelan," I say, doing a twirl. "I take it you approve?"

"You look stunning, Cleo. That shade of blue really suits you," he says as his eyes scan me up and down.

As I sling the black silk shawl over my shoulders, Dillon steps closer until he's within arm's reach. "There's just one thing missing," he says as he reaches inside his pocket. He pulls out a rose-gold necklace with a tear-shaped diamond pendant. "May I?" he asks with a questioning smile.

"Sure, thank you. It's beautiful," I say as I hold my breath.

Dillon steps even closer, still facing me, and slings the necklace behind my neck. Instead of attaching the clasp from behind, he holds his stance and joins the two sides of the necklace under my chin while holding my gaze. I can feel his breath on my neck.

I exhale as the scent of his cologne floods my senses. It's ocean-fresh, but manly. It reminds me of summer vacations on the Greek islands.

I try to stop my heart from racing by placing a hand on the pendant.

"Shall we?" Dillon says, holding out his elbow.

I slip one hand into the crook of his arm, grasping his bicep, while the other hand gathers the fabric of my dress. His muscles tense slightly under my touch, like he wasn't expecting me to hold on quite so tightly.

Like maybe he's just as thrown as I am.

We make our way to the car, neither of us saying a word.

The fire and crackle between us are undeniable, yet we pretend this is just business.

Just one night. Just a dress.

But even I can't lie to myself right now.

My phone vibrates. My sister Tia and her emoji love.

Tia: You're gonna OWN that room, queen! Show them who's boss.

13

Chapter 13: Belle Of The Ball

Dillon

The club dinner's still an hour out, but my brain's already spinning. How to frame the pitch, which version of me I need to present to Oscar, how to keep Cleo from clocking the tension I haven't named yet.

I check my watch again. It feels too quiet, too calm. The lake outside is unbothered by the storm brewing in my chest.

Cleo's been under my skin since that first pitch. But yesterday, barreling down those mountain roads with the windows down, her hair wild, her grin wider than the curve ahead, something shifted in me. I sat there calculating exit strategies, pretending I wasn't impressed, but I was. More than I want to admit to anyone, including myself.

She throws me off balance, and I resent how quickly it happens. I am not built for the unknown, not in business, not in my head, and not in my heart.

Letting anyone past the perimeter feels like a breach in the systems I build for a living. She reads people, and somehow, I have let her read me. Not just the facts. The fractures too.

Cleo Ambrosia doesn't play the game, and something about that makes me forget my own rules. She reads them without judgment, and she never looks away.

It does not feel like exposure. It feels like breathing again.

Part of me wonders if this could work. What it might be like to trust her with the parts I've spent my whole life defending.

I imagine waking up to her laugh, letting her challenge me, ground me, see me not as the CEO, but simply as myself. Someone who does not need to impress her to make her stay, someone she would meet in the dark without demanding a light.

Then the smarter part kicks in, shaped by years of pressure, legacy, and loss. It knows hope has a shelf life, that letting someone in is like handing them the launch codes to everything I have spent my life protecting, and I have built too many walls to give anyone the blueprint now.

Still, Cleo's here. Wearing the dress I chose for her. I think back to that look, that faint, knowing smile. The one that sees through every defense I've ever built. She looks at me like I'm not broken, not dangerous, just human. But for the first time in a long time, I didn't feel like I had to hold it all together.

I shake my head once, as if that could reset me.

If I'm not careful, this weekend stops being strategy.

It could turn into something I cannot control, and that may be the most dangerous part. Distraction is dangerous, and hope even more so. We are here to close a deal, not rewrite the plan. And yet the wanting is louder than the logic.

I exhale slowly. She's here for the weekend. That's all. We're pitching Oscar. That's all. And when this is over, I'll go back to playing it smart. Safe. Detached. Controlled. Because anything else would be lethal.

Then I hear her. Cleo steps into view, and for a second, I can't remember what I was doing. The dress is midnight blue, sleek, made to move with her. It fits like it was made for the way she walks into a room. One glance, and I'm rattled. I expected her to look good. I didn't expect to be rendered speechless.

"Dillon," she says, tilting her head. "You're staring."

I clear my throat. "It suits you."

"Which part?"

"All of it," I say, working to keep my voice even.

Cleo smiles and turns slightly, the light catching the soft wave of her hair.

For a beat, I can't move. Then I step closer before I can talk myself out of it.

I reach for her hand, slow and deliberate.

Her breath catches, and I feel it more than I see it.

I lift it gently, and my lips graze her knuckles.

Her pulse flickers beneath my fingers.

She does not pull away, and I do not let go right away.

When I finally release her hand, she says nothing.

But her eyes search mine like she is seeing past the armor too.

I shouldn't have done that. This isn't who I am.

I told Noah I didn't have room for distractions. Cleo Ambrosia is a walking contradiction. And she's unraveling me one perfectly timed smile at a time.

If I don't pull it together, I'm going to walk into a room of billionaires looking sucker-punched by a woman in heels.

14

Chapter 14: Tango Tipping Point

Cleo

Candlelight bathes the grand ballroom of the Country Club estate in a golden hue. The air is thick with whispered conversations. A live orchestra's delicate sound fills the room.

Ornate chandeliers glisten above, casting shadows over guests in their finest evening wear.

The night hums with glamour and hidden agendas.

As we step inside the ballroom, a few faces stare at us without recognition. Strategists in tuxedos, venture capitalists sipping champagne, power brokers half-hidden behind masks. A predator's playground, polished and polite.

I have a sense of déjà vu.

"Let me get us a drink. Mojito mocktail?" Dillon asks, grinning with pride.

I offer him a warm smile. "Yes, please. Don't forget the mint."

My midnight blue gown hugs all the right places, a kind of

protective armor. I resist the urge to fidget with my purse now that I am alone.

I watch him at the bar. Dillon Whelan, poised to undo me without even trying.

My delicate mask hides my sharp eyes, yet he would recognize me instantly. His eyes track my movements without trying to hide it.

I catch it, the flicker of heat and longing.

I'm undoing him. And that sends a thrill down my spine.

Just when I'm about to step toward him, Oscar Damon rolls in like fog, all charm and bleached teeth.

Dillon intercepts the introduction and places my drink in my hand instead.

"Whelan, nice to see you made it." Oscar beams like the cat who got the cream. "And this is?" He gestures to me.

There is something in the way he says Whelan, as if the name leaves a bitter taste. I do not know their history, but it feels personal rather than professional.

"Oscar, good evening. This is Cleo Ambrosia, my consultant," Dillon says, his tone tight.

"Consultant? Right. You look far too good to be a consultant." Oscar's tone is laced with arrogance.

I notice Dillon's Adam's apple shift.

"Dance with me, Cleo. Let's give Dillon some time to warm up," Oscar says smoothly. "It would be a shame to waste such a stunning dress."

I glance at Dillon. "Actually," I start to respond, but Oscar interrupts me before I can finish.

I feel the moment Dillon sees Oscar reach for me. His expression is unreadable. His fingers are gripping his glass like it's the only thing tethering him. His eyes lock on Oscar's hand with fire, then flick to me. Then he steps in, hand at my back, eyes steady. Possessive and unmistakable in its intent.

He's fighting two wars.

"She promised me the first dance." The words land with precision and weight.

I arch a brow, lips curving. "Did you ask?"

Dillon exhales and offers his hand. "I'm asking."

Oscar pauses, brows lifting in mock amusement. "By all means, Whelan." He tips his glass. "Don't let me stand in the way."

Dillon doesn't wait. He takes my hand and leads me onto the dance floor, his grip secure but not forceful.

"You didn't like that," I murmur. "Jealous or territorial intervention?"

"Both," he replies, his voice rough. The orchestra swells. Then he pulls me into the first step of the tango. It's slow, controlled, intoxicating. Our bodies align as we sync our steps.

"You have a way of reading me I didn't agree to," he says. Each movement becomes a negotiation, his precision against my defiance, his restraint against my invitation.

I turn, challenge him, and lean in just enough to test.

He answers with a twist of intensity that steals my breath.

I pivot again, half a beat too fast. My balance slips.

His arm locks around me, catching me before I fall. Our faces are inches apart. His breath fans across my cheek. He doesn't hesitate.

For a split second, my body braced for the fall. A memory sharp as ice, the snap of cold air, the moment Liam didn't reach for me in time. The trust I lost before I ever hit the ice.

But Dillon does the opposite. He catches me. Holds me

steady.

His grip tightens like he refuses to let gravity win.

"Careful," he says, low and rough. And for the first time in a long time, I let myself believe maybe someone could be there.

"Was that part of the choreography?" I whisper, not trusting my balance, or my heart.

"No," he admits. "But I'm not letting you fall."

The music carries us forward, but something in me wants to linger in that pause.

That unspoken promise.

When our bodies align, the world fades. He's warm. I feel the tension coiled beneath his suit, a storm waiting to break.

"I thought you didn't dance," I breathe, heart hammering.

"I don't *like* to dance," he replies as he spins me close. "Big difference."

Then, quieter, almost to himself, he asks, "Do you enjoy challenging me?"

I almost land against his chest. Too close. I should step back, but I don't.

The steps are different, but the sensation remains the same. Choreographed movements masking the chaos underneath. This time, the audience is one man, and he is watching closely.

Dillon dips me low, one arm locked around my waist, the other steady at my back.

We linger, breathing each other in without moving.

This time, it's not the choreography holding us in place. It's the ache of wanting something too strong to ignore.

Then applause erupts, abrupt and jarring. The moment gone.

Dillon releases me too fast, as if the contact burned.

"You're analyzing this," I whisper.

"I don't know how else to process it," he admits, voice taut.

A hesitant 'maybe' hangs in the air as I glance at him, a flirtatious smile on my face. "Just feel it."

That lands harder than I expect it to.

Something shifts in his eyes, an almost. But then he grabs my wrist, tugging me gently toward the French doors. The moment we step onto the stone patio, the cold hits my skin.

"Dramatic much?" I tease, breathless but not resisting.

Dillon doesn't answer. Just paces. Loosens his bowtie like it's suffocating him. His hands tremble just a smidge.

"What are we doing, Cleo?" he asks, voice rough and unfiltered.

"I don't know how to do this," I whisper. "The push and pull, the signals that mean nothing and everything. I've played this game before, Dillon. I always lose."

He steps closer. "You haven't played it with *me*," he says, like he wants to rewrite that ending. He steps even closer, his thumb brushing over the inside of my wrist, right over the frantic pulse that betrays me. "Tell me I imagined it, the way you look at me."

My pulse answers before my voice can.

I open my mouth. The truth is there, on the tip of my tongue, but I can't bring myself to admit it. Not yet.

Oscar appears out of nowhere with another drink in hand. "Cleo," he calls, stepping onto the patio. "I believe the next dance is mine." He reaches for my wrist without asking, like he's used to getting his way.

My body tenses and my stomach lurches.

I'm not an accessory to be worn. I'm a person to be respected.

I look at Dillon and see it clearly. The fury simmering in

his eyes.

"I didn't agree to anything, Mr. Damon," I say with steady calm.

Oscar leans in. "Cleo, you don't strike me as someone who can be tamed. That must be exhausting for a man like Dillon. I'd be careful with him, he doesn't always see people, only results."

I blink. "Excuse me?"

"You seem like a sharp woman. Don't get caught in the wake of someone chasing legacy," he says with a smug grin.

Before I can step back, a voice cuts through the air.

"Take your hand off her." Dillon's voice is steady and measured, but I feel the storm beneath it. He's holding himself back, barely.

Oscar turns, amused. "Relax, Whelan. It's just a dance."

Dillon offers a thin, practiced smile. He's not frozen this time. He's on fire. "She said no. That should be enough."

Dillon doesn't move closer, not physically, but every muscle in his body is poised and ready. He exhales through his nose, slowly, controlled.

He doesn't want to make a scene or risk the deal he still hopes to close with Oscar.

But I see it, the way Oscar watches Dillon like he's poking a bear to see if it bites.

He doesn't, but his fists are clenched at his sides.

"We're done here," Dillon says quietly.

Oscar raises his hands in surrender. "Didn't mean anything by it. Just being friendly."

Dillon offers me his hand, his eyes flicking briefly to mine, not asking or commanding, just checking. I take it.

"Let's dance," I say, offering Dillon a reassuring smile.

"Dillon," Oscar interrupts, "we will talk later."

Dillon doesn't answer. His eyes never leave mine. We walk away together with no words or apologies. Just clarity between us.

I look back to see Oscar's wry grin, like he's won a game we didn't know we were playing.

As we move through the crowd, I hear murmurs.

Dillon's name, tension, speculation.

Exactly the kind of distraction Oscar thrives on.

But Dillon doesn't react.

He leads me onto the dance floor, hand at my back, jaw tight.

"You didn't have to step in," I murmur.

"I couldn't let that go."

"Even if it costs you the deal?"

He hesitates. Just a flicker.

"There's more than one kind of cost," he says.

And then he pulls me closer.

The orchestra swells, and our bodies find rhythm.

And for once, neither of us is calculating.

We're just here. Moving. Watching. Feeling.

Just for each other, here and now.

15

Chapter 15: Oscar Talks

Dillon

Oscar Damon knows how to command a room. He leans against the cocktail table as if it were designed for him, whiskey glass in hand, charm layered thick as cologne.

When he grabbed Cleo's wrist, it took everything in me not to move. The way Cleo tensed under his touch keeps replaying in my mind.

Right now I need him on my side. I can't afford to lose the deal.

"Dillon, my friend," he says with a slow grin. "You've built something truly remarkable. I can see Lucid Lenses going global, with the right backing, of course."

I offer a nod. "That's the goal. Your proposal is ambitious."

Beside me, Cleo shifts. I don't need to look at her to feel the tension.

The air between us feels brittle, as if one wrong word will splinter it.

Something about Oscar's tone feels off, too smooth, too certain.

I make a mental note to check who's been digging around the Lucid Lenses prototype.

I glance at Cleo just as her eyes lock on Oscar with a quiet intensity I've come to recognize. The kind she uses when she's analyzing something she doesn't trust.

"What's in it for you?" she asks, her tone even.

Oscar chuckles and leans in a little too close. "Smart and beautiful," he says, almost as an afterthought.

She steps away, chin lifted.

"Dillon, you never mentioned your consultant was this perceptive."

It lands in my gut. This isn't harmless charm. It's a line crossed.

She looks at me, waiting for me to react. I should say something.

I already made one move that could cost me this deal. A second might confirm every bias he's waiting to exploit.

So I breathe through it and tell myself it isn't a pattern. A misstep here and Oscar pulls the deal. Months of work. Millions on the table.

I force a tight smile. "Oscar, let's keep this professional."

He chuckles, unfazed. "Relax. Just admiring your team's talents."

Cleo's jaw tightens. She doesn't look at me. Her voice cuts back sharper now. "You've had three companies in the last five years, all of which ended in sudden dissolutions or scandals. What guarantee is there that you won't leave when things get hard?"

Oscar's smile widens. "Business is about risks, darling.

Dillon understands that."

And suddenly, the cost of silence feels heavier than the risk. I glance Cleo's way.

She turns to me, her expression stern. "I need to speak with you. Alone."

I sigh, but nod. "Give us a minute."

Outside, the night air is cool and crisp. It helps. Or it doesn't.

Cleo spins around the moment we're clear of the door. "He did it again—the boundary testing. I know his type, Dillon. And this isn't harmless. You think that dance interruption earlier was a one-off? It's not."

I cross my arms, grounding myself. "Oscar is a proven investor with deep connections. You're letting personal bias—"

"Personal bias?" she cuts in. "That's what you're calling it? Ignoring instincts because they're inconvenient isn't logical, Dillon. It's willful blindness. He manipulates people, and you're walking right into it."

"I make decisions based on facts," I say, jaw tightening. "Not instinct. Not emotion."

She steps closer, fire in her eyes. "Then you're blind. And for someone who built a company on vision, that's ironic."

The words hit harder than anything Oscar's said all night. I built Lucid to bring clarity to the world, to see what others miss. I can't even argue. Because deep down? She's not wrong.

We go back inside. The rest of the conversation with Oscar blurs behind the roar in my head.

Cleo stays quiet, observing, coiled like a spring. As we stand to leave, Oscar gets up with that same slow, deliberate charm.

He places a hand on the small of her back, guiding her

toward the exit.

Oscar raises a smug brow. "Apologies, Cleo. I didn't mean to startle you."

She stares directly into his eyes with a challenging look. "Don't. Touch. Me."

A few heads turn.

The words land like a clean hit to the chest.

I move without thinking. Half a step, hand lifting, heat rising to my face. But then I hear it, my father's voice like a shot between the ribs. *"Never react. Never show emotion. Hold the line."*

And just like that, I'm chained again. Rooted to the ground. Watching her stand alone when I should be beside her.

I should say something, but I don't know what.

Oscar doesn't even flinch. He just smiles, offers a nod, and strolls away, unbothered, unashamed.

Cleo whirls on me before the door even closes behind us. "Did you see it that time?" she hisses. "Or do I need to send you a memo?"

"Cleo—"

"No. This is exactly what I was talking about. He's testing boundaries, seeing what he can get away with, and you just let him."

"I stepped in. But this deal it's months in the making, Cleo. If I push harder, I lose the leverage to finish this."

"Over what I just saw?" Her voice spikes. "Over the very thing you built Lucid to amplify in everyone else but refuse to trust in me because it isn't packaged in code?"

I don't answer. Because deep down, I'm starting to wonder if she's right. And I hate that.

Cleo's eyes bore into my soul for a beat longer, then she

spins and storms toward the balcony, heels clicking on the concrete. She walks away without looking back.

A couple near the bar pauses, watching her retreat.

A waiter glances in her direction, startled by the force of her exit.

My chest tightens. I should go after her. I should explain, or apologize, or something. But my father's voice comes to haunt me. He always told me silence was strength.

Right now, it feels like cowardice.

I've faced thousands of boardrooms, but this silence felt different. Not because of the pitch.

Because Cleo won't look at me.

She used to meet my eyes, defiant, challenging. But tonight, she didn't. And that hurts more than the deal.

But before I can move, a familiar voice slithers up behind me like smoke.

"You know," Oscar drawls, "she's got fire. I like that."

I can't let Oscar know what I'm thinking or feeling. I don't turn to look at him. "She's not interested in your approval."

He chuckles, smooth and unbothered. "Clearly. But I'd be a fool not to admire a woman who knows how to draw blood with a few words."

He claps a hand on my shoulder before I can shrug him off. "Come on, Dillon. Don't let a little friction distract you from the bigger picture."

I catch a glimpse of Cleo just before she disappears. Blonde hair, strong stride, fury radiating off her. She gave me a chance to stand beside her. I did—for a moment. And now I've backed off again. Because I don't know how to hold the line without holding her at arm's length.

Oscar steps around me, blocking my line of sight with that

easy grin. He knows he's won this round. "Listen. I've got a few calls tomorrow with partners on the West Coast. Let's schedule a follow-up. Noon, at my favorite restaurant?"

I hesitate. Every instinct screams at me to hit pause. But logic kicks in like muscle memory. A follow-up is expected, and Oscar knows it. He senses my split-second of hesitation and presses in.

"This thing we're building," he says quietly, leaning just enough to make it sound like a secret. "It's bigger than ego. Bigger than one consultant's hunch. You and I could take Lucid Lenses further than anyone's ever taken emotional tech."

My jaw clenches. "She's not just a consultant."

He raises a brow, then shrugs. "Fair enough. But she's not your CFO either. You need someone who's willing to take risks with you, not rein you in."

"I know what I'm doing," I say, trying to hold back anger.

"Just making sure your development team isn't being steered off course by your new consultant. Don't want this becoming messier than it needs to be. You need partners who think big, not ones who flinch at pressure. Emotional insight is fine for the lab, but don't let it slow you down in the real world."

Every instinct tells me to walk. My muscles stay locked in place.

Oscar feeds the one thing I've built my whole life on: momentum, always moving forward. It's what built iSight Innovations. And the thing that might tear it apart.

"Fine," I say. "Noon."

Oscar's grin widens. "Knew you'd see reason."

He walks off, whistling, his silhouette vanishing into the warm glow of the night lights. I'm left standing there. The cufflink on my left wrist digs into my skin. I twist it, hard. The pain feels earned. Cleo read him the moment he stepped in. I should've trusted that.

Maybe that's the one lesson I should've learned. And I've never felt more blind.

For the first time in years, I know I've made the wrong call.

I won't know how bad the consequences are until it's too late.

16

Chapter 16: Grief Trigger

Dillon

I shove through the ballroom doors as if I'm escaping flames. Cleo's heels echo behind me, each step snapping off the marble.

I spin. "You overstepped back there." It comes out sharp. Too sharp.

I fight to keep the rest of it contained.

Cleo halts mid-stride, eyes flashing. "You let him touch me," she hisses. "And *I'm* the one who overstepped?"

My jaw locks. I know what I saw. One wrong sentence and I lose her.

"I wasn't starting a scene in the middle of an investment meeting," I say.

Cleo steps in close. Heat rolls off her, electric. "So, your deal was worth more than my safety. Got it."

I stay where I am.

"I know what Oscar is. But blowing the deal over a personal

reaction? I couldn't risk it."

She shoves me. Not hard. Just enough to short-circuit everything.

"Stop hiding behind your logic," she grits out. "You want to lead? Then show up when it matters."

Everything stops.

I feel her fire through my suit.

I don't know if it's from anger or adrenaline, or something else I've been too stubborn to name. Restraint wrestles instinct.

"Careful, Cleo," I say, my voice low.

"Why?" she whispers. "Afraid of what you'll feel?"

Yes. I don't say it.

We stand there, the air between us like flint waiting for a strike.

And then, she steps back. The moment breaks. I drag in a breath like I've been underwater.

"Don't. Trust. Oscar," she whispers, her eyes still locked on mine. "That's all I'm saying."

She turns to leave, but I don't move. I want to call her back, to say something, anything, but the words won't come. Instead, I stay rooted.

My mind processes everything I didn't say. Everything I never do.

The music shifts. Nat King Cole. "Unforgettable." My mother's favorite.

The night before her surgery, she swayed barefoot in a threadbare robe. My chest locks. I need air.

I buried the grief under pitch decks and product launches, chasing deals to outrun it.

If I moved fast enough, maybe I'd never feel it.

Tonight, one song cuts through, and I can't outrun it.

I'm ten again, sitting on the carpet, watching her sway barefoot and sing off-key. Her laughter filling the house like sunlight.

Cleo's voice cuts through the fog. "Dillon, are you okay?"

I blink, and I'm back. But the space feels smaller. My lungs tighten.

My jacket feels into a prison. I grab my tie and loosen it.

I grip the balcony rail to steady myself. "I'm fine."

"You don't look fine."

"Sorry. I can't do this right now." I push off the railing, straighten my jacket, and walk away. I hear Cleo call my name, then the sound of heels following.

The cold slaps my face.

I head straight for my Porsche and start the engine. Just as I shift into gear, the passenger door opens. Cleo slides in, breathless.

"Dillon—"

I pull away, harder than I should. She fumbles for her seat belt, silent now.

The city blurs past the windows. I'm not racing, I'm escaping.

Cleo finally says, "You're going too fast."

I grip the wheel tighter. My jaw aches as the memory slams into me. My father's voice telling me I missed Mom's last breath. I was too busy giving a pitch while she was dying.

I blink hard and lock my focus on the road.

There's no use thinking about machines and monitors and things I can't undo.

By the time we reach the lake house, my hands are numb on the wheel. I kill the engine and get out. Cleo follows, close on my heels.

"Dillon, what just happened? Talk to me."

I punch in the code. The lock beeps, and the door swings open. Even the warmth feels like a betrayal.

"Dillon, talk to me."

I whirl around. "Cleo, please. Don't push right now."

I drag a hand down my neck.

I step into the kitchen and open the fridge for something to do.

Cleo doesn't back down. "I'm not trying to fight," she says. "I just I'm worried."

I pour a glass of water and miss the spill.

"You don't get it." My voice drops. "I'm not the guy who talks about things."

She steps close enough to touch. "What if this isn't something to fix?" Her voice is gentle.

My fingers curl around the edge of the counter. I couldn't stop Oscar from brushing past Cleo's boundaries. I couldn't stop what happened to my mom. I couldn't even stop myself tonight.

"Then I break."

My hands tighten on the counter until my knuckles pale.

I don't mean to say it, but it's the truth.

My father built me for logic, not empathy.

And I followed the blueprint, until it failed in the moment that mattered most.

I look toward the lake, focusing on the ripples, trying to center myself.

"That song," I murmur. "It played at my mother's funeral."

Cleo exhales. "Oh…"

I've avoided that song for years. Refused to let it near any playlist, any moment. But tonight, it snuck past my defenses and took everything with it. Despite the setbacks, my mother kept praying. I never understood it. I still don't. But somehow, she came through the fire softer, not broken.

"I don't think about her," I say quietly. "Because if I fail, I can't protect what I've built. I can't protect what I love."

Grief doesn't respect architecture. It found the crack, and tonight, it all came crashing down.

Cleo steps in slowly, like she's navigating a storm. Her hand brushes the counter near mine. "I'm not asking you to fall apart," she says. "I'm asking you not to shut me out."

I look at her. Really look at her.

Her eyes aren't sharp anymore. They're soft, kind. And it undoes me more than anything she could've said. "I'm not experienced with this, being with someone who sees the parts I've buried."

She gives me a small, sad smile. "We all have blind spots, Dillon. The question is whether you're willing to look."

I swallow hard.

I've spent my whole life perfecting how to see what others miss.

Maybe it's time I stopped looking at the world and started looking at myself.

Cleo sees through me in ways no one else ever has.

For the first time in years, I don't feel alone.

She asked me not to shut her out.

For once, I don't want to.

17

Chapter 17: Moonlight Confessions

Cleo

The lake laps against the dock in soft, rhythmic pulses, as if it's breathing. I curl into my sweatshirt, tea in one hand, chin tucked into the other. The moon paints everything silver. The trees, the ripples, even the reflections.

My phone buzzes beside me. Incoming call from Tia. I let it ring, then ignore the text that follows: *"Call me, drama llama."* I want to call her back, to spill everything. But I don't trust my voice not to crack, or my heart not to hope too soon. My mind won't quiet.

I keep looping through everything unspoken between Dillon and me. I came out here in case he was thinking it too. The deck creaks behind me. I feel him before I hear him. My heart stutters.

He hesitates at the doorway, as if deciding whether I'm safe. Whether we are.

Then he steps outside, and the air tightens.

He comes to stand beside me and doesn't sit.

"You disappeared," I say, eyes on the horizon.

"I didn't know what to say," he admits. "That doesn't usually happen to me."

I glance up, studying his profile in the moonlight. He looks tired. Not physically, but emotionally. As if something cracked open and he hasn't figured out how to close it.

"I watched Oscar cross a line," I say. "I waited for you to do something."

He looks at me, searching. I don't look at him.

"You froze."

"I wanted to do something." His voice is low. "But I should've stepped in. I know that. I'm sorry."

I nod. Not because it's okay, but because I understand.

"You see, that's the thing," I say. "I don't get to wait and wonder. I was trained to trust my instincts. To act, not hesitate."

His head turns slightly. "Trained how?"

"I used to work with the FBI. Behavioral analysis. Deception detection. I trained agents to spot lies under pressure."

Dillon blinks. "You're being serious?"

"Yeah." I give a short laugh. "Quantico, joint task force work. It was all very impressive on paper."

"And off paper?"

"Exhausting." I sigh. "Reading motives into every flicker. You stop trusting people and start seeing lies everywhere. Even in people who mean well."

"Is that why you don't let people in?"

The question lands softly, but it doesn't miss the mark.

"It's why I stopped trying," I whisper. "Because once you learn how to profile the world, you forget how to live in it."

He doesn't speak right away. Instead, he steps closer and sits beside me, close but not touching. The heat between us rises anyway.

"So, what changed?" he asks.

I pause. Then meet his eyes. "You did."

He exhales like my answer surprises him.

"I'm so used to reading people. But with you I don't want to analyze. I just want to feel. And that terrifies me." I inhale a breath. "You hide everything behind logic and control and strategic charm. But sometimes…" I swallow. "Sometimes, I see grief behind your eyes. Like you're still waiting to breathe."

He says nothing, but he's listening.

"And me?" I continue. "I built walls after losing everything I thought I could count on. You don't thaw from that overnight."

"But tonight," he says, voice low, "you're here. Letting me in."

I nod. "And you didn't run."

"Not yet." He smiles faintly. "Check back tomorrow."

I laugh softly, eyes stinging.

"So, what do you need now?" he asks.

I don't look at him when I say it. "Someone I don't have to read. Someone I can just feel."

The silence stretches. Fragile, warm, and terrifying. We sit like it's just the moon we're watching. Not each other.

I swirl what's left of my brewing tea. "You look like you're thinking too hard. That's dangerous, you know."

He exhales, his hands rubbing together like he's trying to warm up something deeper than his skin. "I don't think I've stopped overthinking since I was five."

I glance at him. His jaw is tight, like he's chewing on something he doesn't want to spit out. "Is that when you started running calculations on human behavior?"

He breathes out a laugh through his nose. "Something like that." He pauses, then looks down at his hands. "My mother got sick around then."

Everything inside me stills.

"I remember watching my dad," he says, voice low. "Wondering how he could stay so calm while Mom was falling apart. Turns out he wasn't calm. He was just refusing to feel."

I shift so I can see him better. He doesn't look at me.

"At the funeral, people kept saying how gracefully my father handled it. How strong he was." He frowns. "He pulled me aside, squeezed my shoulder hard, and said, 'Pull yourself together. No one respects a man who lets emotions control him.'"

His Adam's apple bobs. He's staring at the horizon, but I don't think he sees it. He's still in that church. Still holding back a sob like it will shatter him.

I want to grab him, hold him. But I don't. Instead, I say quietly, "That wasn't strength, Dillon. That was fear. Your father was afraid of breaking, so he taught you to be afraid of it too."

He doesn't respond right away. When he does, it's quieter.

"Maybe. But it worked. I don't get overwhelmed. I don't break."

My heart aches for him. Not just because of the past, but because of how hard he still clings to it.

"But you don't live either," I say.

He turns to me. His eyes lock with mine.

"And you?" he asks, his voice lower now, almost challenging. "What made you so sure of what you see in people?"

I swallow. It's a fair question. And somehow, the most

terrifying one. But in this moment, with this man, it feels safe enough to tell the truth.

"My father was the overzealous dreamer," I say. "Always talking about big plans and bigger promises. Chasing the next win. My mom believed him every time. We all did. Until the day his 'dream' turned into a federal investigation."

He looks at me with curious empathy.

"He was arrested for fraud. My mom fell apart. My sister was too young to understand. So, I stepped up. Pretended I had it together. Watching people like a hawk became my default. I learned how to spot the cracks before they shattered everything." I exhale. "It's not just instinct. It's survival."

Dillon doesn't look away. His voice is rough when he says, "That's why you don't trust people like Oscar."

I nod. "Because I've met men like him. And I refuse to watch someone I—" I falter. My heart does too. "Someone smart, like you, get used."

The silence that follows feels like standing on a ledge. Dillon leans back. When he looks at me again, I see it. Not logic, not calculation, but something softer.

"You said I don't live fully," he murmurs. "Maybe I don't. But neither do you, Cleo. You see through everyone else's masks. But what about your own?"

I open my mouth, then close it. But something about the way he's looking at me makes it impossible. I recognize the urge to run, to rebuild the mask. I've studied it in others. Emotional evasion. Self-protection disguised as sass. If I were coaching a client, I'd call this a pivot moment. A point where fear meets choice. And I'm standing right in the middle of it, heart in hand.

Time to take my own medicine.

I inhale sharply. "I suppose you're right." The words hit something I didn't expect. Something I didn't realize was bruised.

Maybe it's me, maybe it's him, but suddenly, our fingers brush. Lightly, testing. His thumb grazes my knuckles, the contact feather-light but electric. The world holds its breath. No pressure, no demand. Just presence.

I turn my hand over and let our palms meet. Instinctively, we intertwine our fingers.

No profile. No analysis. Just this.

Real. Unscripted. Human.

We lock eyes. Dillon moves closer. He pauses, with a look that asks for permission.

I look down at his lips, and back at his eyes.

Then, he leans in.

The kiss is soft, careful. Then he deepens it, just enough to erase everything but warmth, ache, and the terrifying sweetness of letting go.

When we part, my breath is shaky. His hand lingers like he's afraid I'll vanish.

I press my forehead to his. "You okay?"

He nods. And for the first time, I believe him. We don't say anything more. We don't have to.

I ease back, just a breath's distance, and tuck a strand of hair behind my ear. His eyes track the movement. He brushes a thumb across my cheek like he wants to memorize it.

Then I force my voice to work. "We should get some sleep," I say lightly, even though my pulse hasn't slowed, and my thoughts are sprinting laps. "Big day tomorrow."

I see his jaw tighten, and that calculating mind of his unraveling. Still trying to catch up. But he doesn't argue, doesn't crack a joke. Just nods.

When I finally stand up, he lets me go. My legs are a little less steady than I'd like. I don't look back, but I feel it. His eyes stay on me until I reach the door. Like he's letting go of something he didn't know he was holding.

I leave him on the dock with the moonlight and walk back inside before I can change my mind.

By the time I slip into bed, the house has gone quiet.

I lie still, but everything inside me is still spinning.

I press my fingers to my lips. Still warm, still his. I've never been kissed like that. It was fleeting but lingering, haunting but electric.

And I know that feeling well.

Dillon didn't just kiss me. He paused the ache, the noise, the fear. For one moment, it was just breath and heat and the slow, trembling possibility of hope.

The lake hums below. Somewhere, a nightbird calls.

Wait, maybe this is spiraling.

I should be listing reasons why this was a bad idea. Why I should leave. Why people who get too close always disappear. Trust has always been a risk I couldn't afford. Like stepping onto the ice for the first time.

But tonight felt different.

Not because the fear disappeared. Because I stopped holding back. I let him in, and I'm still here.

I shift under the covers, heart still racing like I'm back on the dock with him.

What if falling doesn't mean unraveling? What if surrendering, just a little, could feel like freedom? What if love doesn't begin with perfection, but with permission? To be seen. To be held.

Somewhere in the quiet, in the space where fear used to live, something new begins to stir.

Maybe this is what emotional intelligence is really about. Not reading others. Recognizing when you stop running from yourself.

***

By morning, my pulse has calmed, but the questions haven't. The Sisters are already three dozen messages deep by the time I check my phone.

SENSIBILITY SISTERS:

Tia: Just booked a brand tour in Europe, London, Paris, Barcelona. Mild panic. High potential for love story chaos.

Megan: You're going to meet someone who speaks three languages and helps old ladies cross cobblestones.

Tia: Or spills espresso on me and vanishes like a stylish ghost.

Cleo: I'm calling it now. Eiffel Tower. Moonlight. First kiss situation.

Nicole: Remind him you're not into men who post thirst traps and pitch bitcoin.

Shiloh: If he can cook and knows what fresh basil looks like, keep him. Otherwise, no.

Alexa: Don't settle. The right guy will know you're magic and not make you prove it.

Mia: Bonus points if he has a working phone plan and wears pants that fit.

Tia: Can one of you fall in love for me while I eat popcorn in a hotel robe?

Megan: You deserve someone who brings the popcorn,

remembers your coffee order, and knows when not to talk.

Nicole: And understands that "don't touch me" means hands off.

Shiloh: But still warms up leftovers and plays your favorite sad songs without judging.

Mia: Love should feel like peace. Not performance.

Alexa: And if he ghosts? I have a spreadsheet, glitter, and time.

Cleo: Honestly, I'm here for the popcorn plan.

Nicole: You two are literally stepping into romance novels.

Tia: Just waiting for my dramatic meet-cute and minor existential crisis.

Megan: Yours is coming. I can feel it.

Nicole: It's probably already happening. You're just over analyzing it.

Tia: She has been suspiciously soft lately.

Mia: Yeah. Her "no one gets in" firewall might be glitching.

Alexa: Or maybe she's just growing.

Shiloh: She did say someone made her cookies. That counts as intimacy.

Cleo: I'm still processing.

Nicole: Translation: She likes him but hasn't admitted it to herself.

Megan: Just don't run from something good, Cleo.

Tia: Especially if he knows how to bake and doesn't flinch at big feelings.

Cleo: It's complicated.

Alexa: So is healing. Doesn't mean it's not real.

I stare at the text thread for a while.

I laugh, ache a little, love a lot.

Maybe I'm not as alone as I think.

18

Chapter 18: Kitchen Confessions

Dillon

The floor-to-ceiling windows let sunlight spill across the granite counter. The air is crisp with the scent of pine and oak.

I should be catching up on emails about the gala fallout. Instead, I'm staring at the coffee machine, wishing it held answers it doesn't. Neither does the knot tightening in my chest.

A news alert pops up on my phone. A former biotech executive with ties to a defunct AI startup in Prague. The name is redacted, but the timeline overlaps too closely with Oscar's resume. I file it away, meaning to ask Noah.

Fragments of last night replay on a loop. The gala, the Oscar debacle, the walk by the lake. Her lips on mine. *That* kiss.

It started with frustration, turned to defiance, and landed in surrender.

This was supposed to be a weekend. A deal. A contract. A

171

controlled environment.

But Cleo Ambrosia is not a variable you can contain.

I think about the version of me she sees, not the CEO, not the polished product of damage control, but the one who carries a mother's memory like a wound. And still she stayed. I want to tell her about the deals I sabotaged just to feel in control, the nights I stood by that same lake, waiting for the stillness to reach me. But I don't.

My mind spins through the data.

Her working for the FBI should surprise me, but it doesn't. It explains her precision and steel in her voice when she wants answers.

I open the fridge.

My hands move on instinct as I heat a skillet.

I'm not hungry, not really. But cooking gives me something to control, a way to think without spiraling.

I know what it is to measure people, strategize relationships, calculate risk.

But she lives in that space where knowing too much becomes dangerous.

She called me out like she'd read my user manual.

"You hide everything behind logic and control and strategic charm." No one before has seen through my defenses like that.

And yet, when my hand found hers, she didn't pull away. I didn't run. It felt right.

The machine beeps, slicing through my focus. Coffee fills the mug. I lift it, but it's too hot to taste.

Butter pops as I flip the pancake, slightly off-center. It lands cleanly. No surprises, for once.

Then I hear her footsteps. Cleo floats in, rubbing her

eyes. Her hair's a mess, soft curls slipping out of a bun. She's wearing a ridiculous oversized pink hoodie that nearly swallows her whole. She looks unbearably soft.

"You don't sleep much, do you?" she asks softly.

"Too many moving pieces in my head. Quiet feels loud."

She nods like she understands. Blinks like she's recalibrating. "Well," she says, folding her arms. "Didn't peg you as the domestic type. Should I be worried?"

I arch a brow. "Only if you have good feelings about breakfast."

She steps closer, nose twitching. "You made pancakes?"

"They're objectively the best food." I slide one onto a plate and hand it to her. "I cook when I need to think. You follow the recipe. You get a predictable outcome. No curveballs or surprises."

Cleo raises an eyebrow. "Didn't take you for a kitchen philosopher."

I shrug. "My father thought hobbies were a waste of time. Every hour had to serve a measurable purpose. Emotions were a flaw."

I stir the coffee mug, then turn and hand it to her. She takes it from me, and our fingers brush gently.

I turn back to the pancakes. "I was a project to him. A checklist of performance, internships, awards. He measured worth in deliverables. He considered anything less than excellence a weakness."

Cleo steps closer and leans against the counter. Her eyes lock on me, pancakes now forgotten.

"But my mom…" My voice lowers. "She made space for softness, gentleness. She never pushed me or compared me to anyone else. She just showed up."

I line up the measuring cups like soldiers, my eyes fixed on the sugar.

I swallow. I'm on a roll. "She taught me to cook. She used to say love didn't have to be loud to be strong. That warmth wasn't weakness. After a 'lesson' from my dad, usually about something I did wrong, my mom would feed me something warm. She'd sing while she cooked, barefoot, happy, calm. No lecture or pity. Just quiet care, like she was saying, 'You're already enough.'"

Cleo doesn't speak, but her expression shifts. Like she's reading something sacred.

"After she died, I stopped believing in that kind of love. I thought warmth like that was just childhood nostalgia. Not something that could last. Not for someone like me."

"And your dad's version?" Cleo's voice is soft.

"Efficient. Strategic. Always conditional."

We pause, eyes locked.

"And you?" she asks. "Which one do you believe?"

I hesitate. "That's the problem. I learned both. I execute like him. But I crave what she gave me. Maybe that's why I'm always at war with myself."

She picks up a fork but doesn't move. "You cook for people you care about."

I grip the edge of the counter. "Sometimes."

I'm not sure what this means yet. But I know I don't want to stop.

Cleo's breath hitches. For a moment, she looks away, as if anchoring herself.

Her gaze drifts to the kitchen island, and she opens her laptop. I glance over. One column of numbers catches my eye, just enough to recognize the shape of a problem.

"You know your cash flow's upside down, right?" I say gently, careful not to crowd the moment.

She tenses, barely, but then exhales. "Yeah," she says. "Abby's been flagging it for weeks. I've been putting it off."

I nod. "Doesn't mean you failed. Just means you might need a second set of eyes."

Her lips tilt into a wry grin. "Don't suppose you have a spare CFO in your back pocket?"

I grin back. "Only the charmingly unsolicited kind."

She nudges my elbow with hers. "I'll take it under advisement, Whelan."

I motion for us to sit at the bar, side by side. Cleo finally takes a bite of her pancakes. I catch the way her thumb brushes the fork. She does that when she's thinking hard.

There's syrup on her lip. I should look away, but I don't.

"You're staring," she murmurs.

"Observing," I say. "Occupational hazard."

"You're better at it than I thought."

A smile tugs at the corner of my lips. "High praise coming from the human lie-detector."

We fall into a quiet rhythm—syrup, butter, shared silence.

Then she says, "I think I'm bad at trust."

I glance over. Her posture's relaxed, but her voice is tight. "You're the most perceptive person I know," I say. "Brave, too. Even if you don't feel it."

She gives a dry laugh. "You think I'm brave?"

"You are."

She scoffs, but the deflection doesn't reach her eyes. "Recovery's faster when you've been hurt enough times."

"How does that track?"

"I had to become like steel after my dad left and my mom

fell apart. My sister needed someone solid." She pokes at a crumb on her plate. "I trained myself not to be blindsided. When you expect the worst of people, there are no surprises."

"Safer," I echo.

Cleo stands and carries her plate to the sink. I follow, rinsing mine beside her, silence stretching between us.

She turns to me. "And you? What's your excuse?"

I hesitate for a moment. "Control," I say. "I like having it. My whole life's been about anticipating outcomes. Avoiding chaos. Emotions cloud judgment. But then…" I stop as her eyes meet mine. "Then you showed up. And suddenly nothing feels predictable anymore."

She draws in a breath. "People think I'm unshakeable, like I'm always ten steps ahead. But you you don't flinch when I fall apart. Which should be comforting, but it's terrifying."

"I know the feeling."

She dries her hands on a towel. I turn, and in the pause that follows, I step forward and close the space between us. She doesn't move. Her breath catches as I stop in front of her, so close I can feel the warmth radiating off her skin. One curl has slipped loose, skimming across her cheek.

I lift a hand and gently tuck it behind her ear. Her eyes flutter, then lock onto mine, wide and unguarded.

"You talk like you're the only one scared," I murmur. "But you're not."

I lower my head. Not fast or hesitant, just sure.

Then I kiss her.

It starts soft, barely there. A question, maybe an apology. Or hope.

Cleo doesn't pull away. Her lips are soft, tentative at first. Her breath hitches against mine. She curls her fingers into my shirt, anchoring us.

My other hand finds the curve of her waist, pulling her closer, until she presses into me, imperfect but right.

The kiss deepens, slow and unsure. Like we're both tracing the outline of something we hope might hold.

Her hands slide up, fingertips brushing the back of my neck. I let out a shaky breath I didn't realize I'd been holding. This isn't strategy. It's not defense. It's surrender.

When we part, we're both breathless. The air between us crackles with the weight of what just shifted. Her fingers stay curled in my shirt. I feel the slight tremor in her chest, one that mirrors the tight ache in mine.

For a second, neither of us speaks.

"That was surprising," she whispers, voice raw and a little unsteady.

"Not to me." I keep my eyes glued to hers.

We stay like that, forehead to forehead, her breath soft against my skin. She searches my face. I thread my fingers through hers. Then I squeeze her hand.

"I'm not asking you to fully trust me," I say. "Just don't disappear on me."

She nods, but it's slow. "I'll try."

I squeeze her hand. Pulling away slightly, I say, "Come on."

She blinks. "Where?"

I tilt my head toward the dock. "We've got a whole day to relax. Let's go kayaking."

Cleo stares at me. "You're serious?"

I grin. "You've never kayaked with pancakes for power? It's rocket fuel for kayakers."

She rolls her eyes, laughing. "You are infuriating."

"And yet, here you are. Barefoot in my kitchen."

She narrows her eyes, lips twitching. "You really think you can charm your way out of the emotional whiplash you just gave me?"

"Not charm. Just breakfast. And maybe a paddle or two."

She squeezes my hand.

It's a different kind of tension now.

Not pushing us apart, but a powerful pull.

Slightly clumsy, slightly awkward, yet genuine.

I don't have words, but the need to stay right here is palpable.

A part of me wants to hold on longer.

Not out of certainty, but because for once, I don't want to be alone.

Still, a whisper inside me wonders, how long will it last.

19

Chapter 19: Kayak Fall

Cleo

The lake stretches out like liquid glass, a pink blush tinting the mist. It's the kind of morning that begs for peace. And yet, my pulse is in full-blown Olympic trials. Leave it to me to turn a romantic paddle into a competitive match.

Dillon paddles beside me, looking calm and annoyingly competent. It's like he's done this a hundred times. He probably has. There's very little this man doesn't know how to master.

"Race you back to the house. Loser washes dishes," he challenges with a smirk.

I narrow my eyes. "Careful, Whelan. I don't lose pretty."

He grins like he's daring me. "That's assuming you win. Which, let's be honest, is a long shot."

"Oh, it's so on!"

I push forward, arm muscles burning as the kayak slices through the water. The race is fast and breathless.

For a second, we're not two people on the edge of something terrifying. Just strokes and splashes. Almost normal.

The lake sparkles behind me like a postcard. Dillon's laugh echoes across the lake, and I catch myself smiling. Really smiling.

Dillon's kayak cuts the water behind me, steady, relentless, closing the gap. I surge ahead, heart pounding, my grin wide. I'm already imagining his shocked face when I win.

I don't slow down. The adrenaline is a rush, until the kayak tips just enough to wobble. I laugh it off, but the spike of panic clings. At least I'm staying dry and inside the boat.

The kayak scrapes the dock with a satisfying bump. I raise the paddle over my head in triumph.

"Too slow, Whelan," I call out. Victory is sweet.

Instead of reaching for the railing, I lunge forward, water dripping as my fingers brush the slick dock. My bare foot lands on the smooth wood of the steps that lead up to the deck. In my excitement, I forget the golden rule of kayaking: always move slowly getting out.

The wooden steps gleam slick with algae, the bright sun disguising the danger.

The kayak jerks sideways. My foot slips and I'm flung sideways. My thigh slams against the edge of the step, detonating pain up my leg.

And the lake swallows me whole. Water roars in my ears.

Did I break my leg? Hit my head?

By the time I surface, sputtering and furious, I catch sight of Dillon still in his kayak on the edge of the dock.

Dillon's expression shifts into concern the second he sees my face. "Hey, are you okay?"

Heat burns up my neck. I'm mortified that he saw me fall.

I push myself up, brushing at the searing pain in my leg. I glance down at my soaked leggings, the fabric clinging to my thigh. I can't see much, just the swelling. I can't tell how bad it is. No blood. No bone. But the pain's sharp enough to steal my breath.

I check my face and neck for other injuries.

There are none. Only the intense pain in my leg.

I sit down on the deck to steady myself, and dizziness sweeps over me. Nausea quickly follows.

I hear Dillon's kayak bump against the dock before he climbs out with smooth, hurried movements.

"Okay—ow," I groan, breathless. "That did not go as planned."

I force out a shaky laugh as I try to stand up, water dripping from my hair into my eyes. I brace one hand against the dock and try to shake off the shock.

It's fine. I'm fine.

Except, my leg is throbbing. A deep, pulsing ache that makes my stomach clench.

The pain radiates up my side.

This is not how I planned to start the morning.

"Cleo?" Dillon calls, voice light, but I hear the hidden strain. "You okay?"

I open my mouth, but the ground shifts. The light blurs at the edges. The pain spikes. I can barely breathe. I try to muster another smart remark, but the ground suddenly feels like it's sliding out from under me. The bright morning light dims. Heat crawls up my neck.

"I—I'm fine," I mumble, pressing a palm to my forehead.

I try to stand. The second my weight touches my leg, it gives out. The pain burns up my thigh, and the world tilts violently.

"Cleo?" He's closer now, voice sharper.

"Whoa," I gasp, grabbing at the railing—but I miss.

Dillon lunges for me, but he's too late. The trees above me blur. Green against blue sky. I feel myself tipping, my body too heavy, too slow to catch. The ground rushes toward me. My arms won't move fast enough to break my fall.

The pain flashes hot, and the edges of my vision go grainy. It's like the world tilts on its axis. The world cuts out, like someone pulled the plug.

A voice drags me back, muffled like it's underwater.

"Cleo—no. No, no—hey. Stay with me."

Light slices through the haze. Dillon's face comes into focus, close and raw. His hands tighten around my shoulders, steady but shaking.

"Cleo, hey. Look at me—stay with me."

I register the warmth of the damp wooden deck against my skin.

I don't know how long I was out. Five minutes? Five seconds? Time slips.

Dillon's breath brushes against my temple. "Stay with me, Cleo. Please." Then closer. "Cleo—wake up. Please—" His hands tighten on my shoulders, almost shaking now. Like he's trying not to panic but failing. "Cleo, I've got you. But I need you to hold on. Look at me."

What just happened?

"What..." I try to lift my head. My leg screams in protest. The pain is back, sharper now, like glass under my skin.

"Hey, hey," he breathes, relief crashing over his features. "You with me?"

I suck in a breath. "My leg—"

His eyes flash to it. "Is it broken?"

"I don't know." My voice is barely audible.

I press my fingers down along the outside of my thigh, probing gently, then harder. No sharp protrusions. No blood. But the pain . . .

"I can't stand," I whisper.

"Okay, don't move." His hand cups the back of my neck, steadying me. "We're going to get you inside." He shifts me carefully and then pulls out his phone with one hand. "I'm calling 911," he mutters. "You passed out, Cleo. I'm not taking chances."

His voice shakes on the last word.

He leans forward and slides his arms beneath me. "Put your arms around me. Just hold on."

I try, but my limbs are shaky and useless.

"Cleo," he says, firmer now, voice rough with something that sounds like fear.

I cling to his shoulders as he lifts me, cradling me close. My head falls against his chest. He's warm and solid. His heart is pounding fast.

"You scared me," he mutters, voice tight. "One second you're making fun of my paddling, next you're out cold."

I don't respond because I'm trying not to cry. From the pain, from the fear, from the tenderness in his voice. I didn't expect this.

"Let's get you to the house."

No one's ever looked at me like this.

Like I matter even when I'm not fine.

Dillon does.

And somehow that terrifies me more than the fall.

20

Chapter 20: Falling For You

Dillon

As my phone rings against my ear, I tighten my hold. Like keeping Cleo close could somehow shield her.

When 911 picks up, I launch into it. The dispatcher's voice is calm. I give her the rundown: the fall, leg injury, blacking out, and possible head trauma.

"She's conscious but dizzy. Pale. Breathing shallow."

Cleo's curled against me, still trembling, her breath uneven.

"Stay with her," the dispatcher says. "Keep her warm, talk to her, and don't let her drift off. Medics are on the way."

My stomach twists. I press my fingers into my forehead, willing logic to take over. But the tightness in my chest isn't just fear. It claws at old wounds I don't want to touch.

"Check her pupils," the operator instructs. "Are they dilated unevenly?"

I shift, brushing Cleo's damp hair back, gently tilting her chin so I can get a better look. Her lashes flutter, but she doesn't resist.

"No, they're normal," I say, exhaling in relief.

"Good. That suggests any concussion is likely mild. Watch for confusion, excessive drowsiness, vomiting, or trouble waking. If you notice any of that, take her to the hospital."

The thought makes my stomach churn. My grip tightens around Cleo as if holding her closer will keep her safe.

"Sir," the dispatcher says after a pause, her voice softer. "She's going to be okay. Just focus on keeping her stable."

I end the call with a sharp exhale, but my hands are still trembling. I glance down at Cleo. She's colder now. Shivering more.

Body temperature. Skin contact. Dry clothes. Fast.

I swallow, caught between decency and necessity.

"This isn't ideal," I murmur, brushing my hand over her forehead. "But I need to get you dry."

I work gently, trying not to disturb her leg more than necessary. Her clothes are soaked through. She's freezing. I hesitate, then mutter, "Sorry. We'll deal with awkward later."

I peel the layers off gently. Her sapphire bikini catches the firelight, straps thin.

I freeze, a guilty flush creeping up my neck. I tug a thick wool blanket from the back of the couch and wrap it around both of us, then pull her against me, forming a cocoon of warmth.

She's ice-cold. Rigid. Still trembling. But slowly, her body starts to absorb the heat. Her breathing steadies.

I close my eyes.

This feels too familiar. Too close to something I once lost.

My mother used to call it "heart heat."

Love is warmth, and warmth heals.

And here I am now, holding a woman I should've kept away but ache to hold. Willing my heartbeat to steady hers. She's here.

I tilt my chin down and whisper, "I'm not going anywhere."

I slide a pillow under her legs, careful not to jostle her. She stirs, her fingers twitching against my shirt. I rub slow circles on her back, trying to steady her breathing.

"Cleo," I murmur, keeping my voice even. "Look at me."

She lets out a weak huff. "Bossy."

Relief floods me so fast it's almost dizzying. I let out a low laugh, brushing damp hair from her face. "You're just now figuring that out?"

Her eyes flutter open slightly, dull with exhaustion, but she's looking at me. "You carried me?"

"What was I supposed to do, leave you in the lake?"

She blinks up at me, her gaze sharpening just a little. "That would've been the practical thing. And you like practical."

I exhale slowly, my fingers still tracing patterns on her back. "Not with you."

The words are out before I can filter them, but I don't regret them. Because it's the truth.

Cleo blinks at me again like she's trying to process what I just admitted. I don't know what it means.

Only that I feel more than I should.

And that unsettles me.

My lips form a thin line. I reach for the glass of apple juice, gently shifting Cleo so she's more upright. "Drink."

She groans but obeys, taking a small sip. I keep my hand on the glass, steadying it as she drinks more. My grip is firm but gentle, the way I wish I had been when my mother was too weak to do the same.

Cleo exhales, closing her eyes for a moment. "I'm not dying, you know."

Logically, I know that. But my heart still aches. "You scared me."

Her brows furrow slightly, and I know she wants to make a joke, to brush it off, but she doesn't. She squeezes my hand. "I'm okay."

"I know. But I'm still not letting go."

I look at her, *really* look at her. Pale, exhausted, still shivering slightly, but here. Still here.

I bring her hand to my lips, pressing a brief kiss to her knuckles.

Her breath hitches, but she doesn't pull away.

She stirs. Just a flutter at first. Then her head shifts.

"You're warm," she murmurs. "I could get used to this."

I smile faintly. "And you're an ice box."

Her hand slides across my chest, fingers splaying over my heart. "I like this," she whispers. "Being close to you."

I blink, startled. Cleo never says things like that. Not without teasing, not without armor. But right now, she has none.

She curls closer, cheek to my chest. The sound of her breathing breaks my resolve.

"You're safe," she mumbles. "You always act like you're not, but you are."

Something cracks in me at those words.

"Cleo," I whisper, voice catching.

She lifts her head just enough to look at me. Her blue eyes are soft, unguarded. "Why do you look so sad?"

"I'm not," I lie. "Not with you here."

Her fingers skim my jaw. "You care about me," she murmurs,

eyes already starting to close.

I nod, my throat tight. "I do."

Her head lolls against my chest again. She presses a hand to my heart. "Feels good being held like this."

I nod slowly, unable to speak. I've built my life on logic. Formulas. Predictions.

But nothing about her fits an equation. And right now?

"Kiss me," she murmurs as she looks up at me.

I hesitate, then lower my head.

The kiss is soft. Not possession, just presence.

Cleo sighs against the kiss, her fingers tightening on my skin, and for a moment, there's nothing else.

No cold. No fear. Just her pressed to my chest, her mouth on mine.

Cleo doesn't move, but her smile lingers.

My heart stutters.

I shouldn't want this so badly.

I remember the escape room. Her sass.

This is temporary, I tell myself.

But I don't believe it.

And if it isn't, that scares me more than the fall.

When I finally pull back, her eyes drift shut, exhaustion reclaiming her.

She exhales softly.

But her last words echo in my head like a vow.

"You're not who I thought," she whispers. "You're better."

21

Chapter 21: Armor & Echoes

Cleo

I wake to an unfamiliar quiet. The last thing I remember was falling asleep to the rhythm of Dillon's heartbeat.

The medics came and went in a blur. Leg contusion. Mild concussion. No vomiting, no memory loss. Just dizziness and the kind of fatigue that makes your bones ache. Back then it would have been six weeks off the ice.

But my pride took the harder hit.

There's a dent in my thigh, dark plum and bruised blue. Torn tissue, not just tenderness. This won't heal overnight.

I sit up slowly, gripping the edge of the sofa. The ice wrap itches. The swelling fogs my thoughts. I adjust, then freeze as pain shoots down my leg like lightning.

Not broken. But not nothing either.

Sunlight reflects off the lake, mocking the ache beneath my skin. My thoughts spiral faster than the ripples on the lake.

It all comes rushing back. Dillon's kiss. The certainty of it.

The way it quieted everything, like the world exhaled.

It wasn't perfect. It felt real. And that scares me.

The blanket feels too thin now. I finger the bruise and flinch, not from pain, but the memory of my voice. My brain must've glitched when I asked him to kiss me. One soft second where I forgot to armor up. And now I'm exposed.

Like I handed him a map to places I keep guarded.

Brilliant move, Cleo. What were you thinking?

This is how it starts. The closeness. The comfort.

But it always ends the same. I'm not sure I could survive goodbye again.

I survived once when others didn't. That math has never sat right in my body.

I tighten the throw blanket around my shoulders. Not for warmth, for cover.

The door slides open. I tense on instinct, but I already know it's him. His footsteps are soft but sure.

"You okay?" His voice is gentler than usual.

"I'm fine," I lie. The word falls flat. "Just thinking."

He sinks down beside me. The silence hums with everything we're not saying.

"Do you need any pain meds?" he asks in a soothing tone.

"I'm okay. I've been through worse."

"Are you hungry? I can make you something."

"Thanks, but I just need a few more minutes to recalibrate."

We both sit poised on the edge of the sofa like coiled springs.

Dillon doesn't ask again, just waits.

The quiet between us isn't empty. It's full of tension and possibility.

He glances at my leg, then at me. "A penny for your thoughts?"

I arch a brow. "Studied up on your British sayings, I see."

He grins. "So how does a chaos coordinator end up kayaking and racing through escape rooms like an Olympian?"

I smile faintly.

"Would you believe me if I said I was almost an Olympian?"

He blinks. "Wait, what?"

"I fell in love with ice skating at a birthday party. Once I felt that glide, that freedom, I couldn't imagine anything else. I was obsessed. Early mornings. No vacations. I got scouted and relocated to Massachusetts for training."

Dillon leans in. "So, you came to the U.S. for skating?"

"Pretty much."

"That explains everything," he says. "You like being unpredictable. Keeps people off balance."

"Now you're getting somewhere."

"And I'm guessing you didn't just learn to skate; you learned to read people, too."

I shrug. "You don't survive in competitive sports without learning a few things."

I glance sideways at him, catching the curve of his profile in the light. He looks relaxed. I know that stillness. It's how he holds control.

Something stirs in me, fragile and old.

I close my eyes, but memories barge in anyway, uninvited.

The sound of water against the dock tightens my chest. I open my eyes again.

Dillon speaks.

"I used to believe wishing for something hard enough could change things," he says quietly, like it's a confession. "When my mom got sick, I sat beside her bed every night, hoping if I stayed still enough, quiet enough, maybe the pain would stop.

I would've given anything for her to stay."

He pauses. "And she died anyway. I stopped hoping after that."

Some losses don't fade. They just learn to live inside you.

The lake settles into stillness between us.

Dillon doesn't look at me after he says it.

He just watches the water like the answer might still be out there somewhere.

My breath catches.

There's a rawness to his words I wasn't expecting.

Something shifts in the space between us.

"I know exactly how you feel," I say, touching his knee. "I was twelve when my world fell apart. Christmas morning, the police came for my father. There was shouting, officers bulldozing their way into our home. My mother collapsed from shock, and my sister cried so hard I thought she'd never stop. I hoped so hard something would change, but it didn't."

I wrap my arms around myself.

"Because I realized hoping didn't change anything. It only meant you had more to lose."

He looks at me with a knowing glance.

"I stood there. Frozen. Just watching. I couldn't cry, couldn't move. I told myself I had to be strong because no one else would be. I was a child pretending to be bulletproof."

I swallow. "I didn't cry. Not when my mother collapsed, or when my father swore he'd fix it."

I glance at Dillon. Just long enough to feel seen.

"I just remember thinking if I stay strong, if I stay still, maybe it won't fall apart faster."

"After that, I didn't wish for much. Wishing felt like empty words."

"You can't miss what you never let yourself want in the first place."

I glance at Dillon. "I think part of me never stopped pretending."

"You don't have to be strong with me," he says, low, like he's afraid the weight of his words might startle me.

You make strength feel less lonely than it used to.

I swallow hard. "I don't remember what it's like to fall and not brace for impact."

He doesn't flinch. Doesn't fill the space with promises he might break. Just stays there. Still. Steady. Unmoving. Except for the way he holds the space open.

And somehow, that's what undoes me.

Needing someone feels like surrender.

"I get that," he says. "Probably more than I want to admit." He looks out across the water, jaw tense.

"After my mom died, I stopped letting people in. I shut everyone out. I thought if I could just stay focused, stay in control, I'd never have to feel that kind of helplessness again."

I turn toward him, something in my chest tightening.

"I used to think control would save me. Turns out it just keeps you distracted. Sooner or later the pressure gets through anyway."

"Yeah, I get that. I kept telling myself that needing people made me weak," he continues. "But really, I think I was just terrified that needing someone meant giving up the illusion that I could carry it all on my own."

Our eyes meet. Underneath all his certainty, I see it. He's just as afraid of surrender as I am.

"Maybe we're not meant to carry everything alone," I whisper.

The silence shifts. For once, we're breathing in the same rhythm.

I'm longing to reach out and touch him, hug him, like we did when everything fell apart.

The coward in me wins. Self-protection always whispers louder.

"I should go shower," I say.

He doesn't stop me. Just nods.

As I limp away, every step reminds me I'm not made of armor. I pause at the doorway, fingers brushing the frame. Behind me, I hear Dillon exhale. I don't look back.

A memory surfaces.

I was thirteen. My dad had just been released on bail, his voice full of apologies I didn't believe. He stood on the porch step, suitcase in hand.

Tired. Worn. Too rehearsed.

He asked to come back. And even though every part of me screamed no, I said, "Just don't leave again."

He nodded. Promised. Smiled like it was easy. Three weeks later, he vanished in the middle of the night. No note. No goodbye. No explanation.

I never asked anyone to stay again.

The memory of Dillon's voice, his pain, his presence, catches up to me.

For the first time in years, I don't feel completely alone in my doubt.

Just afraid of what it means to let someone stay.

***

I lean against the bathroom door. Still no reply from Mom.

Unease pulses low in my ribs. She always answers, especially after last winter.

I scroll, looking for distraction, and land on Hyde Park during the British Hotpocalypse.

Headline: "Barbie Melts in the British Apocalypse."

Tia stuck to a bench. Megan handing out sunblock like a battlefield nurse. Me, fighting for a rental car when the trains shut down. Brits politely complaining about dying.

It wasn't just heat exhaustion. It was love and friendship, the kind that anchors you when everything else falls apart. We didn't reach Mom for two days. But we had each other.

I blink at my reflection and text her again.

Hey, Mom, just checking in. Call me?

Still nothing. I call. Voicemail. Again. No answer.

I call Tia. "Hey. Have you heard from Mom?"

A pause.

"Not since last week. Why?"

"She hasn't answered my last few texts. And after what happened last winter—"

"Try again. I'll check in too."

I hang up. My heart pounds. The silence isn't normal.

22

Chapter 22: Becoming Undone

Dillon

It's Sunday morning. Two nights ago, I pitched our future in a tux to people who could've bought and sold us before dessert. Yesterday, Cleo was in the lake, her lips blue, her hands shaking, barely able to stand. I couldn't breathe.

The gala's already old news, but Oscar hasn't said a word.

Silence never bodes well when the future of Lucid hangs in the balance and no one is saying why.

I yank open my bedroom door and step into the hallway. The house is quiet in a way that feels watchful.

The lake outside glimmers with the first hint of light. The cold floor bites as I pad toward the kitchen, my hoodie already clinging to sweat.

And there she is, hood up, curled on the couch, like she's trying to disappear into the cushions.

The glow of her phone lights her face, but she's not scrolling anymore. She's staring at the screen, motionless. Lost in

196

something she won't share.

When the floorboard creaks beneath me, she looks up. We lock eyes. That same pulse between us stirs again. Familiar now, but never safe.

"You're up?" I say, surprised. "It's five."

She shrugs like it's nothing. "Couldn't sleep."

My chest tightens. "I'm going for a run." I say it bluntly, not waiting for a response.

I need air. I step outside and take a deep breath.

My legs move before I can stop them.

Maybe if I push hard enough, the gnawing inside me will finally go quiet.

My father never said he was proud of me. Every win was expected. Every failure was a flaw.

Maybe it wasn't disappointment at all. Maybe it was fear dressed up as ambition.

Twenty-five minutes later, the front door shuts behind me and I head straight for the fridge. My lungs are on fire. Sweat clings to my neck, soaking my shirt. I grab a glass, hold it under the spout, and down half in one gulp.

Cleo's at the stove now, barefoot in shorts and a cotton T-shirt, her hair twisted up and secured with a pencil.

Her legs stretch beneath her.

I shouldn't notice, but I do.

Cleo doesn't turn right away. "We only had eggs and feta," she says, flipping something in a pan. "So, I'm improvising."

"Your turn to make breakfast, huh?" I offer with a soft smile. "You sure you want to be up already?" I ask, glancing at her leg. "You could've just told me to microwave something. I've got a black belt in Trader Joe's."

She laughs under her breath. "Trust me, I'd rather cook."

I watch her stir, quick and confident.

"Rosemary Eggs-a-la-Cleo," she says, flashing a smile. "Reserved for special people and doomsdays."

I gesture toward the stool. "Sit. I'll take over."

"I'm fine. Eggs don't bite."

I hover close anyway. She's always been more stubborn than sensible.

"Lucky me," I mutter, settling onto the bar stool.

Cleo pours something warm into two mismatched mugs and pushes one toward me.

"Smells like Christmas in a mug."

"That's because it is. Mint chocolate chips from the apocalypse stash, long-life almond milk, and coffee from the emergency tin." She lifts her mug like a toast. "You're welcome."

For the first time in days, I laugh. Just for a second.

"You surprise me," I admit.

Her eyes glow. "I get that a lot."

We eat without talking, the air heavy, like the moment is waiting to shift.

Her omelet is good. Really good. Sharp with feta, fragrant with herbs.

I watch her, fingers curled around the mug, lips twitching like she's trying not to smile.

It feels domestic. Easy. Too easy. And that's what makes it ache.

"I'm gonna spare you the man smell and go shower."

She nods.

I shower fast, dry off, change.

The tension I tried to outrun is still there.

By the time I wander back to the living room, I hear soft

Christmas music playing. It should soothe me, but instead, it scratches at something raw.

The fire has burned down to flickering embers. One last log crackles as I lean forward, pretending to warm my hands.

But it's not the chill making me shiver.

Cleo's back in the kitchen, humming Sinatra while the kettle hisses. The clink of mugs draws my gaze. She brings over two steaming cups, sits beside me on the couch, and offers that gorgeous smile. The one that disarms me faster than it should.

"Still cold?" she asks softly.

"No. Just thinking." I wrap my fingers around the mug. It's warm and familiar, like her hand in mine after the accident.

She watches me, that quiet curiosity of hers. "What is it, Dillon?"

I should answer. But the silence presses in. My mind isn't here, it's there. Blinding hospital lights. Mom's hand in mine.

"Find happiness, Dillon. Don't let life harden you," she whispered the night before she slipped away. But I never did.

When she died, something inside me went with her. The part of me that smiled, the part that believed life could be more than strategy and survival.

Her funeral was a blur. My father's hand on my shoulder was firm, not comforting. "We don't have time to fall apart," he said. "Work doesn't stop for grief."

And I did. I learned to control everything, to feel nothing, to need no one. That's how I've lived.

I lose track of time, lost in my thoughts. Eventually, I hear Cleo's voice.

"You've been avoiding me."

Because staying near you is starting to feel dangerous.

"Thinking. Not avoiding."

"About what?"

I exhale, sharp and shaky. "About a lot of things. About this."

She looks at me.

I want to be what steadies her.

Something in her shoulders loosens when I stay.

For the first time in years, that doesn't scare me.

The wanting lands heavier than the doubt, and I don't pull away from it.

I've spent so long mastering control, I'm not sure I can be safe for someone who finally dropped her guard.

"Me too. I don't think I can do this."

My jaw tightens before I can stop it. "Wait, why?"

I set the mug down carefully.

She hesitates, like she doesn't want to say it. "I wasn't supposed to be here." Her voice barely makes it across the space between us.

"At the lake?" I ask.

"Not just here. I mean, at all."

My brow furrows. "What do you mean?"

Cleo doesn't answer right away, just watches the steam rise from her cup.

Her body shifts, bracing. She exhales.

I recognize that look.

It's the one people wear when the story finally outweighs the silence.

And the truth slips out before either of us can stop it.

23

Chapter 23: Breaking Point

Cleo

"I shouldn't have made it past seventeen," I say quietly. "Not just here. Not just at the lake house. I mean, at all."

The mug is warm in my hands, but I don't lift it. I watch the steam rise instead, curl, vanish. If I keep my eyes there, I don't have to look at him yet.

"I used to skate competitively. Pairs." My throat tightens. "Liam was my partner. Coach Olga trained us. She ran a pre-Olympic development track. Sectionals were next. Everything we'd worked for was right there."

I swallow, forcing the words forward before courage runs out.

"We'd just landed our first clean triple jump. The kind of moment where the future finally feels real instead of theoretical. Liam joked that I was overthinking the music cut again. We laughed so hard I cried."

I let out a breath that feels like it's been trapped in my chest for years.

"We were supposed to fly home together after training camp." My fingers curl around the mug. "I had a seat on the plane."

Dillon still hasn't moved. He's listening the way people do when they know something sacred is coming.

"I got sick the night before. Food poisoning. My mom insisted I stay back an extra day." I shake my head once, slow. "Their flight took off without me."

The room feels suddenly smaller.

"The plane collided midair with a low-flying helicopter on the return route." My voice lowers. "No survivors."

The words don't echo. They don't have to.

"I remember waking up the next morning and seeing the news across the screen." My chest tightens. "I remember thinking there had been a mistake. That they'd call it off. That someone would say they'd mixed up the flight numbers."

I finally look at him.

"The only reason I'm alive is a bad bag of peanuts," I whisper. "I should've been on that plane. I was supposed to be."

Something flickers across Dillon's face, sharp and restrained. He still doesn't interrupt.

"I told myself it didn't matter. That I could skate through it. That the ice wouldn't care who was missing." My voice wavers. "But every time I stepped onto the rink, there was this empty space where Liam should've been. Where Olga's voice should've cut through the noise."

I press my lips together.

"I quit the next day. I didn't go to the funeral. I didn't say goodbye." A pause. "I couldn't."

The silence stretches, heavy but steady.

"I told myself I was being practical. That it was time to grow up. To move on." I let out a breath that almost becomes a laugh. "But really, I just couldn't survive a world they didn't get to see."

My gaze drops to my hands.

"So I learned something early." I nod once, like sealing it into place. "If you don't let anyone in, no one can leave. And if you're perfect, nothing breaks."

I look up again, meeting his eyes now.

"I stopped skating because flying without a net stopped feeling brave." My voice softens. "And ever since, I've been afraid of anything that makes me feel airborne."

The words sit between us, fragile and final.

"Because falling," I say quietly, "hurts less when you never jump."

The realization lands harder than I expect.

"So, I know how this ends. You let someone in, and they leave, or they lie. Or they take what you gave them and walk away like it never mattered. I've seen it too many times to pretend it ends any other way."

My voice breaks slightly, but I keep going. "And I can't let myself need someone. Because needing someone gives them power. And when they walk, they take pieces of you."

Dillon flinches. He knows what that kind of fear tastes like.

"So that's it? You'd rather shut me out before I even get the chance to hurt you?"

He looks at me like he wants to believe in something. And I want to meet him there. But I'm still stuck in the wreckage of people who didn't stay.

I laugh once, short, bitter. "You say that like you wouldn't. Not intentionally. But you would. Because you don't let people in either, and you never will."

Dillon looks away, jaw clenched so tight I can see it pulsing. "That's not fair, Cleo. You don't know what I—"

"I know enough," I snap. "I know that you see emotions as liabilities. I kissed you. You panicked. And now I'm scared you regret it."

"That's not what I—"

"I can't do this with someone who hesitates when it matters. Not because you don't care, but because you're scared to feel it."

Dillon stands suddenly, the tension snapping off him like a whip. "And I can't be with someone who runs every time it gets real," he says, voice rising. "Who won't take the risk. Who's already halfway out the door the minute it stops being easy."

We lock eyes as time stills.

He swallows hard, then says, quieter now, "You want to know why I shut down? Why I can't always say the right thing?"

I don't move, but something in me softens, just a little.

"The last person who made me feel anything real, died. And the second, my father. He told me grief made me weak. That failure to control meant failure to lead." He exhales sharply. "So yeah. I chose control. I built control. It's all I've ever had."

My eyes burn, but I don't speak.

"Until you."

It's all there: grief, fear, and something we don't dare name.

I shift carefully, my injured leg protesting as a dull ache spreads. I can feel the sharp dent in my thigh as a reminder of how hard I hit the dock.

The bruising from the kayak fall still throbs beneath the

surface, stubborn and slow to heal.

I'd forgotten how pain lingers in the body long after the moment passes. Maybe the heart keeps its own record.

Like grief, deep, invisible, but real. Like scars you learn to hide.

"But the difference is," he continues, voice breaking, "you're still here. And I want you here. Even when it terrifies me."

I blink. The wanting rushes in before the fear can stop it, and that's what scares me most.

"Cleo—"

He reaches for my hand, not gripping, just offering, like he's waiting to see if I'll take it.

"No," I cut in, standing before I can change my mind. "Don't. Please."

I pace toward the window, heart thudding. "I can't do this."

"Do what?"

"Us. I thought I could keep it casual. Maybe even light. But you make things matter, and I don't survive things that matter. You look at me like I'm not a mess. Like I'm not one push away from falling apart."

He rises slowly, carefully. "You're not falling apart."

"You don't know that." My voice cracks. "You don't know what happens when I let someone in."

"I'd like to," he says. "I'd stay."

"But that's the lie, isn't it?" I whisper. "People say they'll stay. And then life happens. Planes crash. Partners die. People walk away."

He doesn't respond. He just stands there. The weight of grief hangs between us.

The moment is fragile.

Fragile things shatter.

I step back. I see the flicker of pain in his eyes. My instinct to run kicks into gear. My armor slips back into place.

"I'm sorry," I whisper. "But wanting something doesn't mean you're ready to hold it."

Behind me, I hear Dillon shift. A sharp exhale. A step forward.

And then, nothing.

He lets me go.

I walk out of the room.

He doesn't stop me, and I don't look back.

He doesn't follow me.

But the silence behind me feels heavier than footsteps.

The air is cool against my skin, but my insides burn.

I turn and shove open the sliding door before I can change my mind. I force myself not to look back.

Except I do. I care too much.

***

I walk to my room, shut the door, and slide down until my knees touch wood. I cry. Not the pretty kind. The ugly, silent tears, with messy snot. The kind that leaves your ribs aching and your throat raw. The kind that reminds you why you stopped skating in the first place. Because once you fall that hard, the ice never feels the same.

My phone buzzes. Again. It's Abby. Her texts are getting more frantic.

Client rescheduled. Payroll delay. Where are you?

I skim, then mute the thread. I don't trust my voice not to crack. So, I say nothing. Pretend it'll hold.

But the weight is stacking, one missed reply at a time.

I stand up and walk to the dresser, ready to pack my bags and leave. My fingers hesitate when I spot a pale-yellow scarf folded at the bottom. My Yiayia's scarf. A last-minute grab you don't think about until it breaks you.

I gently lift the bundle of soft fabric. Holding it to my chest, I close my eyes and remember. The kitchen in our family's old Johannesburg home. Sunlight through lace curtains. My Yiayia humming an old Greek song while I stood on a step stool, sprinkling oregano into the tiropita cheese filling.

"You stir with love, koukla," she'd say, tapping my nose. "That's what warms it."

I had asked her once, "What if someone doesn't love you back?"

She'd kissed my forehead. "Then you still bake with love. Because love given is never wasted."

I've always been the baker, the giver, stirring with love and sacrifice. The one holding the whisk and pretending not to care. But now, I can't bear the weight any longer.

The silence between Dillon and me cuts deep. It's the way Dillon looked at me. Like he saw through the cracks I've spent years patching.

Now I don't know how to stop it. The girl who used to sing while baking with her Yiayia, brushing flour off her cheeks, hands sticky with dough. Who used to believe in big love and second chances and the magic of showing up for someone. That girl danced on ice like she belonged there. She trusted her partner to catch her mid-air, to match her rhythm beat for beat. She flew into lifts like she didn't know how to fall. Until the crash.

Everyone I love eventually leaves, whether it's a coach in a plane, a father in handcuffs, or a friend who turns your secrets into punchlines.

Or someone like Dillon, who makes me feel seen and safe and completely undone.

I don't know what I'm doing, so I hide in my room.

Somewhere out there, Dillon is pacing, thinking. Probably punishing himself for not knowing what to say. And somehow, that makes it worse. But I didn't tell him. I haven't told him anything real.

Not the part where I'm afraid he'll see how much I want this to work, but I have this compulsion to run. Not the part where I need him to fight for me, even if I pretend I don't.

I'm at war with myself.

My throat tightens. I wrap the yellow scarf tighter around my fingers.

Eventually, curiosity gets the better of me. I walk to the window and pull back the curtain. The lake glows under the moonlight, quiet and still.

The intimacy scares me more than anything.

Every glance, every touch, every near kiss that lingers just long enough to make me ache.

He sees past the sarcasm, the strategies, the curated polish. He sees me when I'm quiet. He listens when I don't speak. That kind of attention, it's dangerous.

But history has taught me exactly what trust costs. Every time someone left, I absorbed it. Every time someone died, I blamed myself.

Because love feels like a free fall, and I've hit the ground too many times to trust the landing.

I lie back on the bed, scarf still clutched to my chest. The ceiling blurs as tears threaten, but I refuse to let them fall.

I should go to Dillon. Say something. Anything. But I don't.

Instead, I whisper to the scarf like a prayer I barely believe in, "Help me not be afraid."

Across the house, I hear footsteps. Dillon is wrestling with something neither of us can name. And for once, I don't want to win. But I retreat anyway.

I hear my phone ping with a text message, and the group chat lights up.

SENSIBILITY SISTERS:

Megan: Still alive? Emotionally? Physically?

Tia: Did you kiss him or kill him?

Shiloh: Or both? Iconic either way.

Megan: If you ghost us, I'll stage an intervention. Blazer, clipboard, snacks.

Nicole: And hydrate. Your overthinking brain is working over time.

Mia: Cleo are you okay? Do you want me to call? Or just send tea and cookies?

Nicole: Do I need to book a flight or set a spreadsheet on fire?

Alexa: You don't need to fix this. Just feel it. We've got you.

Tia: Yeah, cry it out, then go back and kiss him again. For science.

Cleo: Still breathing. Trying not to overthink something that felt real. That counts as progress, right?

Shiloh: That's not progress. That's a whole breakthrough. Cue the slow clap.

Megan: Let her breathe. Or spiral. Blanket burrito is also valid.

Nicole: Proud of you.

Mia: And remember, not everyone leaves. Some people stay.

Alexa: Especially when you let them. Vulnerability is strength.

Tia: Emotional bravery is the new black.

Megan: Let him see the real you. That's the part worth loving.

I stare at the screen longer than I mean to. Their teasing makes me smile. But the concern beneath it makes something twist in my chest. Tia always knows when I'm retreating. Megan reads between my silence. Shiloh masks worry with sarcasm. Mia's softness hits like a bruise. Nicole, of all people, is the one who names what I'm doing: hiding.

I start typing.

Cleo: *All good. Just busy.*

Delete.

Cleo: *It was nothing. I overread it.*

Delete.

Cleo: *Tia you were right.*

Delete.

The blinking cursor waits. I don't.

Cleo: Still breathing. Still scared. But it felt real. That counts as something, right?

Tia: It counts as love, sis. Stay with it. Don't analyze your way out.

Megan: Proud of you. And rooting for you.

Shiloh: Let him see you. You're worth being seen.

Nicole: Or at least tell him before someone else does. Men are slow.

I smile through sudden tears. My girls don't just know me. They won't let me forget myself.

And maybe love doesn't start in the grand gestures. Maybe it starts in the text you almost deleted. In the silence someone fills with kindness. In the moment you realize that not all retreat is safety. Sometimes it's just fear in disguise.

The realization hits me: I kissed him. I let someone hold the raw, unfiltered version of me without analysis or performance. Then I put the armor back on, like I never took it off. Because if I let myself believe in him, and I lose that, I don't know how to come back.

I scroll through my texts.

Megan's pinned message is still there, from weeks ago. The one I never replied to.

Megan: Do you ever wonder if we're all just trying to prove we're not like our parents? You're allowed to feel it. You don't have to explain it, fix it, or turn it into data. Some days I think I've outgrown it. Others, I'm not so sure.

I almost reply.

But instead, I set the phone down and curl into the bed like it might hold the version of me I don't know how to protect.

Somewhere down the hall, I know Dillon is there.

But I don't move.

I haven't felt that safe, or seen, in years.

I tell myself it's a recalibration.

Not fear. Not retreat. Just strategy.

But even I don't believe it.

24

Chapter 24: Spiraling

Dillon

Cleo walked away. I should have stopped her, said something to keep her from slipping through my fingers. But I didn't. Instead, I stood there, hands clenched at my sides, watching as she disappeared into the house.

I scrub a hand over my face, but the dread stays lodged, stubborn and sharp.

The same feeling I had at sixteen hits without warning.

Standing by my mother's hospital bed, knowing she was slipping away. Her fingers cold in mine. The machines beeped slow and steady, each sound cruel.

I'd nodded, swallowing the lump in my throat.

When she went, whatever believed in softness went with her.

At the funeral, I stood beside my father, stiff and silent. His hand gripped my shoulder like steel. "We can't afford to fall apart," he'd said. "Get back to work."

That was all he gave me.

So I locked everything down and did what I was told.

The feeling crawls under my skin, pressing against my lungs until breathing feels deliberate.

This isn't just about Cleo. It's about control.

About never feeling that helpless again.

And yet, here I am. Wanting to tell Cleo I don't know how to do this, but that I want to try.

Except if I let her in, she'll see the truth I avoid. That beneath the power and precision, I'm still trying to outrun ghosts.

So I retreat.

I pour a drink I don't need and stare at the fire, trying to feel nothing.

It doesn't work. The second she walked away, I knew I'd already lost her.

She didn't raise her voice. She didn't have to. It was in the look, the one that said she knew I'd disappear.

I proved her right.

I grab my keys and drive.

The trees blur past in streaks of light as the road curves beneath me.

I grip the wheel tighter, knuckles white, trying to outrun the weight pressing on my chest.

I didn't say goodbye. I ordered her an Uber back to the city without seeing her. If I'd looked her in the eyes again, I might've stayed, and told her everything.

Somewhere along the winding road, I pull over and kill the engine. My hands stay locked on the wheel.

This wasn't about the glasses. Or even Oscar.

It was about me standing in the ruins of my own doing, afraid she'd see the wreckage and leave.

It wasn't the first time I'd waited too long to act.

When I was eighteen, my father handed me a stack of printed emails and said, "Read these. Learn what not to become."

At the top was Oscar Damon. The message read:

Subject: Strategic Alignment. High Return. Zero Oversight.

"You want security? Predictability? Play it clean. But if you want dominance, Robert, we have to stop pretending ethics scale."

My father's reply was simple.

"I'd rather build slow and clean than fast and corrupt. We're done here."

I understand it now, with painful clarity.

Oscar lost the approval of the one man who saw through him, and he's been clawing his way back through me ever since.

It wasn't coincidence he appeared in our funding rounds or pitched himself as the bridge we needed. It was a long game. Revenge disguised as opportunity.

And I opened the door for him.

I grip the wheel until my knuckles ache.

Oscar doesn't need scandal. He just needs cracks.

A few missed meetings, delayed reports, a distracted CEO with personal chaos. He's building a case one fracture at a time.

I jab the call button. Noah picks up, voice casual. "What's up, dude?"

"You notice anything off about Oscar lately?"

"Off like hostile-takeover off?"

"Off like he knows things he shouldn't."

Noah exhales. "You think he's gunning for you?"

"I think he's patient."

When I hang up, the silence hums like static.

A board member warned me that Dad's been watching me.

Maybe I've been repeating his pattern all along, letting silence do the talking, mistaking control for strength.

I swore I'd be different. But I'm not. Not yet.

And Cleo saw it. She called it out. When she did, I shut her down.

I don't want to win or be right or pitch another billion-dollar dream.

I just want her. And I was too afraid to believe I deserved her.

The words scrape out of me. "I couldn't protect you. I'm sorry."

Not from Oscar. Not from the fall. Not from me.

I tell myself Cleo was a mistake.

That caring was one too.

But deep down, I know better.

My mother's voice drifts through memory, soft, fading.

I swallow hard.

I let life harden me until she showed up and reminded me how it felt to feel again.

And now I don't know how to fix this.

I can't keep hiding behind what broke me.

Chapter 25: Crossing The Line

Cleo

It's the morning after our fight. Sleep came in fragments. Hope is a gamble I can't afford twice.

It's Monday. Normally, I'd already be back in the city, coffee in hand, halfway through pitch prep.

I arrive at a bougie lakeside bistro that tries too hard to imitate big-city restaurants. The place is all crisp white linens and bread that tastes like nothing. Too sterile for the mess brewing inside me.

The hostess leads me to a private table tucked by the window. It's quiet and upscale, too empty for my liking.

I glance at my phone.

No name. Just a calendar block from a referral-only agency that sometimes connects me with high-level pitch clients. It's the kind of ambiguity that usually sparks adrenaline, not this low drag of dread.

I told myself I was done retreating. That I'd face the future like a strategist, not a scared girl with a yellow scarf clenched in her fists.

And then I see him.

Oscar.

And just like that, I know the test isn't over.

Oscar Damon strides in like the air itself should part to make way for him, as if applause is owed simply for showing up. Cuffed sleeves, designer watch. That same slick, slow grin, like he's always three moves ahead.

My stomach twists. I instinctively take a step back, nearly bumping into the hostess.

His eyes lock on mine, gleaming with smug recognition. "Cleo," he says, stretching out my name like we're something we're not. "Fancy seeing you here."

I recover fast, straighten my shoulders, school my features. "Didn't expect you."

"Surprise," he says, gesturing toward the booth. "Turns out I'm the client."

Of course, he is.

I stay standing, every nerve on edge. "This was a mistake."

Oscar chuckles. "Relax. No contracts. Just lunch. Conversation between professionals."

After a moment's hesitation, I slide into the booth, wary like someone stepping into a trap she already spotted.

His voice is smooth as a sales pitch. "You're sharp. I like that. Most people in this city are playing checkers. But you like to play chess."

He wants a conversation. I want evidence.

I look down at my smartwatch and hit record.

"I don't have much time, so please get to the point," I say curtly.

I'm done faking courtesy with someone who doesn't deserve it.

Oscar swirls his scotch like this is just another casual power play.

"Whelan's brilliant, sure," he says, pausing just long enough for the insult to land. "But he's too soft. Founders get emotional. They cling, and they forget that business isn't about loyalty. Vulnerability like that doesn't scale."

I sit in silence and let him keep talking.

Some alliances run deeper than pride.

"And the board's starting to notice. He can't handle something of this magnitude. You and I both know what comes next."

I tighten my grip on the glass, hoping it hides the tremor in my fingers.

For a second, I consider it.

"iSight needs an experienced leader."

He sips his whiskey.

"We move forward under my lead. Quiet leadership restructure. Whelan exits with a golden parachute, and you stay on to manage perception. It will be a smooth transition with minimal noise."

Another pause, like he's putting on a show.

He leans closer, lowers his voice. "Give it six months, and we'll shift him into a symbolic role. Maybe something overseas. He won't even see it coming."

Oscar smiles, mistaking my silence for complicity instead of revulsion.

"And you? You could be part of it. Vision needs execution. You've got instincts. You knew I was trouble the second I walked in, didn't you?"

I smile tightly. "I just see what's in front of me."

He leans even closer. "Come on, Cleo. Let's not kid ourselves. This isn't about ethics. It never is."

I don't answer. I stare at him.

"You want me to smile while you stab him in the back? I don't appreciate being used."

Oscar chuckles. "Don't be dramatic. It's not personal, it's business."

"You know you're replaceable?" he says, quirking a brow.

"I doubt that."

My jaw tightens.

I pick up my phone and tap the screen, pretending to scroll, buying a second to breathe.

"I think we're done here. My Uber is waiting," I say, calm and final.

He frowns. "That's a shame. I thought you were ready for bigger things."

"I am," I say, steady now. "Just not with you."

If Oscar wants a war, he chose the wrong strategist.

26

Chapter 26: Shields Up

Dillon

The bistro is sleek, polished, and modern. The kind of place where deals are struck and power plays unfold like a game of chess.

I stride through the glass doors, expecting a routine follow-up with Oscar.

Instead, I find Cleo.

She sits across from him, shoulders tight, hands clenched around her purse like she's about to run.

My pulse spikes with something too sharp to name.

Cleo looks up and meets my eyes.

For a second, I see the conflict. Before I can read it, Oscar smiles. That smug grin curls my fists and knots my stomach. He gestures for me to sit down like a kingpin.

"Ah, Dillon," he drawls, spreading his hands like this is all perfectly reasonable. "Glad you could join us. Cleo and I were just discussing ways to ensure your company's future."

He takes a slow sip of his drink, watching me like a predator stalking a trapped animal. "She's quite persuasive. Knows how to soften the opposition with that sharp tongue."

I force my expression blank. I don't like the way he says her name.

My mind jumps to the worst-case scenarios. It always does.

That she's been playing me.

That everything between us was strategy.

I keep my voice level. "Didn't realize I needed a mediator."

Cleo leans forward, urgency in her tone. "I didn't agree to this, Dillon. Oscar asked me to come. I thought he was a new client who needed my insight for a pitch."

Oscar's eyes gleam as he flicks his gaze between us, waiting for the reaction he wants.

Her voice tightens. "I should've asked more questions. I had a feeling something was off, but I wanted to believe it was nothing. And now—"

My fists clench under the table. He thinks she's my weakness. Maybe she is.

"Oh, come on, Cleo," Oscar cuts in smoothly with a smile of superiority. "No need to downplay your involvement. I think Dillon should know just how much you care about his success."

My pulse slows the way it does before a fight.

Oscar tilts his glass, studying me. "You know, Dillon, you remind me of your father. That relentless need for control, that refusal to take a helping hand. Makes a man terribly lonely, don't you think?"

My teeth grind, pressure flaring at my temples.

That's when I know. This isn't a meeting. It's a setup.

Oscar leans his elbows on the table. "The board's been

nervous about your focus, Dillon. With all this emotional intelligence talk, they're not seeing the results. They want monetizable tech. Predictive behavior tracking. Systems that scale. Not your girlfriend's ethics framework. I've already spoken to Coates and a few others. You've lost focus, the strategy's gone sideways, and leadership's failing their financial duties."

I fold my arms across my chest, keep my tone flat. "What is this?"

Oscar exhales slowly, like I'm a child making noise over nothing.

Cleo stiffens.

Oscar clicks his tongue, shaking his head with that fake disappointment he wears like a suit. "Now, now. No need for dramatics. Cleo and I were just discussing how well she executed her role."

My pulse stutters. My chest tightens.

Her role?

Cleo tenses beside him. I see it.

The way her body locks up. The way her face falters for the briefest second before she forces it back into place.

But I see it. And the spiral starts anyway.

Oscar looks at her, his voice low, dangerous. "You really thought I didn't know who was sitting in that seat?"

Her lips part, a soundless protest.

Oscar doesn't even look at me.

I'm just another piece on the board.

"I hired Cleo through her firm. Made sure she'd be at that Pitchathon. I knew you'd push Dillon in the right direction. You just needed the right motivation."

My breath locks.

She looks like she's been punched.

Cleo stares at him, her hands gripping the table. "What?"

Oscar chuckles, watching realization dawn, slow and horrifying, on her face. "Oh, sweetheart," he croons, his grin wicked. "Did you really think you got here on your own?"

Silence stretches.

The rest of the restaurant fades out.

"You were always part of the plan. I just made you think you had a choice."

She doesn't speak. Doesn't deny it. She's putting it together, piece by piece. Her breath shortens. Her gaze flicks around the room, searching for anything to make this untrue. She unravels right there, eyes scanning for an exit that isn't there.

And yet, I can't feel sorry for her. I'm the one who let her in.

"So, what was the plan?" I force the words out. I need to hear her say it.

My voice is colder than I expect. "Keep me distracted while you and Oscar plotted your takeover?"

Her eyes snap to mine, wide, desperate. "No! Dillon, please. I didn't know. I never meant—"

I don't want to hear it. I can't.

Not when the pieces are already falling into place.

Not with Oscar smiling like he planned this from the start.

I shake my head.

I let her in, and I should've known better.

But the part of me that's been betrayed before, who buried his mother and swore never to need anyone again, wins.

I shove back my chair. The legs scrape the tile, sharp and final.

"I'm done doing business with men who manipulate people."

Oscar chuckles. I'm already moving.

"Dillon, please," Cleo calls out, voice tight.

I keep walking, pulse roaring in my ears.

Behind me, I hear the scrape of a chair, then hurried footsteps. Cleo catches up just as I reach my car.

She grabs my arm. "Dillon, wait. Just listen."

I shake her off. "For what, another excuse? Another way to twist this? You walked right into it, Cleo. Even if you didn't mean to."

She exhales, frustrated. "I thought I could outmaneuver him. But I never agreed to any of it."

I rake a hand through my hair, pacing, trying to push past the images flashing through me.

Her sitting across from him. A wicked glint in his eyes, knowing exactly what buttons to push.

The realization hits low, a gut punch I should've seen coming.

"You don't get it, do you?" I growl. "You let him pull you into this, and whether you meant to or not, you let him use you against me."

She flinches like I struck her.

I hate myself for it, but I don't take it back.

"I care about you, Dillon," she says, voice soft but firm. "I wouldn't do anything to hurt you."

I go still.

The words hang there, heavy and unanswered.

"That's the problem, Cleo." My voice sharpens. "When I let you in, I forget how to hold the line. I don't know who I am without the armor."

She reaches for me one last time. "Dillon, please—"

I yank my arm out of her grip and climb into my car.

I start the engine, and I don't look back.
Every mile I drive feels like a door closing behind me.

27

Chapter 27: The Break Up

Cleo

My breath catches, chest pulled tight like a drawn bowstring. I refuse to let the sobs out.

Hold it together, Cleo. Not here. Not now.

Sitting in the back seat of the Uber, I hear music spilling from the restaurant.

Camila Cabello's *Consequences* starts playing low in the background.

I don't need the lyrics.

People keep moving, like nothing's changed.

Like my world didn't just crack open.

My phone buzzes beside me on the seat.

I can't answer. I can't even breathe.

I squeeze my eyes shut, trying to push the pain away. I press the back of my hand to my forehead.

But the moment I close my eyes, I see Dillon's face. His expression when he looked at me like I was another person who let him down.

That's what hurts most.

Not the anger. The disappointment.

He didn't even hesitate to believe the worst.

My phone buzzes again. And again. I reach to grab it. I blink, vision blurring as my heart lurches.

One look at the screen, and it's Tia. My stomach drops. My fingers shake as I answer. "Tia?"

Her voice cracks. "Cleo, it's Mom. It's bad. You need to come home."

Everything stops.

"What happened?" I grip my phone.

"She fell and broke her hip," Tia rushes to explain. "Stress-related, they think, but they're running tests. She goes in for surgery tomorrow morning. I can't get back home right away. I'm in transit." Her voice wobbles, thick with guilt. "I need you to go home to help her. Please, Cleo."

The scenery outside fades.

I should've called and pushed through the silence. That's on me. And here we are again. I'm the pillar of strength. The role I always end up playing.

I stare ahead, forcing myself to breathe past the crushing weight in my chest. "I'll take care of it," I whisper. "I'll book a flight."

I hang up and drop my phone onto the seat, rubbing a hand over my face. I can't fix what broke between Dillon and me.

I don't have a choice. I'm going home.

Why does my heart hurt this much?

I'm ten again, standing in my Yiayia's warm kitchen.

My small hands press into soft dough as she guides me. Her touch is steady and patient as she shows me how to braid the *koulourakia* cookies.

I inhale the scent of oregano, thyme, and rosemary as the *avgolemono* soup simmers.

The familiar smell wraps around me like a comfort blanket.

Yiayia's smile reaches her eyes. She kneads beside me, squeezing my flour-dusted fingers.

"Life's rough, *kopelia mou*. Faith will steady you. Remember that, always."

I believed her. The Easter nights at the Greek church. Standing in a candlelit service, the glow of hundreds of flickering flames stretching into the dark. Each one a prayer for a loved one now gone. The scent of incense and the tender touch of her hand as we whispered prayers together and made the sign of the cross.

Those were simpler days.

The memory never dulled.

Police lights flashed across our windows, sirens tearing through the quiet.

My mother stood frozen on the porch, my little sister sobbing and clutching my arm.

At the door, he turned back and met my eyes, silently mouthing, "I'm sorry."

But sorry doesn't rebuild a family.

An apology can't undo the damage my father left behind.

Our family split apart. Yiayia and Papou were sent back to Greece.

It's the day I learned people leave, and love doesn't stop them.

That trust is dangerous.

Needing someone means handing them the power to break you.

After my father's arrest, faith became harder to hold, like the ground beneath me had turned to sand.

Years later, Megan was the first person who felt steady again.

Glancing in the mirror, I see puffy Gucci bags under my eyes and smudged mascara. I look wrecked.

It doesn't feel like going home.

It feels like running.

I need someone who knows me.

Back then, Megan did.

I remember college. Megan used to hand me a cup of herbal tea when she knew I needed to talk.

She wraps her hands around the mug. "Rough day?"

I nod. "Patrick tried to kiss me in the elevator. Like it was some casual, no-big-deal Tuesday thing."

Her brows lift. "Again?"

"Apparently, no doesn't mean no. It means try again later with cocktails."

Megan groans. "I'm tired of this world pretending hookups are some empowering rite of passage."

"Right?" I exhale. "I want real connection. Not another meaningless almost."

She turns toward me. "I hate that it makes me feel old-fashioned or prudish. Like there's something wrong with wanting to wait."

"I want to save that part of myself for someone who sees me," I say with conviction. "All of me. Not just the parts he finds hot after two drinks."

Megan nods slowly. "For someone who stays when life isn't sexy. Who fights for me, knows my flaws, and continues to stick around."

We sip in unison, a ritual of quiet defiance.

"You think they're still out there?" I ask. "Guys who don't expect you to compromise your soul for chemistry?"

She smiles faintly.

"I think they're rare. But God doesn't deal in crowds. He writes one-on-one stories."

I let her words settle into the ache.

I once believed God wrote mine too.

"I used to pray about him," I say.

"My future husband."

I don't even know if he's real.

"I miss him sometimes. Isn't that weird?"

"It's not weird," she says softly. "It's honorable."

My throat tightens. I don't cry.

Something about this quiet, the knowing, melts me a little.

I used to think I had to become someone different to earn it.

Now I just want to be seen and still chosen.

Megan doesn't say anything.

She just reaches for my hand and squeezes.

Back then, I still believed that love would find me whole.

Tonight, I'm not sure I'd even recognize love if it showed up and said my name.

28

Chapter 28: Resignation

Cleo

My finger hovers over the print icon. This isn't only about Dillon.

It's about protecting myself before someone else fails me again.

Part of me knows he didn't mean to hurt me. He hesitated. He shut down. And maybe that's forgivable. But I'm still bleeding from wounds I never finished stitching.

So I hit print.

I'm not leaving because I want to. I'm leaving because I don't know how to stay without losing myself.

I walk into Dillon's office, fingers tightening around the envelope.

It's not just a resignation letter. It holds every fight, every almost, every unanswered question.

Dillon looks up from his desk, his expression shifting the second he sees me.

The silence between us holds everything we never said.

He sets his pen down slowly, like buying time.

"What is this?" he asks, as a formality.

I slide the envelope toward him. "My resignation. I'm leaving."

Something flickers in his eyes, gone before I can name it.

In a voice too calm, he says, "So that's it?"

His calm tone stings more than I'll admit.

I brace myself, swallowing, arms crossed tight. "Yes. I can't do this anymore. My mother needs me. And you don't need me. Or anyone."

Dillon's brow furrows, a faint crack in his carefully composed face. He hears what I'm not saying.

I wait for him to fight. To stop me, to say this, whatever this is, matters.

Dillon exhales slowly. "If that's what you need to do, then go."

His words land sharply, choking what little hope I had left.

This silence feels like a door locking behind me.

He didn't fight for me. Not the woman, not the partner, not the truth.

My throat tightens.

I nod and turn away, my hand lingering on the door.

I don't turn around.

I feel him watching, not calling me back.

I walk out.

The door closes softly behind me.

Dillon lets me go.

This time, I don't look back.

29

Chapter 29: Revelation

Dillon

The door clicks shut behind her, and I don't move. Not for a while.

I sit at my desk as the screen glows, casting a pale light across the empty room.

The timestamp blinks back at me.

Cleo Ambrosia, 10:42 a.m.

A quiet marker of what I just lost.

Trust withdrawn. Signal lost. Connection terminated.

All I see is her face, frozen mid-expression.

The room feels too quiet.

Reviewing the Lucid Lenses data logs, I see all the things I needed her to hear and couldn't say.

That I needed help. That I was trying, and failing, to understand her. That I was afraid I'd misread something that mattered.

But she didn't see effort. She saw betrayal.

And maybe, she's right.

I built this to outsmart human error. Cleo never fit the model.

Cleo didn't need algorithms. She needed honesty.

Fear finally forced me to see clearly.

I scanned expressions. Calibrated responses.

But I missed the hurt beneath her curiosity.

I didn't see the trust she offered when she let her walls down.

I stare at the data. The numbers mean nothing now. Everything I thought I knew short-circuits against the truth I avoided.

The tech wasn't the problem. I was.

My father's text flashes back. *Ambition draws predators.*

I'd been so consumed with the Lucid Lenses rollout and Cleo that I hadn't noticed the shift in the boardroom. Too many meetings missed. Too many decisions delayed.

And Oscar had filled the vacuum. Backroom lunches with investors. Whispered complaints about my "visionary distractions."

The next few hours blur together.

An email lands in my inbox at 2:13 p.m.

Subject line: *iSight Ethics Framework Revised Proposal*
From: *Cleo Ambrosia*

My fingers hover over the keyboard. I click it open. I read once. Then again. By the third pass, I'm reading it not as the CEO, but as a man who's spent his life hiding behind precision. Not the document. *Her.*

"Emotional intelligence must be met with emotional responsibility."

I'm unarmed.

She saw through me and told the truth anyway.

"Data may be neutral. Its application never is. Trust cannot be assumed. It must be earned and protected."

Every line carries restraint, power, and clarity. Underneath it all is *her voice*.

I forward it to legal with a simple note: "Use this as the foundation. Make it stronger, not softer."

Then I start a new message. One that isn't professional.

> To: Cleo Ambrosia
> Subject: RE: Ethics Framework
> Time: 2:47 p.m.
> This wasn't just policy. It read like the version of us I wish we'd had the courage to begin with. I read every word. And I heard what you didn't say.
> Thank you for not walking away. For choosing to build, not burn.
> I'd follow that framework, and you, any day.
> –D

I hesitate. Then I hit Send.

No regards, no signature block, no deflection. Just honesty.

Cleo walked out. But she didn't walk away. Not really. She left the truth behind and trusted I'd know what to do with it.

And for the first time, I did.

Love isn't always explosive.

Sometimes it lands in an inbox late, unpolished, unassuming.

But exactly when it's needed.

***

Later that evening, I sit alone in my living room, staring at my reflection in the dark window. A hollowness fills my chest, like the air's been pulled from the room.

The doorbell rings. Noah stands on the other side, holding Korean take-out.

"Hungry?" he asks.

"Always."

Twenty minutes later, we relax on the sofa, ready to watch the game on TV. Noah slides his phone onto the coffee table, slow and deliberate.

"Got something for you," he says, low. "Oscar Damon."

That gets my attention.

Noah cues up an audio file and hands me the phone. I click before thinking, and the audio plays. The voice cuts through. The smug cadence mixed with poison, wrapped in charm.

"Whelan's brilliant, sure."

A sip. A pause.

"But he's too soft. Founders get emotional. They cling, and they forget that business isn't about loyalty. Vulnerability like that doesn't scale."

Silence.

"And the board's starting to notice. He can't handle something of this magnitude. You and I both know what comes next."

Another pause.

"iSight needs an experienced leader."

The sound of Oscar moving in his chair.

"We move forward under my lead. Quiet restructure. Whelan exits with a golden parachute, and you stay on to manage perception. It will be a smooth transition

with minimal noise."

Another pause.

"Give it six months, and we'll shift him into a symbolic role. Maybe something overseas. He won't even see it coming."

Shuffling sounds.

"And you? You could be part of it. Vision needs execution. You've got instincts. You knew I was trouble the second I walked in, didn't you?"

Then Cleo's voice comes through measured, but sharp.

"I just see what's in front of me."

"You've been great for this rollout. Polished, strategic, easy for the board to trust. And with Whelan distracted, it's the perfect time to pivot."

Pause.

"Come on, Cleo. Let's not kid ourselves. This isn't about ethics. It never is."

Another pause.

"You want me to smile while you stab him in the back? I don't appreciate being used."

Oscar chuckles.

"Don't be dramatic. It's not personal, it's business. You know you can be easily replaced?"

"I doubt that."

I freeze.

The phone suddenly feels heavier.

Not because I didn't suspect Oscar, but because she recorded it.

Noah nods to his inbox. "Cleo sent it the night she left. No context. Just the file and a two-liner: *Do what you need to. I don't want credit.* That's what got me digging into Oscar."

He pauses. "I think she knew you wouldn't believe her about Oscar unless you had proof."

Noah meets my eyes. "It's not for the board. It's for you."

I'm still reeling from Cleo's voice when Noah adds, "There's more."

I glance up.

"Another recording," he says. "Not from her."

I tense. "Then who?"

He shrugs. "Someone else tipped me off. Someone who figured you'd be too stubborn to listen. Sent it straight to my inbox. "

I stare at him. "Who?"

Noah just raises an eyebrow.

"My father," I say flatly.

Noah's expression shifts, more serious now. "Robert's the one who caught Oscar cozying up to Coates at the golf club. He was arrogant enough to talk so loudly that several people overheard him. Robert dug into his vault of secrets and sent this to me yesterday with a note. 'Use it if you need it. He won't listen to me.' Told me to protect you without tipping you off."

Noah leans in, taps his phone screen. Voice memo queued; seven minutes loaded.

He taps to play it. Oscar's voice slides through the speaker, smooth and smug.

"Whelan's cracked. The girl was the bait. Poor thing thought she landed a golden client. She never would've doubted him if I hadn't pushed the ethics angle. Gave her just enough rope, and she did the rest herself. Now

the board just needs the right nudge."

I grip the edge of the table until my knuckles turn white.

"Once Whelan's out, we move fast. Install a new CEO and clean house."

I stare at the screen, willing the words away.

Noah clears his throat. "You think Oscar's just being Oscar, but all he's wanted is control. He doesn't build; he waits, then hijacks."

My jaw locks. I let that sink in. I should have known.

The realization cuts deeper than the betrayal ever could.

Noah leans back, watching. Waiting for the explosion.

Instead, I set the phone down. Pick up the coffee. Sip once. Set it down.

"The girl," I say, voice flat. Noah nods.

Cleo. Collateral damage in a war she didn't even know she was in.

She sent it to Noah. She didn't just walk away. She made sure I had the truth, even when I didn't deserve it. Even after I pushed her away.

She wasn't walking away to punish me.

She was walking away to protect something I couldn't see yet.

She trusted me not to break it.

Just two sentences: "Do what you need to. I don't want credit."

No fanfare, no demand for validation. Just evidence.

I sit back as shame, and something like reverence, fills my chest.

Cleo didn't just save the company. She saved me.

I breathe out once, slowly forcing the rage into a tighter, colder box.

Not now. Not yet.

Loyalty doesn't always wear a suit and tie. Sometimes it slips in quietly when you're not paying attention.

The realization settles, heavy and immovable.

No more running.

My laptop pings with an email from the board, Meredith Cho, our longest-standing investor.

"The board has grown concerned. Oscar's proposal outlines a more focused monetization strategy. Fewer side projects, tighter leadership controls."

Translation: He'd painted me as reckless and a liability.

I already know what is at stake: my company, my expectations, my heart.

I let out a slow breath and rub a hand down my face.

I expect to feel some emotion, anger, irritation, or maybe even relief.

But all I feel is emptiness.

Then memories flood in.

Cleo.

Her sharp challenge in the boardroom. The way she saw through me, called me out, never let me hide behind my defenses. The way she made me feel alive. Her laughter at the lake.

My mother's voice echoes in my head. Her last words about finding happiness.

I did the opposite. I became hardened, rejecting the only

person who made me yearn for something better.

And now, she's gone.

I open a new email.

> *To: Board of Directors*
> *Subject: Ethics Framework Update*
> *"Effective immediately, Cleo Ambrosia's ethics proposal will be adopted as the operational framework for Lucid Lenses and all future products.*
> *Any narrative suggesting she acted improperly is incorrect.*
> *She acted with integrity when others did not."*

I hit send.

"Get me everything you've got on Oscar," I say. "Emails, contracts, anything he touched."

Noah nods. "Already started."

30

Chapter 30: The Take Down

Dillon

The air is ice-cold. Not from the air conditioner, but from the glint of sharpened ambition around the polished mahogany table. Ten board members sit opposite me.

Oscar sits at the head, already acting like he's claimed the throne. His Armani suit is immaculate, his superior grin measured.

Oscar clears his throat, stacking a printed proposal in front of him like a closing argument. "I've called this emergency session to propose a leadership restructure. Given recent instability in strategic direction, the board deserves to consider the appointment of a more seasoned CEO."

He doesn't glance at me; he doesn't have to. He believes he's already won. "We need a CEO who's present and focused. Not one distracted by internal romances and ethical gray areas. We've lost momentum. Investors are skittish. I've had serious talks with investors about stabilizing leadership and restoring market confidence. If the board agrees, I'm prepared to step in immediately and rebuild confidence. And with the support of three of our major stakeholders, I submit my candidacy for CEO, effective immediately."

A murmur spreads across the room.

For a moment, I wonder if they're right.

Had my obsession with innovation, and with Cleo, clouded my judgment?

Was I still the shark they'd bet on?

I don't flinch. I step forward and place a sleek black folder on the table.

"I second the need for transparency," I say, voice low but clear. "But before we vote, there's something the board needs to see."

I open my laptop and queue the evidence files. My father's audio and the one Cleo sent.

The doors open. Every head turns as Robert Whelan enters. I freeze. Why is he here? I haven't seen or spoken to my father in months.

Now he walks in like he owns the place. Maybe, in some ways, he does. There's no ego in his stride today. Just steel.

Oscar pales. I realize something I didn't see until now. My father didn't come here to save the company. He came to save me.

The room shifts.

Robert sets a USB on the table, then opens the folder beside mine.

"This"—he nods to the screen—"is a call from three years ago."

At the far end of the room, a board member queues up the recording.

"Robert Whelan walked away from the best deal of his life because he couldn't stomach the reality of how business works. And now his golden boy thinks he's above it all? Please."

Oscar's voice spills from the speakers, smug, reckless. Silence stretches as his scheme unfolds.

Oscar bolts upright. "This is illegal," he snaps, his face blanching.

"No," Robert interrupts, calm and lethal. "You were on speaker. It was recorded under our internal compliance policy. New York's one-party consent law makes it legal."

"Dillon's just another idealist hiding behind a legacy. But I've built mine from the ground up. I don't need a last name to get respect. I earn it or take it. Once I get my hands on his patents, I'll flip them before he knows what hit him. So what if I must forge a few signatures to get what I want?"

Robert continues, voice steady. "In addition, I'd like to disclose a few things. Like the fraudulent shell companies and misappropriation of R&D funds. And this, where Oscar admits to forging signatures on a merger proposal I terminated."

The silence that follows detonates.

Robert walks toward the table, calm and composed. His eyes meet mine. Not cold, just knowing. "I didn't just overhear one conversation," he says. "I've been collecting patterns. Financial inconsistencies, conflicting emails, even a whistleblower from Oscar's last firm." He taps the file again. "And there's more. Oscar authorized predictive behavior modeling on beta testers without their knowledge or consent."

I glance at the board. "Cleo Ambrosia's Ethics Framework called it out, page five."

She was right long before I listened.

"If legal hadn't caught it, we'd be wide open to liability."

Robert nods. "And on top of that, Oscar broke NDA protocol with a former investor. Used confidential phrasing from a protected pitch document under active NDA." He looks straight at the chairman. "The lunch with Coates was just the final thread. But the unraveling started long before that."

Oscar turns to the chairman. "This is a setup. You can't prove—"

"We can," Robert inserts.

"Actually," Meredith says, tapping her tablet, "Mr. Whelan submitted the evidence file this morning. We flagged it for an immediate audit. The report came back verified an hour ago."

"Oscar's history with the misappropriation of IP, the lawsuit that was settled quietly in Switzerland, it's all here," Robert says. "You can vote Oscar in if you want. But you'll lose your reputation and your shareholders by morning."

I look at my father. He trained me to fight alone. Now, he's the one in my corner.

I meet each board member's eyes in turn. "You trusted me with this company, and I've made mistakes. But the greatest mistake would be letting a man like *that* lead it."

Meredith sets her tablet down. "This is serious. I'd like to recommend an emergency board vote to formally remove Oscar Damon from consideration."

One board member mutters, "This could sink us."

Another nods.

A murmur of agreement follows.

The chairman glances around the table. "All in favor?"

Hands rise. One by one. Every single one.

I glance at the second file on my laptop. Cleo's audio. The one she sent to Noah that exposed Oscar's whispered betrayal over lunch.

My hand hovers over the play button. I won't play it now; I don't need to. She asked not to get credit because that one wasn't for the board; it was for me.

I drop a final document on the table and stare at Oscar. "Your resignation letter is already drafted. Unless you'd prefer formal litigation."

Oscar's hands curl into fists. But he knows it's over. He shoots up, turns on his heel, and storms out without another word.

After a moment of awkward silence, the board stands to leave. After five minutes, the room is empty. The last door clicks shut. Noah, Robert, and I remain.

I let out a long breath and look at my father. "Thank you," I say, voice quiet.

Robert nods. "You didn't just protect the company. You protected its soul." There's a pause. Then, he says, quieter, "I'm proud of you, son."

I say nothing. My posture softens, like a years-long battle has finally ended.

"I'm not asking you to forgive me," he says, voice gravelly. "But I couldn't sit back and watch him destroy what you built. I made my mistakes. Let this be my way of owning one of them."

We aren't the hugging kind, so we settle for a nod that carries more than words. It isn't a full relationship repair, but it's something. For the first time, I believe he sees me as a man.

My father walks out of the boardroom with quiet resolve.

I loosen my tie and exhale. Relief hits for the first time in ages.

Noah looks at me and shakes his head as if I offended him. "You're an idiot," he says, flat and certain.

I scoff. "Thanks for the insight. But I was expecting applause."

He crosses his arms. "You let Cleo go because you were scared. And now you're sitting here, wallowing in it. So, tell me, was it worth it?"

I don't answer. I already know.

No.

Nothing was.

Not the company. Not the fear that kept me silent when Cleo stood in that doorway, waiting.

Some things deserve a second fight.

I don't argue. What's the point? He's right.

"What tipped you off?" I say instead.

Noah settles into the opposite chair, appearing relaxed. "You," he says, jabbing a finger toward me. "Sitting here like a sad Bond villain after losing the girl instead of doing something about it."

I glare at him. "You think this is about losing a deal or a company?"

Noah laughs once, sharp and humorless. "You lost *her*, man. And you're sitting here waiting for what, permission to fight for her?"

I grit my teeth. "It's not that simple."

"It's exactly that simple," he snaps. "You love her. She loves you. And yeah, you screwed up. So what? Grow a spine and fix it."

I look up, half-expecting answers on the ceiling. There aren't any.

"You think she wants to see me now?" I ask, voice rough. "After what I did?"

Noah stands and braces his hands on my desk. "I think she's scared you'd become exactly who you were afraid of becoming. And the only way you prove her wrong is by showing up."

I close my eyes for a beat and exhale. I built my life around control. Only chasing what I could predict.

But Cleo?

She was never part of the plan.

She was the reason to blow it up.

I shove my chair back. It scrapes as I stand.

"I have to fix this."

Noah beams, clapping his hands, a flicker of approval in his eyes. "About time."

31

Chapter 31: The Lies We Believe

Cleo

York, England

It's only been two days since I left New York, but it feels longer. The house is quieter than I remember. Mom's recovering from a fractured hip. The pain meds help, but they don't touch the deeper exhaustion in her eyes. Even asleep, I hear her labored breathing.

Coming home to care for her felt right, yet something's still missing.

The only light in the room comes from a dim bulb. I sit cross-legged on my old bed, Yiayia's worn photo resting between my fingers. I've traced its edges so many times, it's muscle memory now. Sometimes I wonder if holding it tight enough could keep her with me.

Even the broken parts can build something better, she used to say.

"Real strength, kopelia mou, isn't standing alone. It's knowing

when to let someone stand beside you."

I want to believe her. Right now, I just feel useless.

I lean into the glass and breathe in. Around me, the room is frozen in time. Dance trophies, skating medals, dried-out pens, an unfinished journal entry.

I held it together. Because no one else did.

I fold the blanket over my chair and pause, remembering how Mom used to sit on the rink bench in the freezing cold, watching me practice. Braiding my hair. Driving me to competitions. Sleeping in the car so we could claim early ice time.

My mind wanders in a hundred different directions.

Dillon's nature infuriates me. He's impossible, stubborn, arrogant. He's unshakable. Steady like granite. The only person who's ever really challenged me—not just intellectually but emotionally.

The truth hits hard. Something I always knew and avoided.

I ran.

The thought of him walking away scares me. I've spent my whole life being the one in control, because that way I don't get hurt.

Maybe that's another lie I've been telling myself.

Maybe I was never really living at all.

***

The kettle clicks off, the steam hissing through the spout. I pour hot water into two cups, and the rooibos tea bags steep in silence.

My mother sits at the kitchen table, wrapped in one of my childhood blankets, her leg elevated on a pillow. The same one I used to hide under after the divorce. After Dad left.

"Thanks, love," Mom says softly, accepting the mug.

I sit opposite her, holding her hand.

"You've barely said a word since you got back," she comments. She brushes a strand of gray hair behind her ear, trying for a smile. "You've barely looked up from taking care of me."

"Well, that's what I do, isn't it?" I smile, but it falls short. "I'm here to pick up the pieces and fill in the gaps."

A beat of silence.

"You always were the strong one," Mom says. "Even when you shouldn't have had to be."

My throat tightens.

The tea mixes with the heaviness in my chest.

"I keep thinking about Dad lately. About how easy it was for him to leave. For you to cover for him. For me to believe that men lie and women clean up the mess." I pause. "Every time I try to forget, the memories start to resurface. Forgiving him doesn't erase what he did. The part of me that continues to suffer feels like I'm committing a betrayal by giving him a pardon."

Mom's face stiffens. Her expression shows sorrow instead of defense.

"What?" I ask, sounding sharp.

My mother takes a breath, bracing against a pain no doctor can treat. "He didn't leave, Cleo."

I blink. "I—what?"

"I'm afraid that isn't what happened, Cleo. He went to prison," Mom says, holding back tears. "Not because he was guilty. Because he took the fall."

Her words hit like ice water.

"You're lying," I snap, the chair scraping back as I stand.

My mother straightens the tea spoon beside my cup, as if order might hold the moment together.

Memories snap out of focus. I want to scream, want to believe it's a lie, but something in her voice, in her eyes, tells me it's not.

"You said he was a liar," I whisper. "That he stole. That he walked away."

"I told you what I thought would protect you." Mom's eyes turn glassy. "What would keep you from asking questions. From putting yourself in danger."

I tighten my grip on my teacup.

"We left in a hurry. Your father's arrest wasn't the only reason. His partner threatened all of us," she continues. "I didn't know how deep it went until your dad was behind bars."

Tears burn. "Why didn't you tell me?"

"He was arrested in France, and the authorities kept it quiet. There was no public trial, only a plea deal behind closed doors. He took it to buy us time, Cleo. Time for us to disappear."

My chest tightens.

"I was trying to keep us alive." Mom's voice breaks. "We moved, changed names. I thought if I could keep that part of him hidden, you'd grow up with one good parent instead of none. I didn't know it would make you feel abandoned by us both. By the time it was safe to tell you, too much time had passed. I didn't know how to undo the story you'd built around him. And part of me was ashamed that I let it happen. Besides, your father begged me not to say anything to you girls."

"Where is he?" My voice cracks. "He's alive?"

Mom nods. "Living on a Greek island under a different name. After he got out, he vanished. Said he'd done enough damage. That the best way to protect us was to disappear."

I stand and pace, breaths quick and shallow. "All this time, I thought he abandoned us. I thought he walked away. I've been living life as if every man walks away. That's why I felt I had to be strong!"

Mom's trembling. "I know. And I'm so sorry. I thought I was protecting you, but I see now that I was wrong. I left you with a story that broke something in you."

I sink into the chair, fingers trembling.

"He loved you, Cleo. He didn't want your childhood burdened by what he'd done to protect it."

The truth slips in like light through a crack, too bright to hold at once. I don't know what to do with it yet. Decades of anger don't vanish because the story changed. Part of me wants to believe her; the rest of me is still twelve, still furious.

The quiet stretches out between us, heavy and raw. I let the tears fall. I wanted justice. But maybe what I needed was release. A way to stop bleeding every time his name came up.

"I've hated him for years."

"I know."

"I've hated you, too, sometimes."

"I know."

Her face crumples, but I can't stop. Rage rushes through me, blinding and electric.

"Do you know what it did to me believing that he abandoned us? That I wasn't worth staying for?"

She tries to open her mouth to either defend herself or apologize. I don't allow myself to wait. I grab my jacket from the hook by the door and throw it over my shoulders. "I just can't do this right now."

I'm outside, gulping damp air like it might wash the betrayal out.

I'm twelve, sitting in our living room, when mom tells me everything will get better after the divorce. She says it like she believes it, but I know better. The house slips into quiet chaos. Stacks of unpaid bills. Laundry piles. The fridge is half-empty.

Mom's trying, but she's overwhelmed. So, I step up. I take care of Tia. Help with homework. Track the doctor's appointments. No one at school sees how bad things really are. All they see is my stern face that says don't mess with me.

High school. Tia crying on the school curb, backpack clutched to her chest. Mom forgot to pick us up again.

"Some kids dream of being stranded at school," I joke. "Adventure, right?"

"It's horrible," she whispers. "I'm scared."

I sling an arm around her shoulders. "Ice cream," I say. "But don't get used to it. I have a reputation as the bossy older sister to uphold."

Her watery smile keeps me breathing.

***

I don't remember leaving my mom's house. Just the weight of the door handle. I don't remember crossing into York city centre. In the Museum Gardens, people sit on the grass watching boats drift along the River Ouse.

I need motion to outrun the echo. Anger still scorches the back of my throat. But beneath it is something heavier: grief.

I know the truth now. It doesn't erase the pain, but it changes it.

My mom didn't lie to hurt me. She lied to protect what was

left of our family.

And my father didn't run. He took the fall to protect us.

And suddenly I wonder if I misunderstood Dillon too.

But silence wasn't the same as love.

The knowing isn't forgiveness.

It's just a new kind of ache, the kind that demands time. Maybe healing isn't about flipping the story overnight. Maybe it's about learning how to live with both versions until one feels true.

Inside, anger burns because I'm exhausted from holding everything together.

But I get it now. They were imperfect, yet they remained human. But now I'm just tired of carrying this weight.

The buzz of a text startles me. I glance down. For a second, I think about ignoring it. But then I glance at the screen.

Mom: I'm sorry. I should have told you everything sooner. Love you always.

The years I spent in anger can't be erased. But maybe it makes forgiveness possible. Maybe those skating-school care packages meant more than I let myself believe. They did what they could with what little they had.

I wasn't ready to call it forgiveness, not yet.

Maybe someday I'll try to write to him. For now, it's enough to stop letting their silence write my story for me.

Maybe I didn't grow strong, I grew hard. There's a difference. I'm finally ready to unlearn it.

My phone rings. It's Megan. I hesitate, then swipe to answer.

"He—hello," I say, flat.

"Oh, Cleo darling, what's the matter?"

"Sorry. I'm spiraling."

"I had a feeling."

"Wow. Inspirational talk. You should be a life coach."

"Sarcasm noted. But honey, I know you too well." Her voice is warm, steady, like a hand on my back in the dark. "You're scared, right? And now you're throwing yourself a pity party." She sighs. "As much as I love a good party, you know that's not one with cake or flowers."

Despite myself, my mouth twitches. "You're hilarious."

"I'm serious, love. I know exactly what this is. You ran. Told yourself it was for the right reasons. But deep down, you know that it wasn't."

Silence stretches. I don't fill it. I can't.

"You let him go because needing him felt dangerous. And now you're calling it strength."

My throat tightens. It's not just what she's saying. It's how she's saying it. Like she's holding my heart and knows not to squeeze.

"You've always been the strong one, Cleo," she says softly. "But strength doesn't mean never needing anyone. Sometimes, it means letting someone in."

A knot rises in my chest, thick and sharp.

"Was it worth it?" she asks, voice like velvet. "Walking away?"

I swallow.

No. Not my pride. Not the fear.

Not this need to prove I'm fine alone.

Because I'm not. Because I need him.

And for once, I don't care what that says about me.

I breathe in. Then out.

And say the only thing that matters. "I have to fix this."

"Then go, darling. Choose the thing you were always so

afraid to want."
I hang up.
The truth smacks me in the face.
I don't want to be alone anymore.
But I know what matters.
I don't need a plan; I just need him.
My feet are moving.
This time, I'm choosing love over fear.
I lift my face to the sky and let the rain fall.
The lie finally breaks.
I'm done running.

32

Chapter 32: Reflection

Cleo

York, England

After several sleepless nights, I needed to move. The rink is mostly empty, just a few kids on the ice, all bundled up. Toddlers cling to the wall, an older couple glides through a slow waltz at center. I disappear into the perimeter of the space.

No makeup. No audience. No Dillon. Just me and the cold.

The sound of my blades scraping the ice becomes a steady rhythm. The first few glides feel stiff. I don't try to impress. Skating has a way of cracking things open, whether I want it to or not.

I move toward the end of the rink and shut my eyes. After the funeral, I couldn't sleep. I'd be at the rink at five a.m., lights off, the sun still asleep.

The first time I skated after the crash, I thought it would break me. But the ice was the only place that made sense. The only place where my legs knew what to do, even when my heart didn't.

So I skated every morning until my lungs burned and my muscles trembled.

It wasn't beautiful or brave. Just survival.

The spin became a prayer, the ache in my feet the only proof I was still alive.

Then I'd put on fake smiles and pretend I was fine. What other choice was there?

I blink, breathing hard. A tear slides down my cheek. I skate faster. Crossovers, a spiral, and into a lunge. I don't need choreography because my body remembers.

This time, the grief goes beyond what happened. It's about dad. It's about Dillon. What we almost had. What I walked away from. Because it felt too close to losing myself.

But skating taught me something else, too. You fall, but you get up, again and again. Sometimes you get bruised, and sometimes you bleed. But the only way to move is forward.

I stop at center ice. Chest heaving, hair damp with sweat, tears on my jawline. But I'm standing. Still here. Still Cleo. The little girl who used to believe in magic on ice. The teenager who lost everything. The woman who learned to bury it. And now the one who might be ready to feel again.

I spent years training myself to detect every tiny detail. Reading facial expressions, speech, and behavior like I'm on high alert every second. I have entered boardrooms and courtrooms and family interventions with the ability to foresee what was coming because I could read the signs before they happened.

No one tells you that making a career out of reading minds means sometimes missing the heart.

But Dillon Whelan short-circuited every assumption I had.

The version of Dillon that I couldn't read might have been what attracted me to him. The glitch in the algorithm. He showed me his true nature in his unexpected way.

He saw me. Or at least, I thought he did.

Now, I don't know what was real.

Which parts of our conversations were instinct and which were code. The smiles he gave me versus the smiles that served as data collection.

And I hate that it matters. I hate that I care. I hate that I left. I hate that part of me already misses him.

Maybe I am the same.

I use intuition as armor to see pain before it hits.

But love doesn't work like that.

It refuses to be predicted or managed.

There's no chart, no model.

Love doesn't follow equations. Sometimes it turns into disappointment, and sometimes it keeps going anyway.

My throat tightens. I press a hand to my chest.

I left thinking I'd protect myself. Clear my thoughts.

All I feel now is the dull pulse of loneliness and regret.

Dillon hadn't left me. I left him. And now I'm alone.

Our kiss went beyond any strategic plan or tagging system or recording process.

That's what scares me most.

I can't fix the past. But maybe I can stop letting it define me.

***

I sit on my bed and shift my weight. A dull ache shoots down my thigh. The same leg that hit the jetty steps. Pain that lingers under the surface. Invisible, still real.

Kind of like everything I'm trying to say.

I open the voice recording app on my phone. A soft beep. "Okay. So. This is stupid. But I'm talking to my phone because I can't talk to him. Not yet. I skated today at my home rink for the first time. I kept meaning to go, but I couldn't. Not until today. It felt terrible and perfect, like relief tangled with suffocation."

I pause.

"Skating wasn't my escape. It was how I survived. It was the one place I didn't have to pretend. And Dillon, he saw through the charade. I hated it at first. Then I needed it. Then I ran. He didn't leave. I did."

I pause.

"I keep thinking about that night in the lake house. The way he held me like I wasn't too much. Like I wasn't one moment away from shattering. I was scared because he made me feel again. Maybe feeling isn't the threat. It's the beginning."

I let out a deep breath.

"I don't know how to fix this. But I think I want to try. Loving Dillon, even if it ends, doesn't mean I'll lose myself."

I close my eyes, letting the tears fall.

"Maybe I'm not skating alone anymore. Maybe love isn't something to master. Maybe it's something to let move through you, just like skating."

I save the recording but don't listen.

I don't know if Dillon will ever hear this, but I needed to say it, just for me.

Setting my phone aside, I wipe my cheeks. I pour myself another cup of tea, hoping and praying that someone hears.

From my lips to God's ears.

***

Later that afternoon, I sit on the floor of my mother's flat, surrounded by tea mugs and sticky notes. Tia's out filming something glossy and charming and unmistakably her.

The silence here feels thicker than usual. And I know exactly why.

The email arrives at 2:47 p.m. I don't open it right away. I take a sip of my tea, then click the message.

> *Subject: Re: Ethics Framework*
> *From: Dillon Whelan*
> *You didn't just write policy. You wrote the version of us I wish we'd been brave enough to start with. I read every word. And I heard what you didn't say.*
> *Thank you for not walking away. For choosing to build, not burn.*
> *I'd follow that framework, and you, any day.*
> *–D*

I read it once. Twice. Three times. I don't cry.

My instinct is to protect myself, pull back before it hurts. But something in me settles. Not the fierce, self-protective part of me that wants to stay detached, but the softer, smarter part that knows staying detached isn't strength.

I pull my laptop closer and start typing.

Not everything's fixed. But maybe everything doesn't have to be to take one step forward.

> *Subject: Re: Ethics Framework*
> *To: Dillon Whelan*

Time: 3:07 p.m.

Thanks for reading between the lines. I didn't know if this version of me, the one who feels before she calculates, would be welcome. But your message? It made me want to keep writing. Not just frameworks, but futures.

Ready when you are. Let's build something worth keeping.

—Cleo :)

I hover. Breathe. I hadn't planned to send anything. The Ethics doc wasn't about fixing us. But maybe doing the right thing leads somewhere good anyway.

I hit send and close the laptop.

For the first time since I left New York, I don't feel like I'm running.

***

Watching the sunset in York, Tia and I drink kombucha from champagne flutes and eat tapas like it's a ritual. The lights glow, illuminating the city in the background.

"I swear," she says, flopping into a patio chair, "if one more client calls me 'ambitious' like it's a personality flaw, I'm going to throw my phone into the river."

I lean back beside her, raising a glass. "To ambition. The double-edged sword."

We clink glasses. Fizz bubbles. We nibble on what's left on the tapas tray.

"You ever wish you could just stop? Take off the brand, the wins, the curated vibe, and just be?" I ask.

"Every day."

I glance at her. My sister, golden, glowing, always performing like it's a stage she can't step off. And yet, the exhaustion in her eyes is real.

She leans over and lights the patio candles. "I built this agency from my living room," she says quietly. "Now I'm coaching people who pretend they've got it all together, while I haven't had a real day off in six months."

"Same," I whisper back. "We're the daughters of chaos, remember? We never got to rest."

We fall silent. Memories of slammed doors and broken promises hang between us.

"I think that's why we work so hard," she adds. "Because no one stayed to take care of us. So now we take care of everything."

My chest tightens. "And what do we do with the part of us that still wants to be taken care of?" I ask. "That craves softness and real love and safety?"

Tia looks out at the skyline. "We hide her. Post her behind confidence filters and business cards. And pretend she doesn't exist."

"Maybe that's why we're still single," I muse.

"Or maybe we're just waiting for someone who can love the girl behind the armor."

I nod, throat tight.

That girl is tired. She's hopeful.

"I'm proud of us," I say softly.

Tia leans her head on my shoulder. "Me too. Even if we're hot messes."

"High-functioning hot messes."

"Trademark it."

33

Chapter 33: Thirty Thousand Feet

Dillon

The apartment hums with the low static of the city. I didn't sleep, running angles to fix the mess I started. Not tired, just hollow.

I sit at my desk, staring at the glasses.

My creation. My shield. My downfall.

Cleo's voice echoes in my head. *"You built a machine to feel for you."*

She was right. I thought I was protecting myself. Instead, I built a wall so high I missed the life on the other side.

I pick up the glasses, their weight heavier than ever.

All the data, the algorithms, the precision. None of it caught the real things. The tilt of her smile, the stubborn glint in her eyes, the laughter that cracked something open in me.

None of it needed translating. It just needed to be seen.

I set the glasses down. Across the room, my reflection stares back.

Black tee, sharp watch, clean lines. Cool on the outside. Chaos inside.

All I could see was her. Cleo, walking away. Betrayed, tired, gone.

Like I proved every lie she believed about men.

Maybe I had.

I grip the counter like it might anchor me. It doesn't.

Noah was right. I spent years chasing wins like they would patch the holes. Like success could undo what I lost.

It never brought my mother back. It never made my father stay. And it sure didn't stop me from losing Cleo.

I shut my eyes and breathe in slowly.

For once, I don't plan the next move. Don't run the chessboard. I just stand there.

And let it hit me. The grief. The regret. The guilt. And something else. Something small, dangerous, new.

It feels like surrender.

Maybe Cleo had been right all along. Maybe love wasn't precision. Maybe it was faith.

Her email hits at 3:08 p.m. Short. Unpolished. Unapologetically her.

> *"Ready when you are. Let's build something worth keeping."*

I read it once. Then again. Everything else, the numbers, the deals, the timelines, fades.

I drop her framework straight into the iSight system. No redlines and no edits. Then I forward it to the executive team.

She was the future too. Not as an acquisition.

Cleo's message still glows on my screen.

"Let's build something worth keeping."

I take one last look at the Lucid lenses sitting on the desk. They can stay right there. I don't need them anymore.

My heart pounds. I know what I have to do, and I pray it's not too late.

I remember what she said when she quit, about her mother needing her, and that her mother lived in York, England.

It's a long shot. But it's the only one I've got.

No plan. No speech. No guarantees.

One truth louder than anything else: if there's one thing I know, I can't lose Cleo.

Not like this. Not ever. Even if it means risking everything.

I grab my duffel bag, shove in clothes, my passport and laptop. I book an Uber.

An hour later, I'm standing at the ticket counter at JFK Airport.

"One ticket to London," I tell the agent. "Next available flight. I don't care about the seat."

"Business or personal?" she asks, eyeing me.

"Both," I say.

I don't have flowers. I don't have a speech. Just a feeling I can't shake, and the woman who finally made me want to stop running.

I realize sometimes love doesn't wait for perfect. It books the next flight, walks through customs half-dead with jet lag, and shows up anyway.

Not with answers, but with presence.

***

The hum of the engines fills the cabin, but I barely hear it. I plug in my earphones and hit the music player. The opening chords land sharp, right beneath the breastbone.

I don't usually get emotional over music, but this one gets me every time. "You Are the Reason" by Calum Scott plays on loop.

The title says more than I could.

I look out the window, wondering if I've done the right thing. It's cliché, but here I am, crossing the ocean to be with Cleo.

I stare at the panel above me, but all I see is her. Smiling across a stage, calling me out in a boardroom, seeing right through me.

I exhale hard, jaw tight.

I told myself it was better this way, that she was safer without me. That I couldn't afford to care. What a lie. I cared the moment I met her, and now, I can't imagine my life without her in it.

My mother's voice drifts through the static of my thoughts, clearer than I expected. Maybe I'm finally starting to understand. I replaced love with logic. Control with silence. And where did it get me? Thirty thousand feet in the air, chasing the only thing that ever mattered.

I swallow against the ache pressing against my ribs.

I notice a voicemail I missed before takeoff. Robert Whelan. Yesterday. 11:03 p.m. Even on airplane mode, I can still listen to it. I should delete it. But I hit play instead.

His voice crackles through my earbuds, low and rough around the edges.

"I know I wasn't the father you needed. Maybe not even

the one you deserved. But you made yourself into a man I'm proud of. Always have been. I was just too proud to say it."

Silence.

Then the soft click of disconnection.

I stare at the screen in front of me. My hand stays clenched, white-knuckled on the armrest.

No one else would notice. Inside, something splinters.

Not anger. Not regret.

Just grief for what we never said sooner.

But somewhere deep in places I buried long ago, something fragile stitches itself back together.

I breathe out slowly.

No flash of certainty, no big thunderbolt.

Just a quiet loosening of something inside me.

I don't have all the answers.

And for once, I'm okay with that.

By the time we land, I know exactly what I must do.

I just hope I'm not too late.

34

Chapter 34: The Grand Gesture

Cleo

York, England

I sit tucked in the corner of the small café across from York Minster. The cathedral looms with centuries of secrets. I watch the mist roll across the streets like a living thing, my cold hands wrapped around a chipped mug of tea.

The ancient Jorvik cobbles beneath my boots have outlived centuries of change.

England's original capital, York, inspired the naming of New York.

Living in both cities taught me that even when things change, some truths don't.

I was running.

Trust wasn't my instinct. It was a war fought in a thousand small battles inside my chest.

Every betrayal carved caution into my bones.

Dillon stands at the heart of that battlefield. He holds

nothing but empty hands.

I close my eyes, feeling the cold seep through the windows. I hug my sweater tighter around my body, and I realize something.

Maybe faith is choosing to stay when you can't see the ending.

I press a hand to my heart, breathing deeply.

I toss a few pound coins onto the table before stepping outside.

The bells chime low as I push open the café door. The spires of York Minster stretch toward the grey sky. A light mist dusts the limestone walls, unmoved by time. The bells grow louder as I approach, reverberating through the afternoon air.

Walking past Betty's Tea Rooms, the afternoon tea trays glow in the windows.

Betty's has been welcoming visitors since 1919.

Cold air brushes across my cheeks, and for a second, I forget to breathe.

I hadn't expected to come here today.

But after that email, after Mom's crisis, after Tia's quiet nudge, I needed more than answers.

I needed stillness. Something sacred.

I step inside the cathedral and inhale sharply.

My eyes lift to the ceiling, and calm settles in.

My hands tighten around the edges of my coat.

And then—

"Cleo."

His voice. Low, urgent, raw.

I pivot, my heart slamming against my ribs.

Dillon.

He stands at the entrance, disheveled from travel, his coat

undone, his hair wind-tousled.

But it's his expression that unravels me. Unguarded, stripped of every layer of control he's ever wielded.

He looks at me like I'm the only thing tethering him here.

"You flew across an ocean," I whisper.

"Wasn't far enough to stay away," he says.

"But how did you know I'd be here?"

He glances up at the cathedral. "Your mom didn't give me details, but she said you'd gone looking for stillness. You once told me York was the only place that ever felt like home. So I took a chance."

Something inside me opens. Like light spilling into a dark room.

I step closer. "You didn't come to fix this."

"No," he says. "I came to stand in it."

"With me."

He nods. "Only with you."

Then slowly, he takes a step toward me. "I love you."

The words land stark and bare against the sacred backdrop, igniting everything I've been trying to smother.

He swallows. "I've spent my whole life controlling everything, every outcome, every risk. And then I met you. Suddenly, none of it mattered if I didn't have you. I was an idiot for pushing you away, for thinking I could handle losing you. Because I can't, Cleo."

His breath shudders. "I don't want to do life without you."

My throat tightens.

The words crash over me, knocking down every wall I've built. Fear still lingers in the cracks.

I force myself to speak, my voice barely above a whisper. "Dillon, I don't know if I can trust you. I'm not sure you know how to let me in. How to not shut me out when things get hard."

He nods like he expected that answer.

Then, without hesitation, he reaches into his coat pocket and pulls out a folded piece of paper. His hands tremble slightly as he presses it into mine.

I unfold it, my eyes grazing over the words. Oscar's resignation. Dated, signed, effective immediately.

I look up sharply. "You fired him?"

Dillon's jaw flexes. "He didn't go quietly. But the moment I had proof, I gave him a choice: step down or be exposed. He chose the quieter exit. But he's done, Cleo."

His voice softens. "I don't expect you to trust me today. I just needed to show up for once, not as the CEO, but as the man who let you down. This isn't a pitch. It's a confession. I was wrong. Not just about Oscar, but about how I handled you. You didn't just deserve honesty, you earned it. And I failed."

He swallows hard. "And I'm done protecting people who never protected me."

He reaches for my hands. "I was ready to hold onto my pride, everything I thought made me who I was. But none of it matters if I lose you in the process. I don't need control, Cleo. I need you. And if that means letting go, trusting something bigger than myself, then I'm ready."

I swallow hard to force the lump down my throat.

This wasn't a gesture for show. It was truth, weighty and costly.

He didn't just choose me, he chose integrity.

Behind us, the cathedral doors creak open, and a choir's soft harmonies spill into the air, rising like a prayer.

I exhale shakily, my heart hammering in my chest. "You'd walk away from everything?"

Dillon's lips twitch into a small, soft smile. "For you, in a heartbeat."

Something inside me opens.

For the first time in my life, I let myself trust.

I reach for his hand, threading my fingers through his, and his grip tightens as if he's anchoring himself to me.

Then he kisses me.

Soft, searching, yearning.

"I stopped running the moment you arrived." I say, pressing my cheek against his.

We intertwine our hands. And as the bells chime again, I lean into him, my forehead against his chest.

I choose love over fear.

***

We're quiet for a long time as we wander hand in hand through the cathedral like a pair of tourists seeing it for the first time.

"I'm not afraid anymore." My voice is muffled, but I know he can hear every word.

Love, the real kind, doesn't demand proof. It shows up. It stays. It waits for your pace. And when you're ready, it stands beside you.

"I trained my whole life for something I never got finished." I meet his eyes, my heart hammering.

Tears start to blur the ancient stonework behind him, but I blink them back. "I thought if I stayed away from dreams, stayed away from anything I couldn't master, maybe I wouldn't have to survive that kind of loss again."

I press a trembling hand against his heart, grounding myself.

He places his reassuring hand over mine. "But standing still felt like another kind of dying."

For a moment, Dillon says nothing. He watches me, his gaze fierce and soft at once, like he's memorizing the way I'm stitched together with old scars.

Slowly, he lifts a hand and cups my cheek, his thumb brushing reverently over the curve of my cheekbone. He doesn't tell me it's okay. He doesn't try to fix it. He just holds me like I'm something sacred, not broken, not fragile, just real.

And somehow, without a single word, I know he sees all of it. The dreams, the wreckage, the pieces I thought were unlovable. And yet he's not afraid of any of it.

I think of my mother. She did the best she could. I still love her.

Maybe that's where healing begins. Maybe that's where I begin again.

***

At twilight, we wander the streets of York. The quiet hum of the city wraps around us. My hand is still in his, the warmth grounding me in something I'm finally allowing myself to believe in.

For the first time in weeks, I don't notice the ache in my leg. We slow our pace, stopping by a weathered wooden bench near the old city walls.

Dillon tugs gently on my hand, guiding me to sit. "I need to show you something," he says, pulling out his phone.

I watch as he taps through a few screens, then holds out the device between us. The screen flickers to life. Oscar's voice fills the air, smooth, smug, poisonous.

Oscar (on audio):

> *"Dillon thinks he's in control, but after the board vote, he won't have a company left to control. The fool played right into my hands."*

My stomach twists. I glance at Dillon, but his expression is steady, calm, resigned.

> *"We have to move fast. Once the patent is officially filed under his name, we lose control. But if we strike before then, it's ours. He won't even see it coming."*

Dillon stops the recording. "I already knew before I came to find you," he says, his voice low but steady. "Noah sent it to me. Actually, my father tipped him off."

I blink, surprised. Dillon's mouth tilts in a wry smile.

"Robert set the whole thing in motion," he goes on. "A friend of his from the golf club overheard Oscar ranting. He was part of the conversation and decided to record it. He passed it along to my father. Said he thought I deserved to know. My father sent Noah the old files and proof."

I shake my head. "Sounds like your father had a chess move you never saw coming."

He exhales slowly. "Turns out loyalty doesn't always look the way you expect."

For the first time, I don't envision a man who failed me. I see one who stood in the shadows, guarding me anyway. Maybe it's not too late to return the gesture.

"And the company?" I ask softly.

Dillon smiles a small, steady smile that feels earned. "Still mine. For now. Noah's ensuring the final patent claim is finalized."

Relief crashes over me in slow, gentle waves. I squeeze his hand. "You're going to be okay."

He leans closer, pressing his forehead against mine. "I wasn't. Not until you."

I blink back the sting of tears.

He brushes a strand of hair from my face, his touch achingly tender. "You were right about him. About everything."

My voice comes out as a whimper. "I just didn't want you to get hurt."

His smile deepens, almost reverent. "Cleo. You saved me."

I reach for him, threading my fingers through his, feeling the weight and the solidity of everything we fought for.

"We saved each other."

Dillon tugs me against him, wrapping his arms tight around my shoulders.

I close my eyes, breathing him in, the solid beat of his heart, the warmth of his body, the fierce steadiness of his love.

"Still think I'm a robot?" he says.

I look up to meet his gaze.

"Nope. Turns out even steel hearts melt."

The bells of York Minster ring out into the night.

I know this with certainty, this is where we're meant to be. Together.

35

Chapter 35: Wholehearted

Dillon

Golden light bathes the ballroom at the New York Glasshouse. The skyline glitters through floor-to-ceiling windows, wide and luminous. Voices hum and glasses clink as the buzz builds momentum.

Weeks later, the echoes of York still follow us. Between red-eye flights, board meetings, and rebuilding trust in real time, we learn how to build slow. To stay steady when life stops testing and simply asks us to show up.

Tonight I'm not just launching a product, I'm stepping into something bigger.

I scan the crowd, taking in the sea of press, investors, and tech insiders all waiting to hear about the Lucid Lenses microexpression glasses.

Then I see Cleo standing near the stage. A vision in a sleek, midnight-blue fitted gown. Her eyes are bright, filled with a love I never thought I'd deserve.

Cleo catches my gaze and tilts her head slightly. She smiles like she knows what I'm thinking because she knows me.

The event coordinator gives me a nod. I straighten my tie and step onto the stage as the murmurs settle. I'm not trying to prove anything, just telling the truth.

I grip the podium, scanning the audience before settling my gaze on Cleo.

"When we started this project, I thought I knew what success looked like. Numbers. Strategy. Control. I built iSight Innovations on the idea that progress is about precision. About eliminating uncertainty."

I pause, my chest tightening. "But I was wrong. Real progress, the kind that changes lives, doesn't come from control. It comes from collaboration. From people who challenge you, push you, and make you better."

I let my gaze linger on Cleo for half a second longer. She gives me the tiniest nod, her lips curving in encouragement.

"This project was never about replacing human intuition. It was about enhancing it with clarity and integrity. We've implemented privacy-first safeguards, clear opt-in features, and robust ethical oversight. Because technology should never outpace trust."

I draw in a breath and continue.

"Lucid can scan a face, track micro-expressions, read physiological signals. It can tell when someone's afraid, curious, or overwhelmed. But it missed the one thing that mattered most."

I pause. Let the room lean in.

"It doesn't see what human connection does to the heart."

A hush hangs in the air now. No click of a camera. Just stillness.

"That's the thing. No matter how advanced the tech, it can't replace what makes us human. Emotion. Forgiveness. Love."

I glance back at Cleo. "This isn't about predicting feelings. It's about honoring them. About giving people the courage to see and be seen."

Our eyes meet with understanding. She nods in approval.

"This technology should bring people closer, not tear them apart. It bridges the gaps in understanding and helps us see each other in ways we never have before. It gives a voice to the uncertainty. Ladies and gentlemen, welcome to the new era of human understanding."

The room erupts with applause, but the steady beat of my heart drowns it out.

As I step away from the podium, Cleo strides toward me, pride evident in her eyes.

She's the only thing I see.

When she reaches me, she doesn't hesitate. She cups my face, whispering just for me, "That was perfect," and gives me a quick kiss.

I lower my gaze with a cheeky smile, brushing my thumb over the back of her hand. "I had the best editor."

She laughs, eyes shining. "That's right. And don't forget it. Lucid can scan a face," she whispers. "But it takes love to read the heart."

I lift my gaze. "I had to learn my heart first."

For the first time, I don't feel like I'm standing at the top of the world alone.

I feel like I'm where I'm meant to be. With her.

I feel a touch on my shoulder and turn to see my father, face beaming. "Well done. I'm proud of you, son," he says with a rawness I've never seen before.

"Thanks," I say, almost apologetically.

"Despite Oscar's tricks, you did what you do best."

I quirk a brow. "Oh, and what's that?"

"You did the right thing. I can't say that about myself, I'm afraid." My father pauses. "I know I let you down in the past, and for that, I'm sorry. I hope you can find the bandwidth in your heart to, um, to to forgive me."

I blink. Wow.

Did *the* Robert Whelan just ask *me* for forgiveness?

He extends his hand with the invitation for closure, but I step forward and embrace him in the biggest hug. He startles at first, but leans in and hugs me back.

For the first time in my life, I feel a genuine connection between us.

And I know we're not going back, only forward.

***

The music shifts, soft jazz humming through the speakers as the gala transitions from speeches to celebration. I step away for a moment, needing air, needing a second to process how much everything has changed.

As I lean against the terrace railing, the city stretching out beneath me, the lights aglow, a memory surfaces.

I'm eight years old, barefoot in our kitchen, my mother laughing as she spins me in an impromptu dance. She twirls me, her hands warm and steady. "Dillon, life isn't just about what you build. It's about who you dance with."

I laughed, embarrassed, rolling my eyes at her sentimentality. "Dancing's not important."

She smiled, pressing her palm against my cheek. "Love is.

One day, you'll understand."

I close my eyes, the memory settling like an ache and a balm. I understand now.

I turn back and find Cleo, laughing at something Noah said. She radiates confidence, light, and joy.

The fear of loss and failure had been my constant companion for so long. It's gone.

Replaced with a contentment I never knew was possible.

Love isn't control. It's trust. It's faith. And I choose it. Every single time.

I make my way back to Cleo, sliding a hand around her waist as I murmur, "Dance with me."

She raises a brow. "You hate dancing."

I grin and press a kiss to her temple. "Not with you."

And as she lets me pull her onto the dance floor, the past and present collide in a way that feels divine.

I know now this is what my mother meant.

Cleo snuggles against my neck; I inhale her scent. Jasmine mixed with something softer that settles me.

This is what she wanted for me. Not power. Not control. But love.

✳✳✳

The next evening, Cleo and I sip hot chocolate at the Rockefeller Center ice rink. The crisp air wraps around us like a comforting blanket. The festive Christmas string lights give off a warm, romantic glow. I hold her close, pressing my lips to her hair and breathing in her scent.

"You've run three pitch decks, two board meetings, and a launch. You have eaten nothing that wasn't catered since

Monday," Cleo says. With a huge grin, she waves two skate wristbands in front of my face. "You need ice therapy."

I raise an eyebrow. "That's not a real thing."

"Of course it is. Like brunch, we like it. Come on, Mr. Control Freak. Trust me for once." She skates backward, hands locked in mine, her eyes never leaving my face. "You don't have to know how to lead," she whispers. "Just let me guide you."

I laugh, but my legs shake, my heart pounding, and it's not because of the ice.

Letting go of control feels liberating.

Cleo moves closer, tilting her head up. "So what now?"

I grin like my heart is about to burst. "Well, I was thinking of a vacation."

She snorts. "You? Taking time off?"

I run my fingers down her spine, slow and deliberate. "For you? Anything."

Her expression softens; we just breathe each other in. She leans her forehead against mine. The kind of closeness that says more than words.

Then, she bites her lip. Her eyes flicker. She hesitates. "There's something I need to tell you."

I draw back enough to see her fully. She cups my face with both hands, holding me steady like she's grounding herself. Her gaze darts between mine, like she's searching for something.

I frown. "What is it?"

She exhales, and a warm smile creases her eyes. "I love you."

The words crack something open in me. Not because I doubted. But because I needed to hear them from the one person who sees through me without blinking.

I press my hands over hers, sealing them to my jaw. My voice barely comes out. "Cleo…"

"I want us to do the next thing together," she says, glowing now. "Whatever it is. Wherever it leads."

My pulse trips. "Next thing? Like what?"

She slides her arms around my neck, and suddenly we're close enough to feel the heat between us shift.

Cleo swallows hard. "Fancy launching an iSight and Calypso combo in Europe?"

Her eyes dance with delight. I just want to savor this moment.

A thrill thrums beneath my ribs. But this time, it isn't about scaling or strategy.

It's about her. It's about us.

What we could build, not just in business, but in everything.

I raise a brow. "Now I'm intrigued. Do tell."

She hesitates, then adds softly, "And maybe you help me fix what I've been avoiding. Calypso's growing too fast. I'm good with people, with vision, but not numbers."

She lifts her eyes to meet mine, vulnerable but sure. "I don't need rescuing. I just need a second set of eyes. Yours."

My heart kicks. Not because she's asking, but because she trusts me enough to. "I'm in," I say, pulling her closer. "Let's build something that's not just brilliant, but something that lasts."

She exhales like she's been waiting to hear it all along.

Our hands find each other's, fingers interlacing tighter.

The rest of the world blurs.

And then, I close the gap.

The kiss is slow, reverent.

Like we're sealing something sacred.

Her lips meet mine, warm and sure, and everything clicks into place.

The push and pull, the questions, the walls.

It all dissolves into this moment.

This kiss isn't about sparks, it's gravity.

Choosing the same direction at the same time with the same heart.

When we break apart, our foreheads rest together.

"This," she whispers. "This feels right."

I smile. "You feel like home."

And just like that, the next adventure begins.

Chapter 36: The Proposal

Cleo

Lake Como, Italy

The yacht rocks gently beneath us, the scent of lake water and citrus drifting through the warm air. It smells like a love letter sealed with sunlight, a kiss after the rain. The sky blushes pink and molten gold as the sun sinks behind the mountains.

Several months have passed since that rainy doorstep moment in York. Months spent learning to speak honestly, to argue with care, to rebuild from the inside out.

It feels almost too perfect.

Our feet brush as we sit side by side on the cushioned deck, but it's his gaze I feel most. Like I'm the only thing anchoring him here. Warmth curls in my chest, not from the sun, but from the way he looks at me.

"You're staring, Mr. Whelan," I tease, tilting my head.

There's a naughty glint in Dillon's eyes.

Dillon leans in, the corner of his mouth lifting just enough to make my heart trip. "Can you blame me? I'm sitting next to the most brilliant woman I know. And I've closed billion-dollar deals, so I don't say that lightly."

I laugh, shaking my head. "Says the man hopelessly in love."

"You always know how to ground me." He exhales softly. "The first time you told me no, I knew winning wasn't the point. You were. We make a great team. And besides, doubling the company's growth in one deal? Kind of a big deal."

In four months, we merged Calypso and iSight. Now we are building our first European office in Paris.

My throat tightens. "We built something. Not just the company. Us."

"And we're just getting started," he says. "But today, nothing else matters. Just you. Just this."

My chest tightens with overwhelming certainty.

Dillon takes my hand and slips it into the pocket of his linen pants. My fingertips brush something cool. My breath catches as my trembling hands pull out a white gold ring with a heart-shaped diamond. It's delicate and elegant, catching the last rays of sun like memory and moonlight.

I stare at it, my pulse loud in my ears. "Dillon, what—?"

He takes the ring from my palm. Then, before I can process what's happening, he drops to one knee right there on the deck, the lake stretching wide and luminous behind him.

I hold my breath.

"I've spent my life making decisions, closing deals, winning battles," he says, voice steady, but filled with something rare and vulnerable. "But the greatest decision I'll ever make is choosing you, every day, for the rest of my life. Cleo Ambrosia, will you be my partner for life?"

The words slam into me, breaking through fear, doubt, and the part of me that thought love needed protection.

I press my hand to my mouth, and for a beat, the world tilts. Not in fear, but in wonder. My hands shake uncontrollably. Every cell in my body says yes, quieting the small voice that wonders if it's too soon.

When I finally find my voice, I reply, "Can I keep it?"

Dillon's laugh is rich, unfiltered, like sunlight. In that sound, I hear my future.

I wipe away my tears and laugh. "Tell me you didn't hide the ring in your presentation clicker."

He grins. "Tempting. But I figured you'd still try to steal it."

"Only if you were mansplaining again."

He grins. "So always?"

He cups my face, thumbs brushing tears I didn't know had fallen. And when his warm lips meet mine, my breath catches.

It's not just a kiss. It's a promise.

Steady, warm, and everything I never believed I could have.

Dillon slides the ring onto my finger. I can't look away from him. Not just the man, but the life he's offering.

I once thought love was something to earn, like a pitch to perfect.

Maybe real love begins when the armor drops.

When you stop performing.

When you stand uncovered and say, This is me. Still messy. Still worthy.

And love proves itself and stays anyway.

I wrote a letter to my father a few weeks ago with no expectations. I feel free.

Tia's thinking about writing one too. Maybe that's how we start, one letter at a time. It's not closure yet, but it's motion.

And for now, that's enough.

Maybe forgiveness doesn't always mean reunion, but it does mean release.

I blink, and behind us, laughter rises all at once. I spin around, heart skidding sideways, to find Tia, my mother, healthy and glowing in a pale blue dress, Megan, and Noah grinning like they've been planning this for years.

My vision blurs for a second.

This is real. They're all here.

For so long, I carried it alone. The fear, the hiding, and here they are, my sister, my mother, my friend. Proof that I was never as alone as I believed.

Tia rushes forward, wrapping me in a hug. "Surprise!" she squeals. "Also, I may have brought some dresses, just in case."

I gasp, pressing a hand to my chest. "You—what?"

She grins. "What can I say? I've always been better at wardrobe than words. But I knew this one would fit."

She shoots Dillon a wink. "Turns out I've been helping Dillon for longer than you realize. Remember the gowns for the country club ball? That was me. He hired me to dress you without knowing we were sisters. Once I put two and two together, I knew you were meant to end up here."

My sister has been part of our love story all along.

I turn back to Dillon, breathless, heart pounding.

I press a gentle kiss on his lips. "I love you."

His grin warms my heart.

I finally understand.

This kind of love doesn't wait until you're ready.

It waits until you're real.

And then it stays.

That's the kind of love we chose.

And this time, we're not running.

He takes my hand, and together, we step forward into what comes next.

This time, the pitch is personal.

And I'm keeping the clicker.

37

Chapter 37: Epilogue

Cleo

The sun filters through linen curtains as I curl deeper into the villa's chaise lounge with a romance book. I'm still getting used to mornings without pitch decks or caffeine-induced anxiety.

Dillon's laughter echoes from inside, probably teasing the chef about making breakfast "strategically."

I smile and reach for my phone, ready to ignore the world for one more hour.

Two unread emails appear on my lock screen.

One from Megan. One from Tia.

My sister and my best friend, both in France, suddenly emailing like something has shifted.

My heart does that familiar skip it always does before something changes.

Whatever this is, it feels like a beginning.

I open Megan's first.

To: Cleo

Subject: Monet's Gardens are Magic.

Cleo, my love, you were right. Paris and Giverny are even more beautiful in person. Violet ice cream. Flowers everywhere. It smells like peace here. Funny thing, though, I ran into a guy inside the gardens. Tall, casually brilliant. Had a laptop sticker with a code language I recognized. We joked about the security vulnerabilities of the house Wi-Fi.

He said something about "finding beauty in the cracks." I haven't been able to stop thinking about it, but it's probably nothing. But then again, you always told me Paris had a way of opening people up.

M

Email from Tia.

Location: Paris

To: Cleo

Subject: Um. We need to talk.

I just finished the Eiffel Tower shoot, and you are not going to believe this.

My photographer, The Grump, is basically a walking existential crisis in boots.

Silent. Broody. Definitely judging my outfit. And yet, I think he's either brilliant or completely unhinged. He caught a photo of me mid-laugh that made me pause.

Like he saw me. The real me. I don't know what to do with that.

Also, he stole my croissant.

Tia

P.S. How do you say "emotional sabotage" in French?

I stare at the messages, a slow smile curling at my lips.

Tia never lets her guard down that easily.

Megan doesn't flirt with strangers unless they speak code and carry meaning.

Maybe Paris really is working its magic.

Whatever is unfolding for them feels like the start of something wonderful.

This time, I get to watch their stories unfold.

One messy, magical chapter at a time.

And somewhere in Paris, two new stories are just beginning.

Return to the Sensibility Sisters

Cleo and Dillon's story may have found its quiet landing, but the Sensibility sisters are only just beginning. The next story follows Megan Mercer, whose careful, well-ordered life begins to shift during a work assignment in Paris.

Among the gardens of Giverny, a chance meeting with a stranger who feels unexpectedly familiar begins a connection neither of them planned. Paris, late-night conversations, and a love that grows quietly through observation and trust await in the next Sensibility story.

Continue reading with the opening chapter of Braided Roses (Sensibility Romance Series Book 2)

Chapter 1: Monet's Gardens

Megan

Monet's Gardens, Giverny, France
Standing on the narrow stone ledge Monet once painted from, I stop, closer to the edge than I realize.

The air feels cool and damp against my cheeks. Green in a way that feels like a temperature, not a color. It traces along my collarbone, slips beneath my sleeves, easing into places I did not realize were still braced.

This place feels familiar, like something I have already visited but never lived.

I step closer to the water.

The stone beneath my soles is damp, holding warmth longer than expected. Sun filters through the branches, landing in slow patches across my skin.

My mother would have moved through a place like this without slowing. Always forward, always curious.

Just a little farther, she used to say, there is always something worth seeing next.

I raise my DSLR to my eye, framing the lake and trees the way my mother taught me. It feels less like photography and more like keeping her close.

I step forward, closer than I should, focused on the frame, and then a firm grasp closes around my waist.

"Careful, you might not like a cold plunge right now."

I lower my camera and let it rest against my hip, then turn over my shoulder to see.

His gaze is on my footing, not my face. His grip is steady. Warm.

"Oh, thank you. I was so distracted by the view I did not notice the edge," I say, straightening myself.

He is solid where his hand steadies me, posture relaxed, practiced. He is close enough that I notice a faint crease at the corner of his mouth.

His loose dark curls frame a face that looks relaxed until you notice how closely he is tracking everything.

But it is his eyes that capture me.

Story continues in Braided Roses

Author Note

If you're here at the very end, thank you. This story has been a journey of love and the courage to put my heart on the page. It's a story of logic meeting vulnerability, ambition colliding with love, and two fiercely guarded people learning to choose connection over control.

Writing *Mind Reader* was more than a romance. It was an exploration of what it means to risk being known, even when the world tells you to protect your heart.

Cleo's story is deeply personal to me. She's smart and sharp and driven. But like so many of us, she's also quietly scared of needing too much, of trusting too far, of being let down again. Her journey to trust Dillon wasn't about surrendering her strength. It was about redefining what strength looks like.

And maybe that's where you are too. Maybe you've learned to succeed by staying ahead, staying guarded, staying in control. Maybe you've been told that independence means not needing anyone.

But the truth is, real love, the kind that stays, doesn't shrink you or ask you to be less. It meets you exactly as you are and invites you to breathe a little deeper.

Whether you're chasing your own version of a big dream, picking up the pieces of your past, or standing somewhere in the middle of your story, I hope Cleo and Dillon reminded you that healing is possible.

That you can be brilliant and soft at the same time.

That you are not too much.

And that love, when it's real, is worth the risk.

Love was never the opposite of logic.

It was what gave it meaning.

The moment I stopped trying to read every sign and simply chose to stay, I finally understood what faith feels like.

In the end, love wasn't something to solve.

It was something to trust.

And when I finally stopped running, I realized it had been waiting all along.

Even the smartest code can't replicate what the heart knows instinctively.

No algorithm can learn the language of love—the kind spoken without words, only understanding.

My hope is that you find love in your own way, in your own time.

Thank you for spending time with these characters. Thank you for reading all the way to this page. And most of all, thank you for believing in stories where grace, growth, and wholehearted love win.

With all my heart

Mimika Cooney

P.S. Wear the dress. Take the leap. Choose love over fear. And yes, you can be both the CEO *and* the woman who cries during romantic scenes!

Before You Go

If this story made you smile, breathe a little easier, or stay up past your bedtime, would you leave a few words for the next reader? Reviews matter as they help other readers find books they'll love. They tell me what resonated so I can write more of it. Your honest thoughts are perfect. A single sentence is enough. Not sure what to say? Try one of these quick prompts:

- The feeling you were left with at the end
- A favorite moment or line
- Three words you'd use to describe Cleo and Dillon
- Why this worked for you as a closed-door romance
- Who you'd recommend it to

How to leave a review in under a minute:

- Open the store where you got the book.
- Tap "Write a review."
- Add a line or two, press submit. A simple star rating helps but your words travel farther.

About the Author

Mimika Cooney writes emotionally rich, closed-door contemporary romances about intelligent women, meaningful work, and love that grows through restraint, timing, and choice.

Mimika wrote her first book idea on a typewriter at the age of ten. It took her forty years and four career changes to finally come back to her first love of storytelling. She believes love and faith go hand in hand and every good romance deserves a little heartbreak, a lot of healing, and one unforgettable happily ever after.

An award-winning author with a global perspective, Mimika was born in South Africa and now lives in the United States. She speaks three languages and brings a love of travel, culture, and observation to every story she tells..

Her stories blend warmth, wit, and emotional depth, pairing slow-burn romance with real-life professional stakes. Set in cinematic locations such as Paris, New York, London, Europe and beyond, her novels focus on connection built quietly, personal courage, and the moments that change how a life is lived.

Rather than relying on high drama or spice, Mimika's romances are grounded, character-driven, and emotionally intelligent. Faith appears gently in her work as interior grounding rather than a plot driver, woven with subtlety and respect.

A hopeless romantic, Mimika has been married to her teenage sweetheart for thirty years. Together they share three children: two independent young adults and a witty teenager.

When she is not writing or planning her next writing travel trip, she will be found on the ice practicing her spins as an adult figure skater. She also enjoys stabbing people for fun (without getting arrested) as an amateur fencer.

Get on the VIP list for the inside scoop and claim your **Mind Reader Book Bonus!**

https://www.mimikacooney.com/mindreader

You can connect with me on:

https://www.mimikacooney.com

https://www.facebook.com/themimikacooney

https://www.instagram.com/mimikacooney

Subscribe to my newsletter:

https://www.mimikacooney.com/sensibility

Also by Mimika Cooney

The *Sensibility Romance Series* is a collection of clean, emotionally rich contemporary romances following a circle of friends whose lives intersect through work, friendship, travel, and the long work of becoming whole. These stories center on capable, accomplished women who have been holding it together for a long time and are ready to feel understood.

Each book follows a different character through a season of change, exploring what it means to invite love, be loved, and build a life that feels true. Romance unfolds quietly through presence, patience, and connection that is earned rather than rushed, as ambition, friendship, and intimacy learn to coexist.

Every novel stands alone, yet the series is connected by shared moments and overlapping lives, tracing distinct paths toward love, courage, and self-trust. Set against elegant global backdrops, these slow-burn romances offer complete emotional arcs and a sense of quiet satisfaction, inviting readers to slow down, exhale, and stay awhile.

Written for readers who value lyrical intimacy, emotional depth, restraint, and clean, closed-door romance with no explicit content.

Get your free copy of the Sensibility Series Guide when you subscribe to Mimika Cooney's newsletter. Receive special offers, new-release details, and a welcome gift delivered straight to your inbox.

https://www.mimikacooney.com/sensibility

Mind Reader (Sensibility Book 1)

https://www.mimikacooney.com/mindreader

For the woman who learned to read everyone else so she wouldn't have to risk being known. Cleo decodes emotions. Dillon built a device to understand them. When their rivalry turns into a reluctant partnership, sparks fly. In New York's high tech startup world, can love be the truth they both need?

Braided Roses (Sensibility Book 2)

https://www.mimikacooney.com/braidedroses

For the woman who is good at holding herself together, but isn't sure how to let herself receive. She's a guarded marketing exec. He's a charming coder. When a surprise encounter in Paris sparks instant chemistry, Megan and Noah discover their anonymous online connection runs deeper than they imagined.

Supernova (Sensibility Book 3)

https://www.mimikacooney.com/supernova

For the woman who's been praised for being extraordinary, but secretly wonders who she is without the spotlight. An influencer with a plan. A grumpy photographer with trust issues. Tia and Leo are stuck together on a six-week brand tour across Europe. When sparks fly, staged smiles give way to something real.

Salt & Light (Sensibility Book 4)

https://www.mimikacooney.com/saltlight

For the woman who brings warmth and hope to everyone else, but has quietly forgotten how to let herself be held. A no-compromise foodie blogger. A guarded Catalan chef in Barcelona. Shiloh agrees to be Mateo's fake girlfriend to get his family off his back, but between sizzling dishes and stolen glances, fake turns real.

Last Love (Sensibility Book 5)

https://www.mimikacooney.com/lastlove

For the woman who believes love has already passed her by, and is learning that staying open is still an act of courage. They were everything to each other, until life tore them apart. Years later, Mia and Micah reunite in Italy. He's never stopped loving her. She's not ready to believe it's real.

Barefoot Vows (Sensibility Book 6)

https://www.mimikacooney.com/barefootvows

For the woman who has built something beautiful for everyone else, and is finally deciding she's allowed to want it for herself. She's a buttoned-up wedding planner. He's a charming pilot. Alexa is all business until a work trip throws her together with free-spirited Dustin. Opposites attract, but can they trust what's real under the sun?

Thawed Christmas (Sensibility Book 7)

https://www.mimikacooney.com/thawedchristmas

For the woman who learned to survive by staying composed, and is discovering that tenderness is not a liability. One ski lodge. One studio apartment. One blizzard. When perfectionist ex-figure skater Nicole is forced to share space with laid-back ski instructor Connor, winter collisions melt into something unexpected.